Sinister Sanctuary

Caroline stood shivering, breathless in the darkened room. She was safe at last. *He* would never look for her here.

She moved, and her foot struck something soft. She stared at the dark shape on the floor and her fragile sanity seemed to be trying to rip away from its moorings. It couldn't be, it *couldn't....*

Caroline leaned over and her fingers touched the forehead, the nose, the slack open mouth, and she wanted to scream.

Then she heard the heavy footsteps coming up the stairs outside, and knew that the murderer had come for his next victim....

DARK INTERVAL
was originally published by
Doubleday & Company, Inc.

Joan Aiken

DARK
INTERVAL

PUBLISHED BY POCKET BOOKS NEW YORK

DARK INTERVAL

Doubleday edition published 1967

POCKET BOOK edition published April, 1974

L

Standard Book Number: 671-77730-0.
Library of Congress Catalog Card Number: 67-14713.
This POCKET BOOK edition is published by arrangement with Doubleday & Company, Inc. Copyright, ©, 1967, by Joan Aiken. All rights
reserved. This book, or portions thereof, may not be reproduced by any
means without permission of the original publisher: Doubleday & Company, Inc., 277 Park Avenue, New York, N.Y. 10017.
Cover illustration by Lou Marchetti.
Printed in the U.S.A.

Prologue

Harry Lupac was waiting for the girl he was going to murder. He was on edge with expectation, like a bride before her mother-in-law's first visit, glancing at himself nervously in the mirror, emptying an ashtray, rubbing needlessly at a spot on the table. He had never planned a murder before, and planning made him fretful, it was not his way to work things out beforehand: only sheer necessity was making him do it now.

He stared out of the window at the track up which she would come.

Nobody yet.

Would she be pretty? He didn't know. It would be odd if she were. At this thought, which had not occurred to him before, intent as he was on the bare details of the operation, a sort of excitement took hold of him and he walked across the room and looked at himself in the glass again, pulling somewhat complacently at the dark green tie complemented by the pale green shirt. He had a long, mobile face, airily haggard; red, pouting lips; hazel eyes; a lock of hair fell over his forehead constantly, and was constantly thrown back.

"My dear young lady," he said to the mirror. "How do you do? I am so sorry that our first meeting must be our last. I regret it especially now that I see you are a lady of so much beauty and charm." He began to giggle, and then stopped, scowling at the sound of his voice in the empty cottage, crossed to the window, and consulted the silent road again. Of course he would say none of these things.

There was no sign of her. Reassured, he threw himself on to a chair, cocked his legs on the table, and went on, gazing at the ceiling.

"But as you *have* to die—and this, I am afraid, is quite essential—is there any little celebration, any treat that would sweeten your last moments, mmh? It would be the least I could do for you. A martini? And let me pin this bunch of violets on your lapel."

There were no violets but he removed a scabious from a rather charmingly arranged bunch of wild-flowers in a vase and flourished it at his invisible companion. "What is this you say? You don't see the necessity for dying? You don't understand? Ah well, in that case, let me explain. It was that truly unfortunate occurrence, you see, last Sunday . . ."

But the real beginning had been much, much longer ago than that.

She was running through the woods stealthily, like a hunted thing; she looked over her shoulder as she ran, and warily all round her, and paused sometimes to listen for footsteps. She would have seemed conspicuous enough, had there been any observer, for an unseasonable April snow had flecked the whole valley with white. Bare oaks, and birches with only a scanty covering of green stood silhouetted, white tracks crossed and diverged like scars on the steep tree-hung slope, and the solitary running figure was plainly visible for hundreds of yards. But her tracks were obliterated behind her by the falling snow; she took comfort from this.

Half her caution was a delicious pretense—for it was not really *very* probable that her mother or sister, let alone Cousin Flora, would be found up at this end of the valley in such weather, even when exercising the dogs —but half was real enough. Suppose they did find out? What would the reactions be? Anger, outrage, malicious amusement? Wincing from the thought she fled even faster through the dazzle of white and green. Her progress was like a graph drawn at lightning speed from one point of cover to another: diagram of a young girl running to meet her lover.

Quick as she had been, Tim was there before her.

At the head of the Tebburn valley a disused railway emerged, briefly, from a tunnel, to cross the snowy, wooded depth on a viaduct and disappear again into the nearer hillside; by the tunnel opening stood an abandoned signalman's cottage. Tim's old motor bike was already tucked in between the woodpile and the wall, camouflaged with a bit of snow-furred sacking. No one was likely to pass here, but she had begged him always to hide it and, laughing at her, ruffling her short hair, he had promised.

Now, silent as a drifting flake so as not to let him down by exercising less care than she had demanded of him, she stole along the wall until she could look in at the little parlour window. Most of the panes were cracked, all were grimed with dirt, but she could just see him; her heart gave a great joyful bound of love and astonishment because during each time of separation she found it impossible to believe that ever again in her life would she have the prodigious luck and happiness of seeing him again.

But there he was.

The little front room was dark and damp because of the overhanging hillside and crowding untrimmed trees, but they had managed to make it comfortable. Aghast at her own daring she had slipped off to an auction of second-hand furniture in Bridpool, missing a piano lesson (old Mr. Monsell would never think of ringing up to inquire where she was) and, with money Tim had given her, bought two chairs, a battered table, and a roll of moth-eaten old carpet, bright pink roses on a green ground.

"Just right for a love-nest," Tim had teased.

"Oh, Tim, don't call it that! Love-nest's a horrible expression. This is a refuge—no, a *sanctuary*. I wish we dared light a fire, though."

"Never mind, the oil stove does a perfectly adequate job."

He had the kettle on it now, she saw; a thread of steam wavered from the spout. He must have been quite a long time ahead of her, long enough to spread out his books on the table and become engrossed in work. He had not seen her yet, he was frowning with concentration, his head propped on one fist, fingers pushed up through his hair. For the first time, as she watched him, a strange maternal pang touched her—he seemed so young and vulnerable, absorbed in his studies. Hitherto she had always looked up to him as a protector. "Don't fret your head, Carinney, I'll fix it somehow," he used to say, over some problem that seemed to her desperate and insuperable. But now, like anguish, the thought struck her: he has so much to worry about, his finals, and his father's illness, and the family business—is it fair to load him with the burden of this concealment as well?

At the moment he looked up and saw her and smiled; the effect was like a sudden burst of sunshine in a rocky landscape. In two strides he was up and had the sagging door open; she ran through into his arms.

"What were you doing standing out there in the snow, you old silly? Why didn't you come in?"

"I was sending waves of love through the window."

"It feels better in close-up," he said, pressing his cheek to her dark hair. "You're terribly late; what kept you?"

"People came to lunch—"

"Friends?"

"We haven't any friends," she said. "No, people who wanted to buy a deerhound. I had to stay and lead the dogs about; I thought I'd never get away."

"Never mind, you're here now." Already they had settled into their usual position; he in his armchair, half his mind back among the textbooks, the other half encircling her with love; she settled on a cushion on the floor, leaning against his chair, silent in her happiness.

"I'll make tea in a minute," she said presently.

"Not just yet—let me finish this—" He was lost again,

wrestling with symbols that were incomprehensible to her, but she did not mind. She was proud that she did not distract him, that he could work so intensely in her presence. "It helps, having you there," he said once. "You're a catalyst."

At last he surfaced and shook off the entangling formulae of his problem and smiled at her. She returned his look seriously, and then jumped up and began to move quietly about, taking mugs out of a damp cupboard, and a teapot, and a tin of tea.

"I brought a cake."

"Good," said Tim. He stretched. "Concentrating makes me hungry. I've done a lot. Shan't be able to work nearly so hard back at Oxford."

She turned away from him, bending over the kettle so that he shouldn't see the anguish that made her face haggard at the thought of parting. Every term when he went away it was worse; this time she really didn't see how she was going to bear the deathlike darkness of life without him.

"Cheer up, Carinney," he said, gently, turning her chin towards him with a finger. A tear sparkled on her lash; shamefacedly she wiped it away. "Only two months, remember? And then, if you really don't want to brave your mother—"

"No. No!"

"—We get a special licence and disappear off to Weston super-Mare or Walton-on-the-Naze—"

"Stow-on-the-Wold." She achieved a shaky smile.

"Somewhere they'll never think of looking, anyway, and get married and send a postcard to say so, and I'll find a job in Azerbaijan or Chimborazo, and next time your dear family sees you you'll be a sophisticated matron with a tropical tan and a habit of clapping your hands for the butler and calling 'Ho! Chota-peg! Brandy-pani-da!' "

"Ass! I'd like to see Hudson's face if anyone clapped their hands for him. He'd just about have apoplexy. Actually, after living with the way Mother treats servants, I never want to have any as long as I live."

"I'm afraid you'll have to get used to a whole retinue," Tim warned her solemnly. "Or the other memsahibs will think you are letting down the dear old flag."

"Oh goodness, must I? I'd much rather do the work myself, I'd soon learn. I wish your job wasn't likely to take you to such true-blue outposts of empire. —No I don't, I don't care *where* we are, or if I have to boss around fifty servants, as long as we're together and away from here. I can always mend your socks."

"Terylene," Tim said, grinning. "Never go into holes. Better play house now, while you have the chance."

"Here, then." She pushed his books to one end of the table and spread a cloth over the other, before laying out plates and mugs. "I even remembered to warm the pot."

"Did you put any tea in?" He peered sceptically and nodded to her suddenly anxious expression. "Cordon bleu standard by the time I've done my finals."

"No chance to practise while you're away," she said mournfully.

"You could come up here on your own. Or with Hilda."

"Oh no, I'd hate to. This is our place, not anybody else's." She looked round her with love, thinking: I'll never be happier than I am in this fusty little room with the pink roses on the floor and the mildew patches on the walls. If I live to be a hundred and spend every day of my life with Tim, still I'll always remember this.

No premonition touched her; no warning of another day, not far distant, when she would sit in this homely room eating and drinking not with Tim but with an enemy, a smiling stranger who was calmly and ruthlessly planning her destruction.

"Dee—Hilda's home again, did I tell you?" she remarked. "There was a frightful row when she suddenly arrived two days ago; you know she'd been a sort of paid-companion-cum-kennel-maid to those titled people in Scotland? Mother's furious because she got the sack for kissing the laird's son behind a haystack."

"Poor Hilda. Why couldn't she marry him?"

"I suppose he has to marry money, or someone respectable. Our family's hardly adequate. Mother was in a fearful rage; she said if Hilda couldn't play her cards better she must just stay at home and help now, she washed her hands of trying to get her launched in decent society. And Hilda said she'd sooner go on the streets than try to climb into decent society by way of its kennels. She was savage. She loathes being back at home."

"Is she taking it out on you?" Tim said gently.

"A bit." She looked away from him, out of the window. "Never mind. Don't let's think about my horrible family. Tell me about yours. How is your father—is he any better?"

Tim's young, plain face looked suddenly drawn, and ten years older. Troubled, noticing again the nervous tic that had begun to affect him lately, she put a hand against his cheek.

"No, he's not too good, actually. In fact, the specialist was pretty frank last time he came over—they don't have much hope that he'll make a full recovery. Which might mean that, instead of being able to flip off and get a wildcat job in Cotopaxi, I have to buckle down and go into the old firm a lot sooner than we'd expected."

"Oh, darling!" Dismay and concern moved equally in her face. "Your poor father! How awful. And here I've been, selfishly talking about my troubles—"

"Don't worry, my precious love. Perhaps it's not as bad as they think. The old boy's devilish tough really, like me. I expect he'll pull through."

"Oh I do *hope* he does. I do hope he's better by the time you do your finals."

By the time we run off and get married, she did not say. "Is there any more tea?"

"Masses." When she brought back his cup he took her hand, drawing her down until she knelt by him and he was able to put his arms round her.

"Don't be frightened," he said. "I'll always be around to look after you, whatever happens. We're so fantastically lucky to have each other—"

She glanced up, wondering why he had stopped

short, and heard the creak of the door, felt a cold draught lift the tiny hairs on her skin.

Tim's face, looking over her shoulder, went suddenly blank, with the taut, guarded look of one who sees a pile of masonry topple and waits for the crash.

"Well, *well!* Two lovebirds in their nest!"

The husky, scoffing voice of Lady Trevis cut between them like a fretsaw. Neither spoke, and she went on, "So *this* is where you get to in the long afternoons, Caroline? No wonder you didn't want to be a Brownie leader. — Don't you think my daughter's a trifle young for this sort of fun-and-games, Mr. Conroy? It is Tim Conroy, isn't it?"

Tim's hand slipped from Caroline's shoulder as she slowly turned, rising, and faced her mother, who stood leaning against the doorpost. Lady Trevis was halfway through her forties and just on the point of letting her appearance go hang; but at the moment, wearing narrow trousers and a yellow silk shirt, put on for the benefit of the dog buyers, she contrived to look almost within range of elegance—sportingly indulgent of the childish squalor in which she found her daughter.

As always in her mother's presence all Caroline's self-confidence evaporated; her hands hung awkwardly, she stood mute. Tim was astonished at the change, seeing his love who, when alone with him, seemed almost airborne, incandescent with happiness, transformed to a sulky juvenile. For the first time he became fully aware of the justification behind her desperate wish to get away from home.

"Well?" Lady Trevis repeated on a rising note. "Neither of you anything to say? Cat got your tongue, Caroline?"

Then they both spoke at the same moment. Tim said, "It's not the way you—"

Caroline said, "Tim's working for his finals. It helps him to concentrate when I'm with him." She spoke in a low voice, looking at the floor.

"Oh yes, I'm sure!" Lady Trevis, bored with the minor key in which the scene had been played so far, made a sudden theatrical switch from sportswoman to fish-wife. "I can just about *imagine* the sort of concentrating that gets done here. You must think I'm a fool." Her glance, destructive as a flame thrower, swept about their dolls'-house paradise. Stridently she demanded, "Where's the bed? Or do you make do with the floor?"

Tim was pale now, but keeping his temper well in control.

"Lady Trevis, you've got it all wrong. I promise you I haven't seduced Caroline—" He felt, too late, the pomposity of the phrase, and saw Caroline wince as if a screw had tightened.

"Seduced!" Lady Trevis jeered. "My, my, what a big word to use!" She added coarsely, "D'you expect me to believe that? D'mean to tell me you got this place all fixed up just to *study* in? That's just a bit too good to be true!"

"All the same it is true," Caroline muttered.

"Very likely! If it's true, why come all the way up here to Whistle Cottage? Why doesn't Tim ask you to his home? Why hasn't he ever been to Woodhoe? I suppose you're ashamed of us? You've been mighty secretive, I *must* say—still waters certainly run deep! I hardly knew you were acquainted with Tim Conroy, let alone popping into bed with him in this charming little—"

"We are *not*—" Caroline began angrily. In the same breath Tim said,

"We're going to get married. As soon as I've done my finals." He heard Caroline's sharp breath as Lady Trevis retorted,

"Oh you are, are you? May I remind *you,* miss, that you're a minor and need my permission before you jump into matrimony. And I can tell you this—you're *not* going to get married after Tim's done his finals"—she raised her voice as Tim moved forward protestingly—"you're going to get married next *week,* so you can put that in your pipe and smoke it. I'm not having any bastard grandchildren, I can tell you that. The people round here are toffee-nosed enough as it is. And you may think yourself lucky I don't take you before the courts, Tim Conroy!"

"For heaven's sake," Tim said, holding on to his reasonableness with an effort, "Caroline's nearly eighteen, she's an adult—"

"Ho, Caroline an adult? Don't make me laugh! She's still wet behind the ears. You'll have your hands full with her when you're married, I can tell you *that*—secretive, obstinate, sulky—"

"We can't get married right away!" Caroline burst out. "Don't you understand, Tim's got to work! This is his last term, he's got his final examinations coming up, and his father's ill too—it's out of the question."

"You should have thought of those things before you started messing about, my lady! It's a bit late now! I must say, this is a fine gratitude for all that classy, expensive schooling. It's just as well your father's dead and doesn't know—"

Here, remembering, perhaps, the circumstances of her husband's death and realising that this was hardly a felicitous line of approach, Lady Trevis came to a halt.

Tim said gently, "Very well, we'll get married next week. I'll see about a licence straight away. And I'll find some digs for us both in Oxford. And now perhaps you wouldn't mind leaving us alone for a little private conversation—"

Suddenly he felt sorry for Lady Trevis, poor stupid woman, trying to batter her way into the enclosed circle of their happiness. There she stood, with her triumph round her ears, like a child that has broken another's toy in grabbing, and is left with only scattered beads and bent wire. She seemed suddenly much older, tired, blowsy. She snapped,

"Your college airs don't cut any ice with me, my boy. I'm not having the two of you putting your heads together behind my back and planning how to get out of it. Caroline's coming home with me this minute."

"No I'm not," Caroline said quietly. She looked white, sick, and drained; Tim was appalled at the damage the scene had done her; yet even his love and pity could hardly comprehend how completely her self-respect and security had been shattered. But he dreaded

the effect of a further half hour's tête-à-tête with Lady
Trevis, walking home through the woods. Thank heaven
at least the other daughter had come home, he thought,
to act as a buffer. . . .

"I'm bringing Caroline home on my pillion. I'll take
care of her, I promise," he said, putting a hand on Lady
Trevis's shoulder and propelling her gently out of the
door. For a wonder she submitted, even gave him an
arch, flirtatious look and said,

"I suppose you think you can get round me with your
smooth Irish tongue, Tim Conroy. I know your ways!
But I warn you, I'm a tiger where my daughters' interests are concerned. I'm going to see that you do take
care of her!"

Tim winced at this roguishness. He waited until she
had whistled up a couple of Sealyhams, who burst out of
the snowy bushes, and taken her way downhill before he
went back into the cottage and shut the door.

Caroline had not moved. But when Tim came in she
began to wander slowly about, collecting the cups and the
teapot, dull-eyed and listless, like a person in shock.

"Well, one thing, that's over," Tim said, trying to make
a joke of it. "No blood shed, but she's got a fierce
tongue, hasn't she, your mother!" He put his arm round
her, holding her with her head under his chin to avoid
the tragedy in her eyes. "Don't look so stricken, Carinney, maybe it's all for the best. I can see it certainly will
be a good thing for you to get away from her. —What's
the trouble now, don't you want to marry me after all?"

"No, but"—she spoke into his chest, her anguished
words were partly muffled by his corduroy jacket—"now
you're *saddled* with me whether you want me or not.
The whole thing's ruined from the very beginning. Oh,
God, how I hate her for doing that!"

"Heavens, what's a couple of months?" Tim said easily over her head. "And, you know, I was never too
keen on all this cloak-and-dagger concealment—" He felt
her quiver and hurried on, "Just concentrate on our being together for good. I'll find rooms with some cosy old
landlady, and you can fry me eggs for breakfast and

see I get off to lectures in time. You'll like that won't you, mm?" She nodded piteously, a faint life beginning to move behind the frozen mask of her face. "And once we're married you need never see your mother again if you don't want to."

"That's true." A long, trembling sigh broke her immobility. She added with resolution, "And what's more, I never will. Oh, Tim—I'll make it up to you, I swear, for your having been forced into a shotgun wedding. I won't be a worry to you, or keep you from working."

"I know you won't, Carinney," he said quietly.

She leaned against him in defeat, knowing that she should have found the strength to set him free from this tangle, knowing that she never could. Presently she sighed again, turning her head to look for the last time through the green, grimed panes of their window, and said in a childlike, pondering voice, "How ever in the world did she think of coming up here? It's not like Mother to go for long walks by herself. I wonder what put it into her head. . . ."

They had a suffocating day for the wedding—which did not, after all, take place until June because Lady Trevis decided that Caroline and she could not be rigged out fittingly as bride and bride's mother in under a month.

It seemed as if all the damp heat of that miserable summer had gathered itself together into one steamy, torrid, twenty-four-hour space. Caroline, who had submitted to her mother's dictates over clothes and wedding arrangements in silent, uncaring passivity, was sullenly glad that the costume Lady Trevis had decided on as suitable for her was too hot; she accepted her discomfort as a deserved punishment from the gods.

They had a registrar's-office wedding in Bridpool; Lady Trevis's fierce, long-standing feud with the vicar had put the Woodmouth church out of the question, and Caroline was glad of that too; a penance must be severe for real atonement and surely this dusty, impersonal ceremony was penance enough to placate avenging Providence for the fact of her marrying Tim too soon, too young, and perhaps against his better judgment. She trembled superstitiously when the Registrar, a woman ("How very odd!" Lady Trevis had whispered, much too loud, "Can it be legal to be married by a woman? I shouldn't fancy it!") said to them, "How lucky you both are to know your minds so young. I'm envious of you two!" She meant it, too; Caroline crossed her fingers and hoped the Fates hadn't been listening.

Mrs. Conroy, Tim's mother, had of course been invited but sent a telegram of excuse; Tim's father had had another stroke the day before and she was spending every minute by his side in the nursing home. Tim's eyes, in general so quietly confident, had a look of strain, his skin, stretched too tight over his cheekbones, was grey with the pallor of exhaustion. But he held Caroline's hand close in his the whole time and that was a small comfort, a crumb of reassurance.

Since neither Caroline nor Tim had suggested inviting any of their own friends, all the guests were Lady Trevis's choice, a random selection from her theatrical past, and the wedding lunch, hectically gay, took place at the Nabob Hotel, Bridpool's biggest before the whole party went on to complimentary matinée seats at the Playhouse. Often, afterwards, Caroline wondered what play they had seen.

When it was all over and Lady Trevis, lachrymose and rather tipsy, had been put into the hired car, had leaned out of the window and cried for the last time, "Mind you take care of her now, Tim, remember she's my baby!" and the rest of the revellers had gone off somewhere else, Tim and Caroline stood exhaustedly in front of the hotel.

"What shall we do now?" Tim said in a flattened voice.

"What would you like to do?"

"I don't know—I promised Mother I'd ring the nursing home at six; it's only four now. I hate Bridpool on Saturday afternoons, don't you? It feels like a dead place."

"Let's go to the movies." Caroline surprised herself by the immediacy of her decision. She knew it was really only a postponement; what she dreaded was the arrival in Oxford, the need for integration with Tim's life there, the thought of his finals next week. An interlude in the cool, cushioned dark would stave it off a little longer.

"Good idea," Tim agreed relievedly, and they turned into the Metropole without even bothering to find out what was showing. Something about the Himalayas, Caroline thought; she half dozed against Tim's shoulder while the film ran its course, avalanches thundered and blizzards raged. At six they wandered out again, back towards the Nabob: "We seem to have spent the whole day on this bit of pavement," Caroline said. "We might as well build a log cabin and settle down here." "What you need is twelve hours of sleep." Tim turned for the first time to survey her concernedly. "You look like a ghost."

Caroline thought with a pang, "He isn't my lover any more. I'm a weight round his neck now, a responsibility to be worried about."

As he opened the door of the telephone box she stepped a pace or two away.

"Don't you want to come in?" he said. "There's room——" But she shook her head, certain that he would not want her distracting him just then.

She saw his face tighten as he listened; then he turned away from her; there was another brief interchange. When he came out and looked for her she moved forward.

"Oh there you are," he said unsmiling. "thought you'd wandered off."

"Is it—how does——?"

"He's sinking. I'll drive over to Reading right away. The problem is, what do we do with you?"

Trying to combat the feeling that she was being rapidly walled up in a cell of ice, Caroline said, "I'm coming with you."

"I don't think——"

"Oh, not to see him." One does not—unless gifted with consummate self-assurance—ask to meet one's reluctant father-in-law for the first time on his deathbed. "I'll just stay around somewhere—I suppose they have waiting-rooms—or sit in the car."

"I'd much rather you didn't," said Tim and plainly meant it. "Haven't you anywhere I could take you—any friend?" She shook her head. "This may be all night, you know—it won't help to think of you shivering on some damn bench."

From somewhere she found words.

"Look, darling, we've just promised to share everything, haven't we? What sort of a wife would I be if the very first time you have to face something like this I run away and hide under the blankets?"

"All right," he said briefly. "We won't waste time arguing. The car's still in the Nabob car-park—are you coming with me to get it?"

But when they were driving out along the A.4 he leaned over at a traffic light and gave her a quick kiss.

"I'm sorry this is being so bleak for you, darling. Not an ideal wedding night."

"Oh, Tim!" she burst out. "Why do you have to behave so well?" With an effort she kept herself from adding, "When you know his stroke is probably a direct consequence of our wedding."

"Well," Tim said with chilling matter-of-factness, "it wouldn't help if I cursed and wept, would it?"

They finished the drive in silence. In silence he parked beside the laurel-girt, red brick nursing home and ran up the steps. "I'll wait here for now," Caroline called, but he was already inside.

Searching for distraction—he had taken his keys, and all their luggage was locked in the boot—she found a technical magazine in the glove compartment and settled down to read. "Most of the high melting-point body-centred cubic metals such as iron, molybdenum, niobium, and tungsten show a sudden transition from ductile to brittle behaviour as the temperature is lowered . . . A material that is normally ductile at room temperature can become completely brittle after irradiation. . . ."

"You've got a letter from Caroline, dearie, isn't that

nice? I told you it would be a good thing to write to her for their first wedding anniversary. Now we *must* persuade her to come home for a visit; it's high time that silly old quarrel with your mother was tidied up. What does Caro have to say?"

Cousin Flora, who never let herself be impeded by any false delicacies, sat back and attentively watched every movement as Hilda spread marmalade on toast, drank some coffee, and finally opened her letter. Flora had the annoying habit of getting up and breakfasting before the rest of the household at Woodhoe; as she then remained to observe them eat and extract any interesting matter from their mail, the air of virtue she assumed for her early rising seemed hardly justified. She was in her early seventies, small, pixyish, with a head of snowy curls, an innocent pink-and-white complexion, unusually large feet, and serene, guileless eyes which gave no clue to the strong vein of practical sense beneath.

She had come to live at Woodhoe House three years before Caroline's marriage, on the death of an aunt whose dutiful companion she had been for many years. The income from the resulting legacy would have been sufficient for independence in a labour-saving flat, but Cousin Flora was symbiotic, sociable, and also had a horror of fire: "I prefer to be in a nice big house with plenty of doors and windows," she explained frequently, without adding that she also preferred the status of residence in a baronial mansion, however tumbledown. "And I'm accustomed to making meself useful; I like to think that besides paying my whack I can be a help to your dear mother in plenty of little ways." She made a confidante of Hilda, since Lady Trevis, while not despising nine extra guineas a week, generally received Flora's attentions with something less than grace. Hilda was a realist, and sometimes found it useful to avail herself of her elderly cousin's wish to please.

Now, concisely, "Caroline's had a baby," she said. "Born in March; punctual, isn't it. Nine months after the wedding, just about to the day. Ostentatious, I call it."

"A baby! Ohhh!" Cousin Flora gave vent to an extraordinary warbling coo. "How thrilled the Conroys must be."

"An heir for all those oil wells, you mean? An atonement for the trouble she caused them?"

"Now she *must* come home! How I'd love to see the dear little thing!"

"Well your wish isn't going to be gratified because she's taking it out to the Persian Gulf almost at once. Here, read for yourself." And Hilda tossed the sheet across the table.

At this point Lady Trevis tottered in, haggard and yawning. "What d'say—Caroline gone to Persia? Y'not serious?" she demanded, putting out a blind hand for the cup of coffee that Flora solicitously poured and passed her.

"Taking the baby too," said Hilda, laconic.

"Baby, what baby? First I heard of a baby."

"Dear Caro's had a little baby—isn't that wonderful news?"

"Three months old. A boy. You're a grandmother."

Lady Trevis received the news without joy. "Take a three-month baby out to Persia? The girl's mad. Mad. It'll get dysentery or enteric and die of *course*—they always do in the tropics. Anyway, what's she want to go to Persia for?"

"Tim, who seems to be a big shot in the firm since his father died, has to go and solve some crisis connected with oil wells." Hilda's tone was dry. "So Caroline, naturally, as a good wife, accompanies him."

"Stark, staring barmy! Why, Caroline doesn't even know how to look after a baby in England, let alone out there in some godforsaken spot. I shall write and tell her so at once. I don't want this muck, Flora—you know I always take it black." She pushed her coffee away with aversion, rose, and trailed out of the room, ignoring Flora's protest, "Oh, but cream's so *good* for you—"

"Save your breath," Hilda said. "And Ma might as well save hers; if she does write it'll be the surest way of making Caroline do the opposite thing. . . ."

"Fancy, though! They must think highly of Tim." Cousin Flora was eagerly reabsorbing every scrap of fact from Caroline's short note. "Caro's a dear girl, of course, but *rather* introverted and uncommunicative—and she's so young to be the wife of someone in a responsible position . . . I wonder what salary he draws. Oh dear me! It's useless to regret, I know, but it does seem a tiny bit of a waste that, as things turned out, Aunt Prue's legacy went to Caro and not to you—you *needed* it so much more. Specially as Caro simply invested it all in Tim's family business. I suppose she thought it was the least she could do, as her marrying Tim brought on the stroke that killed his father, but still—"

· She picked up the cup of cold coffee Lady Trevis had left and thriftily drank it, thus missing the look of almost uncontrollable dislike Hilda gave her.

"If you'd had the money you would have been able to start your little photography business," she mourned. "Doing portraits of people's dogs would have been so suitable and taken you out and about . . . What's become of that young man you thought of going into partnership with?"

"He got a job on a national daily and went up to London," Hilda said flatly, and looked at her watch. "Oh well—exercise the bloody dogs, I suppose." She stretched, staring out with boredom at the romantic view of rocky river and tree-hung valley beyond the window, then stood up, remarking acidly, "However you look at it, Caroline's marriage was a most unfortunate piece of mismanagement. If you hadn't found out she was meeting Tim and told Mother, he'd probably have gone abroad when his father died and forgotten all about her."

"Oh, but how were we to know your dear Mother would take it the way she did and make them get married?" Cousin Flora looked hurt; her mouth drooped like a baby's. "Naturally I thought—so young as dear Caro was—that Gloria would forbid them to meet. After all, she didn't know about Aunt Prue's little legacy to whichever of her nieces married first."

"No, but *you* knew. As you'd told Mother so much you might have told her that."

"But it was supposed to be kept a secret, dearie! Ohhh!" said Cousin Flora guilelessly. "Do you think if Gloria *had* known about it she might have behaved differently? You're her favourite, but she's always seemed equally keen on getting you *both* married off. D'you really think—*if* she'd known she might have felt that, as the elder, *you* should have first chance for the money? Was that what you meant? Oh dear me! I suppose a little bit of capital might just have made all the difference with that young photographer?"

Hilda returned her innocent gaze with one of deliberate indifference, and she went on comfortably, "But a young man who was put off by your losing a legacy wouldn't *really* have been a very good choice, dearie, would he now? I'm afraid he must have been a little bit of a fortune hunter perhaps—I believe you said you had mentioned to him that you had expectations? *What* a pity. I suppose it would have been better if I'd never told you about Aunt Prue's will, but we've always been such chums, haven't we? You were *my* favourite from the first. I'm afraid I'm no hypocrite, could never hide the feeling that Caro is rather selfishly *reserved*. Never mind, dearie, there's as good fish in the sea, they say; and you'll be getting the tiny nest egg that Aunt Prue left me, by and by; reward for a kind girl who stays at home to keep her poor old cousin cheerful." She gave Hilda's hand several quick little pats, and added reflectively, "Dear me, no, this house would *not* be such a pleasant haven for me if your mother and I were left alone together; I fear I might get on her nerves a tiny bit. I've always wondered, really, why she stayed here."

"Inertia," said Hilda. "The place belongs to her. And it's easier to stay than move. Who'd buy this old heap of mildew? Unless *you* would, Cousin Flora—you seem very fond of it," she added lightly.

"Gracious no, dearie, the responsibility would worry me to death! No, this arrangement suits me perfectly; we're very cosy together, aren't we, and I'm sure you

don't begrudge giving a few years of your young life to
a poor old woman in exchange for a little windfall later
on. I only wish my rheumaticks hadn't got so bad now
that I can't take the doggies out for you and help a little
more. Why, bless my soul," she added humorously,
"*look* at the time, and I haven't even started me jobs
yet!"

Hilda moved to the door without reply.

"As you go, would you mind telling Hudson," began
Flora, whose ill fortune it was constantly to have people
walk away before she had finished what she had to say.
But since Hilda left without apparently hearing, she fru-
gally ate up the last piece of toast before summoning
Hudson, who was aged, cross-grained, unkempt, but still
undeniably a butler.

When he hobbled in she said kindly, averting her eyes
from the unwashed yellowish white hair straggling over
his collar and the grease spots on his alpaca jacket,
"Oh, Hudson, you can clear away now. And will you
polish the silver today; it's badly tarnished."

Scorning to reply, Hudson sniffed, and began stacking
the breakfast things with maximum clatter. Cousin Flora
stood up in a leisurely manner to demonstrate that she
was not afraid of the sardonic gleam in his old eye,
bright as a toad's under its pouched lid.

"Such a lovely piece of news today, Hudson! Miss Caroline's had a little baby."

"Ho, she has, has she," he grunted. "Not lost much
time, neether; safe bind, safe find." Raising the butter-
dish lid he sourly surveyed what was underneath.

"And she's going out to Persia."

"Can't put too far 'tween her and home, eh?"

He scuffled a handful of cutlery together, adding, in a
disconcerting falsetto, *"The ship drove fast, loud roared
the blast, and southward aye we fled."*

Flora said feebly, "I suppose so"; she had never become used to Hudson's habit of quotation.

"Suppose so! You oughta know, you fixed it, didn't
you? You grassed. Proper old cuckoo in the nest. Ask
me, them rheumaticks of yourn was sent as a judgment."

"I can't imagine what you mean." She moved towards the door with dignity. "Don't forget about the silver now."

"Well, one thing's for certain," muttered Hudson. He swept some crumbs carefully off the table with his sleeve and ground them into the carpet. "Now she've got away she won't be coming back if she can help it. Not for a long, long time."

A long, long time . . .

Caroline had been dreaming—some interminable, uneasy dream about Woodhoe. Sometimes she felt she would never entirely escape it. Even after the birth of her child, married life, four years away from home, the dark house and clambering woodlands still had power to grip her sleeping mind; a defensive mechanism generally helped her to forget the details before she came to full consciousness, but at least twice a week she recognised the after-symptoms on waking: a dark oppressive cloud of tension and distress, slow to disperse until she had talked to Tim, gone into the nursery, checked over the components of her small household. It was as if she still feared to believe in her present freedom and happiness —which, nevertheless, seemed to gain value from the contrast. Each day after a dream of home came as a brighter, more precious gift.

Yet, they had worked for their happiness too, she and Tim; carefully, breathlessly weaving the fabric of their marriage, strand by strand, from those first desperate weeks when so many things seemed bound to destroy them: his father's death and the ensuing trouble in the firm which, coming just before his finals, had spoilt his chances of a good firstclass degree. He had told her that didn't matter. Work in the firm was what counted now, he said, and he *had* worked, while she had helped him in every way she knew how. And he was grateful to her; they had been cautious, tender, and forebearing with one another like two convalescents recovering from a serious illness.

Blessed Tim, she half murmured, turning to seek his

hand; I don't deserve you, but oh, I'm grateful for you; no words will ever really express my gratitude.

He was not there; he must have got up already. She tried to shake off the clinging fragments of her dream. What time was it? Surely it must be very late? Panic! The silence seemed unfamiliar. No whine and creak from the faulty fan, no small voice humming wordless, tuneless songs in the next room, no slam of drawers as Tim dressed. She must have overslept, and what about breakfast? Then she relaxed, remembering with relief. It must be Sunday, Ahmed Abdullah's day off. Sunday, of course. Old Miller the timekeeper would be coming along presently for the ritual Sunday walk. And meantime, Men's breakfast. The two of them, her family, with much important, whispered confabulation, would be in the bungalow kitchen, putting orange juice and toast on a tray, would presently appear in the doorway and go through the accustomed dialogue as she pretended to stir sleepily and wake.

"Well, this is a very handsome breakfast that you and I have put together, mate, but for the life of me I can't remember who we made it for. Was it for me?"

"Had yours, Daddy!"

"Was it for you, then, I wonder? Rigged up so grand in your red-and-green shirt?"

"*Course* it wasn't!"

"For Dingopuss?"

"No!" Bursting with laughter.

"For Ahmed Abdullah?"

"No!"

"For old Mr. Miller, perhaps, before he takes you for your Sunday walk?"

"No!"

"Then I give up—can't think *who* it was for."

"*It's for Mummy!*"

And the two of them sitting on her bed while she ate it.

Sunday. And—now she remembered—a special Sunday. Old Mr. Miller was coming an hour early because of the Birthday. He had had his own plans for celebration.

"You will let me take him down to the rig, won't you, mum? I'll see he don't get too near or come to harm. I'll be ever so careful."

"Well—" she had been doubtful. "Don't you think he's a bit young, Mr. Miller? Just three? It won't mean very much to him, surely? Of course I know you'd be careful—"

"He knows all about it, mum, he's as bright as a button, he wants to see, don't you matey? And it's a grand, gradely sight, as not many little lads has seen. Make a wonderful birthday treat. It'd be something to remember all his life."

All his life.

They must have gone off already. Better get up and begin making the birthday lunch; they'd be hungry when they got back. But why wasn't the fan working? For some reason this tiny departure from the usual pattern troubled her profoundly. Full of apprehension she started to push herself up into a sitting position.

And found she could not move.

"Just take it easy," a voice said. "Relax. No sense in struggling."

I've been kidnapped!

Her eyes flew open. Someone in white walked across the room—Arabs?—a ransom note?—Tim—a bag of fingers sent to the British Consul at Aden—

Oh God, I'll never see either of them again.

"Like a cup of tea?" the voice said. That was no Arab. She felt the rim of a cup against her mouth; she gulped, without meaning to, quite a lot of the warm, sweet stuff. A large pink face swam into her vision, swam away again.

Where are my arms? Why can't I use them?

"Don't thrash about, dear," the voice said mildly. "Just lie back comfortable."

"My arms!"

"They're all right now, just about better."

An isolated flash of memory came to her—from a time that had never been, it seemed. Bandages all over her arms and hands, Tim sitting by her bed, white as death.

Somehow I burned my hands badly? How can I have done that?

"Am I in hospital?"

"Sure," the voice said. "Beginning to remember now? Took long enough."

"Where am I?"

"In pack, dear."

The word was meaningless. "No, I mean, what hospital?"

"The Beaumont."

Beaumont?

But, she thought, that's not in Aden? What do I know about the Beaumont Hospital?

The words had a faintly familiar, faintly frightening ring. From childhood. Somebody went there—no, people didn't just *go* to the Beaumont, they were *committed*—mysterious, frightening term—Millie, the housemaid who began having delusions, had been sent there. But that had been in England, five years, thousands of miles away.

"Funny," she said nervously, "there used to be a Beaumont Hospital in Bridpool, not far from where I lived."

"That's it. On the ball today, aren't we? Matron will be ever so pleased. Takes a real interest in you, she does. Says you went to the same school as her."

Nothing made any sense. I must be dreaming. But this is a worse dream than any about Woodhoe. I hope I wake up soon.

"Time to take the temperature now," the voice said.

She opened her mouth automatically, but the thermometer never came near. Instead she followed its course downward, saw, with mystification, a cocoon of whitish-grey swathings where her body ought to be. Bandages all over? What has happened to me? *What sort of hospital is this?*

"One degree under," said the voice, and laughed inexplicably.

A vast roaring filled her ears. Warm water flooded down from all sides. It's the river. It must be. The Tare, coming down in spate, pouring into the Tebburn; mother

always said one day the house would be washed away
. . . What a joke on Cousin Flora, flood not fire. Help,
help, somebody! For god's sake, get me out of here!

Tim, where are you? Tim, I'm drowning!

She went down, gasping, into the dark.

One

Thursday, August 19.

Bridpool, in its saucer of wooded hills, lies sweltering under a warm grey sky. Dust and grit underfoot. From the dockside a ship lets out an impatient blast, as if maddened by flies. Happy ship—a week's sailing would take it to the Persian Gulf. Oil and tar sweat in the heat, the docks are black with the grime of centuries, where cargoes of spices, tobacco, sack, and malmesy were once unloaded for merchant adventurers under the Tudors.

But among the spacious houses on the encircling hills, away from the smell of commerce, all is clean and green enough. Here, as the merchants prospered, they built their mansions. Here, now, nicely balanced midway between professional and residential, is the area known to estate agents as Pill Acre. Nursing homes, convalescent homes, clinics, hospitals in their trimly kept grounds. The Astor, the Clifton, the Beaumont. Glossy black railings, beautifully whitened doorsteps, satin-bright brass plates with lists of doctors (something almost absurd in the length of these lists: Doctors Kimbolton, Trenchard, Forticue, Howard, Galbraith, Forrestier, Tudor-Rhys—which will you have, take your pick?). Each house is full of doctors, bristling with doctors. Rollses, Bentleys, and Daimlers, many chauffeur-driven, glide in and deposit their freight of well-dressed over-anxiety and neurosis, glide away again to smoke a cigarette and read the Bridpool

Evening Chronicle at the nearest vacant parking meter till the end of the fifteen-guinea session. Panelled front doors softly open and shut receiving and discharging cargoes of tense, prosperous figures who have come to the town for its mineral springs and reputedly salubrious air. Hundreds of patients, ill in body or mind, are seated trembling in those spruce houses, waiting in hope and terror. Faint but recognisable behind the neat façades, in the soft summer air, is the scent of fear.

Fear.

Climb the stairs (thick carpet in a cheerful shade of blue) sit in the waiting room. Armchairs, fresh flowers, gas fire, *Vogue, Tatler, Queen,* and *Country Life.* All so calmly English. Nothing to remind one of that other life.

An unfurnished consulting room in this district can be rented (Cousin Flora, who knows a myriad of useless facts, once told you) for £300, including use of waiting room and receptionist. Say thirty patients a day, at an average of ten guineas each, what will you pay in super-tax?

Caroline's mind flinched from the sum, but it returned maddeningly to tease her. You can't work it out, can you? Fool, fool, can't do her arithmetic, doesn't know her tables. Secretive, obstinate, sulky, young for her age. How any child of mine could grow up so abysmally ignorant . . .

The door opens—no matter how gently, you jump as if you had been shot. The white-coated receptionist gives you her calm, professional smile.

"Dr. Galbraith will see you now, Mrs. Conroy."

Familiar routine by now.

In a dressing room at the Bridpool Philharmonic Hall, Hari Lupac talked to his friend and manager, Dominic Tree. Or rather, Dominic talked and Hari leaned back in his chair, eyes half closed, completely relaxed, with his irritating air of not quite bothering to listen. In fact this was merely a pose as Dominic well knew; Lupac was very sharply aware of all that went on around him.

"Oh, by the way, Harry, young Gerald Brodie from

the *Chronicle* wants to talk to you about an article with pictures for their color supplement," Dominic was saying.

"When? I can't see anybody just now, you know quite well."

"No, no," Tree said pacifically. "After the recital, I told him. Just a couple of minutes to fix up times and places. This will be an excellent thing. We need to do some image-building."

Dominic was one of those pale, cold, intelligent young men, entrepreneurs by birth, who, reaching their early thirties, settle there permanently and never grow any older. His eyes, opaque as grapes, seemed to observe nothing, actually observed everything. He had a slightly fanatical look, like Henry V, but was in fact earthily shrewd; although their acquaintance had been fairly brief he had already acquired a strong respect for Lupac as a marketable commodity.

He added, "Brodie's very harmless and juvenile; he'll be overawed at meeting you."

"Oh, very well."

"There was a message from Fernanda Chumley. An invitation to her father's cocktail party at the week end."

"In London? Or here?"

"Here. At the Nabob. And stay on for dinner afterwards."

Harry said, frowning a little, "I do not much want to go to this party."

"It would be sensible not to offend them, Harry. Among conductors, Sir Horace is exceptionally rich and influential—he created the Bridpool Philharmonic Orchestra from scratch, you know."

"I do not need to lick the boots of rich, influential conductors. Let them lick my boots if they want to! And if I did need to, still I should never do such a thing."

"All right, all right, relax! There's a difference between boot-licking and common civility. And Fernanda's a pretty girl—I daresay she'd marry you like a shot if you asked her. Why don't you take her out?"

"Why, Dominic—you schemer!" Harry smiled slowly. "What am I supposed to do—go to bed with her?"

"Certainly not—if you don't want to."

"I do not at all want to," Harry said with sudden brisk-ness, his faint accent becoming more apparent. "Fer-nanda bores me. I should be bored before I even began. She is insipid."

"Too pretty?" Tree suggested drily. "She might put you in the shade; you wouldn't like that."

Harry laughed, though with a shade of annoyance. "Rubbish! Pretty? You see a dozen girls like her in any English street—thin, dark, inhibited. I have always dis-liked thin, dark girls."

Dr. Galbraith is thin, dark, nervy-looking, rather cross; hardly a good advertisement for himself? But this is because he is so successful, has to see so many patients. He has an arm in a sling; broken playing polo. It makes him less godlike—why should a psychiatrist feel the need to indulge in such a snobbish diversion as polo? Or is that how he meets his titled patients? "When we've fin-ished this chukka, old man, I'd be awfully glad if you'd give me a bit of advice about m'daughter, Her-mione, y'know, the younger one. Been a bit queer since she came that purler when she was out with the Quorn. . . ." "Why, of course, Lord Orville, I'd be de-lighted to have a chat with her."

Dr. Galbraith says, "Well, Mrs. Conroy, how are we today?"

He looks as if he were thinking, "My dear young wom-an, if you can afford to pay *my* fees you must be so rich that you need not have a care in the world; I feel no sympathy for you whatsoever. The price of that ring alone (but it is too loose now, it keeps sliding from her finger) would keep a family in Stepney for a year."

What you don't realise, Dr. Galbraith, is that Tim's family are paying your fees, an obligation so heavy, after the harm I've done them, that I feel I must economise frantically elsewhere, walk rather than bus or taxi, buy no clothes, cut my own hair . . . Don't you know, Dr. Galbraith, that Tim won't accept a penny more than a junior executive's salary, although it's the family firm?

That's their tradition. Don't you know how scrupulously, how desperately I tried to budget during the four years of our married life? You should know, heaven knows enough details have been laid before you, everything I can remember.

But it's the things I *can't* remember that frighten me. The time after the birthday. I still don't know how long it was. And this feeling I have now . . .

Dr. Galbraith, can't you tell me if it is true, as I believe, that someone, out of the people around me, hates me so much that he is working all the time to prevent my recovery? Can't you tell me who it is?

"I'm all right, I suppose," she said shortly.

"That's good." He chose to answer the words, not the tone; he went on in smooth transition, "I'm glad to hear that, because I've decided that this shall be our last consultation for the present; I think I have now done for you all that can be done from outside. You've had your breakdown and recovered from it, and come out of hospital. Now it's up to you to carry on by yourself."

"Last? You mean I'm not to come to you any more?"

She trembled on the edge of an abyss; his expression, like a spear point, kept her from falling forward into it. What has happened to you, he seemed coldly to be asking, that has not happened to scores of other women, yes, in equally dreadful circumstances, if not worse; why should you, with your quite limited experience of suffering, waste any more of my time?

But wait, please wait! Caroline wanted to cry in panic. I'm not ready to stand on my own yet! How can I go on by myself if I am still not clear what happened out there at Ras al-Abdan? Or what has been happening since?

The thought of Woodhoe House without the weekly escape to Bridpool was a terror in itself. You don't know my circumstances at all, she felt like saying, you've no means of knowing them unless you come to that airless dark cleft in the wooded north coast, unless you see the ruined bulk of Woodhoe House for yourself, the rutted, breakneck drive, the way the trees hang crowded together up the valley sides, over the rocky stream. I'd sooner be in Brixton jail. And that's no lie.

"So we'd better make this a clearing-up session," he said briskly. "Ask me anything you want to now."

"It's not being able to remember what happened—"

"That will come back in time as I've told you repeatedly. You can't hurry it."

"Shan't I be able to see you again?"

It is humiliating to have such dependence on this knife-like man; can he, perhaps, be right? Will it be better for me to step off by myself into the void?

"Of course you can make an appointment to come and see me if you're specially worried or upset about something." His voice was impatient. Just you dare try it, that's all, the black waspish eyes seemed to warn, I have enough bona fide cases without pandering to idle, wealthy hypochondriacs. You ought to be earning your living, my girl.

But, Dr. Galbraith, I'm almost sure someone doesn't want me to do that. And what I want to know is, why?

Caroline took a deep breath.

"Well then," she said, "I'd like, just for once, to try and make you see the whole background . . ."

He pursed his small, tight mouth. "I should have thought we'd already been over all that fairly thoroughly. However, go ahead, you've got"—he looked at his watch —"forty minutes. . . ."

"I should never marry a dark girl," said Harry. "If I ever did marry—which I do not think is at all likely, I greatly prefer my freedom—it would be somebody really striking and decorative, who would be a good foil to me."

He smiled, thinking of Hilda; she would never be a rival, her features were too irregular, her attraction lay in gaiety and brilliant make-up, which was what he enjoyed; he would have said that he preferred art to nature. But just the same, he had no intention of marrying her.

"Nevertheless, I think you ought to be civil to the Chumleys."

"Why?" said Lupac coldly.

"This smear campaign in the Soviet press is bound to do you some harm. You need all the friends you can get."

Harry began to laugh. "On the contrary, my dear friend, the smear campaign is to my credit! Naturally they are annoyed, over there, that I choose intellectual freedom with the capitalist hyenas—what do I care for their spite? They can say I have committed adultery with my grandmother in Vienna, tortured a bank manager in Budapest, and killed half a dozen children in Prague. I do not worry! It is all sour grapes. The English will take no notice. I have not decapitated any dogs."

"I suppose it will die down," conceded Dominic. "But still I think you ought to be polite to the Chumleys. It wouldn't kill you to take out Fernanda a few times; you might even find she improved on acquaintance."

"My dear Dominic, you sound as if she were a product in which you had shares. Very well, I go to this party, but beyond that I make no promises."

"You seem very confident of your success in this country."

"You may be sure I am," said Harry, laughing. "Their slanders over there will not last. Supposing I were to publish my side of the case. Escape? I could say that this so-called escape across the Iron Curtain was a carefully planned long-term manoeuvre to plant an agent where he would be least suspected. But what happens? So soon as he is over the fence that naughty agent turns and thumbs his nose at them."

"Is that the truth, Harry?"

"I will not answer you yes or no," Harry said coolly. "It is better if you are left in doubt."

"But they always keep hostages in such a case."

"Hostages? My young sisters, two boring little girls that I am glad to see the back of. Ever since our parents died, they are round my neck like milestones. I must be responsible for their food, their clothes, their education. And now, freedom!"

He stopped, glanced carelessly at Tree, and added, "That is, supposing I do not invent the whole story."

Tree's expression was half horrified, half unwilling respect. "You are a callous devil, Harry; sometimes it surprises me that you are such a fine musician."

"You think morals are to do with music? That is an English attitude. Besides I am not a *musician;* I am music itself."

"It must have been a Marxist attitude too; they can't have expected you to act as you did or they would have used safeguards of a different kind."

"That is the secret of success," Harry said smiling, "always to have one less principle than your adversary. And now that they know, over there, what I am really like—now they realise I do not care *that* for those tedious girls—very likely they will not bother with reprisals. What would be the use? If it is not already too late," he added calmly.

When you have to condense the story of your life into forty minutes, where do you begin? With the moment when the bankrupt baronet staggered weeping away through an autumn downpour, crying, "Ah, you bitch, you mercenary bitch, Gloria, curse your selfish middle-class soul, and may you rot in a smug little suburban hell that's specially tailor-made for you with doilies and toilets and serviettes!" After which he reeled off between the puddles and pot-holes of the drive, disappeared into the dark, and was not heard of again until his death, three weeks later, in the arms of the widow who ran the Sun Inn at Bere Stickleigh, five miles away.

How can I describe the awful oppressiveness of that house, so utterly lacking in any characteristic of home? Beautiful scenery, oh yes, if you like precipitous gorges and a river hurling down at breakneck speed, falling a thousand feet in four miles of steeply tilted woodland. I can see that I too might have loved it in different circumstances. But why did he ever bring mother there? Why did she ever come? You'd think one sight of the house, built by some mad Victorian forebear, dark and damp on its plateau of rock between the Tare and the Tebburn, would have been enough to send her flying back to the bright lights of Bridpool and her nice safe job as bit part actress at the Playhouse. But no, the notion of being a baronet's wife must have seduced her until it was just too late, till the honeymoon was over and there she was, trapped by a title and a family mansion, and just enough to live on, and the never-ending sound of falling water.

"Oh, this perpetual bloody roaring," she used to cry, her hands over her ears. "I'll never get used to it, never. It makes me want to scream!"

I remember Father quoting that bit of Wordsworth about beauty born of murmuring sound and her bursting into derisive laughter. But a lot of my childhood he was away in Africa or somewhere, trying to retrieve our fallen fortunes with groundnuts. Then, when he did come home, he was mostly drunk, or shambling-hungover and railing at our accents.

"For God's sake, Gloria, you were on the stage, can't you teach them to pronounce their O's? I deeont kneeow," he mimicked savagely. "Gar-ahge, child, not garridge. Who the hell will ever care to know you if you talk like that?"

He was a tall, ruined-looking man with tearful blue eyes and the remains of fair hair, and broken blood-vessels in his nose; he had been handsome once, there was an angelic, romantic portrait of him in wartime Air Force uniform. That was when he met Mother "on the catch," he used to shout at her, in the W.A.A.F. At the time he may have seemed a good bet, I suppose, gay, and with a little money, and specially when his elder brother was killed and he came into the house and the title. But Gloria must soon have realised that she'd put her money on an also-ran. Where *she* came from before the Bridpool Rep. remains an impenetrable mystery; occasionally she'd say that her family were artistes; of the music-hall stage, Father would suggest when drunk and acrimonious. The friends who began to turn up occasionally after he died are always careful not to allude to the past. But they are strident and raddled and gay.

Funds and tempers running short, she pushed him abroad to the groundnuts; then he failed and came back again. No money now to send us to what Father considered "decent" schools, so Dee went to his cousins the Carrewes and had the benefit of their girls' governess. It was bloody, she told me once, in a rare moment of sisterly confidence: poor-relation treatment from the start, Mansfield Park wasn't in it. From the Carrewes she learned and passed onto me the fact that Father was known as the Bankrupt Baronet.

We never had much to do with one another, Dee and I; she was five years older, and we were so different. And Father, when at home, favoured me because he preferred my looks. "My beautiful daughter," he used to call me when he was hazy and swaying with drink, it made me squirm, "she'd better get rid of her common accent somehow and marry a rich man, it's the only hope for this family." Dee didn't like that; you couldn't blame her. It was a pity she was slightly lame, not real lameness but one leg a little shorter so her walk was uneven; Father said there wasn't any money to have it put right.

He never had any dealings with the local people; at first he was away, and then too drink-sodden. Grandfather Trevis had given garden parties and endowed the village school with challenge cups, sat on boards and committees; he was a JP and read the lessons in church. Or so Hudson used to tell me. Father didn't do any of those things and Gloria couldn't care less.

"What, me?" she'd scream satirically. "Be president of the Women's Institute? Go and sit in a chilly shed that stinks of paraffin learning about crochet and missionary work in Tonga and having to fork out double everyone else's subscription? No, thank you *very* much, I'm no Lady Bountiful. You don't catch me trailing round with jelly and benevolent soup to the grateful parishioners."

So we weren't liked in Woodmouth village. And it's a lonely part, the coast all cliff and nothing but moors inland for twenty miles; it isn't surprising we had no friends.

Yes, all right, Dr. Galbraith, can't you see, I'm just trying to explain? It may seem ordinary enough to you. But if I don't go into detail, how can I convey to you the terror of that world, the darkness and friendlessness, the utter lack of help or comfort?

I hoped I'd left it for ever.

And, don't you see, the terror is *still there?* Still there now I'm back. Things happen that I can't explain.

I was about eleven when Father came back from some timber venture in British Columbia, trembling, bloodshot, more ready than ever to snarl at the food, the faded covers on the furniture, the peeling paint, and our general subtopian accents; he discovered that my knowledge of arithmetic was about equal to that of a child of five.

"It's degrading to have a child in such a state of abysmal ignorance. Is she stupid, Gloria? Or what?"

"It's no use," Mother said, flicking cigarette ash on to the carpet. "She's hopeless at sums, that's all. She's too like you, Godfrey, that's the fact of the matter."

Mother had never made any secret of her preference for Dee.

So for a fearful period Father tried to teach me arithmetic. By the end of the sessions he'd be hoarse and sweating, with suffused eyes and bulging veins, an empty brandy glass on the floor beside him, while I was limp, speechless, exhausted with terror, my mind completely numb.

"Merciful heavens, Carey, eight times eight. *Eight times eight!*"

I could only stare at him, speechless, blank.

"I give up," he declared then. "The child's subnormal. I wash my hands of her."

Not long after this, I suppose, Mother finally lost patience and kicked him out. He came back and she kicked him out again and three weeks later he was dead. Mother had been breeding dogs a bit, and now she started doing it professionally. From the life insurance (it turned out that, with her canny streak of self-preservation, she had made him over-insure his life to a ruinous and crippling extent) there was enough to send me to boarding-school; Mother was delighted to rid the house of children. She sent me to a good school so that, she said, I could make useful friends. But I didn't. It was too late for Dee; she had already been sent to help a titled family with their horses and dogs because, of course, Father's daughters couldn't work at office jobs.

Only one good thing happened to me in my childhood. I met Tim. If I hadn't—

Forty minutes *can't* be gone already.

But, Dr. Galbraith, I was just getting to the important part. To my marriage.

Yes, I see. Yes of course.

Thank you.

Yes, I will. Yes I expect you are right. Goodbye, and thank you again.

Goodbye.

And so, off into the abyss.

In the little outer room she has just presence of mind to summon the shy, friendly politeness (learned, ah, how gratefully from Tim who by example has managed to break down some of her terrified reserve with strangers) and say to the secretary, "I may as well settle up my last account now, mayn't I? It will save you sending it to me?"

She fumbles in her bag for cheque-book, pen. Her ring slides off again and she tucks it into the pocket. There is a bad moment signing a cheque: after the horrifying total has been announced she pauses, her fingers tense on the ballpoint. Name? What name? What is your NAME? Think! Try not to remember Hilda, scornful, impatient, snatching a grocer's cheque away from you— "For God's sake, look what you've written! Well, that's twopence wasted," as she tore it up. "If I could write cheques for thousands, I'd take a bit more care, I can tell you."

What is your name?

The secretary looks at her inquiringly.

"Just trying to remember the date," she excuses herself and has it pointed out on a calendar two inches away from the cheque-book. And an appointment book open, thank heavens, showing *Mrs. Caroline Conroy, 11:45.*

With inexpressible relief she signs Caroline Conroy and is away down the plushy blue stairs, out into the sunshine of Cabot Street. Unseeing, she walks past the Doric porticos of Rollses, her mind a wash of turbulent memory now, tossing frustrated against Dr. Galbraith's closed sluice gates.

Down the sunlit length of Cabot Street and into Bridpool's main square, where Georgian architecture gives way to nineteenth century Gothic, opulent on the profits from cotton and chocolate. The Playhouse, the Philharmonic Hall, the Nabob Hotel and, a later addition, the Metropole cinema. She moves on hastily, looking at her watch in self-defense against a stab of memory. Two o'clock, too early by a couple of hours for the appointment with Miss Hume. What about an afternoon concert: TODAY, proclaims the blue sticker across a poster of a violin recital: a blurred, much-blown-up photograph of a man with fair hair and eyes reduced to black pinpoints by the coarse print; the sticker obscures his name.

Inside, buying a ticket, she sees the same poster, this time without sticker. Hari Lupac, of course, the violinist who escaped. Hilda was watching him on television the other night; odd, for Hilda, who takes no interest at all in music, but she said she was waiting for the news. An uncommon face, so mobile, with those cold, detached eyes and the strikingly blond hair; he certainly looks like a musician.

An usher beckons her impatiently; obedient, Caroline goes forward down the hall and slips into a seat on Row Two.

Harry glanced at his watch, stood, stretched, and picked up a violin.

"I had better go in. God, I hate these afternoon recitals; it is a murderous time of day to play to an audi-

ence." He moved towards the door, whistling the allegro
movement from Brandenburg No. 4 with great precision, stopped just in time, and walked out onto the platform. The rather sparse audience clapped in a reveren-
tial, subdued manner.

Harry gave them an unsmiling survey, waiting for a
couple of late-comers to scurry to their seats. He was not
interested in audiences and this one was in no way remarkable: the usual matrons in for shopping and lunch
at the Nabob, taking the opportunity for a little culture
and to get off their feet for an hour; the Bridpool University students, earnest long-haired boys and girls. Thin,
dark English girls. His eye flitted past them indifferently,
passing over a girl in a grey shirt in Row Two. He began to play, forgetting audience, Dominic, the Chumleys,
his dark little sisters (already almost out of mind in that
faraway homeland) and the forthcoming interview with
the Bridpool *Chronicle*.

First and foremost, Harry was a musician.

The music was no comfort to Caroline: a Bach partita
in E major. Like black coffee, it pricked, it prodded, it
stimulated; instead of slipping into a comfortable haze
her mind began to range feverishly back over the past six
months. So much there was that she could not remember
at all—the time of merciful unconsciousness when,
drugged, bandaged, inert, she had been flown home to
England for skin grafting. Then came a period of slow
recovery during which visitors were allowed and, with
the gradual return of strength, anguish began to grow
and grow, quickened by external circumstances—the
friend who hadn't been briefed and who asked, "You've
got a little boy, haven't you? Where is he—with your
mother?"; Tim's letters, brief, sapless, conveying nothing of what was in his mind; and then the culmination,
the first day she had been allowed up for two hours in
an armchair; Sister Griffin's entrance, all smiles: "Well
now, *here's* a visitor who'll do you good, my dear!"

Lady Trevis's eyes darting appraisingly round the
room. "Good God in heaven! What this place must

cost! Still, I suppose the Conroys can afford it." Next, studying her daughter, "I must say, *you* don't look up to much. Well, Caroline, of course I'm sorry it happened, but I can't say I'm surprised. I did warn you, didn't I?"

That was the last memory Caroline took with her into a world of darkness and confusion, of terror and despair, from which, irritably urged on by Dr. Galbraith, she at last made her hesitant return into the light of day.

And so, back home to Woodhoe House.

"This is Gerald Brodie from the *Chronicle*," Dominic Tree said.

Harry nodded; he was rubbing his forehead and neck with a towel; his eyes still held the glazed, absent expression that came into them when he played.

Young Brodie was like a large Labrador puppy, all wagging tail, big feet, and enthusiasm.

"Mr. Lupac, may I say what tremendous personal pleasure your music has given me!" he began at once. "Even though, of course, one has heard you on the radio and on records, one has no conception of the power, the immense authority—"

Harry nodded again, bored. "Can we give the gentleman a drink?" he said to Dominic. "Can you drink vodka?"

"Won't you both come out somewhere and be my guests?"

Harry glanced at his watch. "Kind of you but I have a date in twenty minutes. Another time. Now, what did you want to know?"

"Everything, really!" Brodie said, a little quenched but still volatile. "Naturally the public is dying for some background, and we want a profile of you to use during the Bridpool Summer Festival. You know, you're almost a legendary figure—this escape to the West is still news. We'd like pictures of you in your home, and perhaps in some well-known spot, Stonehenge or somewhere like that, pictures of you engaged in your favourite hobbies and pursuits . . ."

"They want to build up an image," Dominic said, giving Harry an admonishing glance past the vodka bottle.

"Don't you think the articles in the Soviet press have created sufficient image?" Harry smiled, not very pleasantly. He carefully inserted his violin into its case.

"Oh, good heavens, we take no notice of those! No, what I want is the intimate, domestic side of you, at ease, off duty. Do you play any games?"

Harry's face, turned away, was twisted into such a cynically mocking grimace that it was perhaps as well young Mr. Brodie could not see it.

"I do not occupy myself with sports, no. I have too much respect for my hands. And I have no home."

Dominic began a protest, but then checked himself.

"No home?" Mr. Brodie looked disconsolate.

"I live in digs—out of a suitcase. I am always moving," Harry said coldly. "I do not like ties—even the ties of place. However I am often in my friend Dominic's apartment—I make curry in his kitchen. I daresay he will not object to your photographer taking pictures of me there, will you, Dominic?"

"No—no, of course not," Tree agreed, and gave Brodie the address.

"Then have you no hobbies at all?" Brodie asked, baffled.

"I play chess—when I can find a worthy opponent. I walk in woods."

"Which woods?" Brodie pounced.

"The forest of Clun," Harry replied without the slightest hesitation. "I often go there—do I not, Dominic?—when I want to get away from crowds. I hate to be followered and pestered—this has no reference to you, Mr. Brodie, of course."

"It would be fine if we could get a few pictures of you in the forest of Clun. Where do you stay when you are down there?"

"Oh—sometimes at one place, sometimes at another. I may rent a cottage."

"Shots of you in a cottage, now—"

"Oh—kay," Harry said indifferently. "Dominic will fix it, will you not, Dominic? Find a nice picturesque cottage. After my Philharmonic Hall concert, for the festival opening."

"Not before?" Brodie said, disappointed. "We'd hoped for a piece to tie up with that."

"I am sorry."

Brodie looked so downcast at this rebuff that Tree gave Harry another warning glance. With a sudden complete change of manner Harry began talking in a friendly, almost caressing way to the young man, made a number of jokes, told some nonsensical stories about his childhood, and spoke ardently of the artist's need for political freedom "which you are most happy to have in your country," he congratulated Brodie, who was quite charmed with this unexpected warmth and began to think Lupac an extremely sympathetic character. When Harry said, "My Bach is worse than my bite," he laughed so loud that he might have been hearing the joke for the first time. Tree, examining his fingernails, breathed a faint breath of relief.

"My friend Dominic will tell you what a recluse I am," Harry said to the gratified Mr. Brodie. "Why, I am so scared of being recognised and spoken to by strangers that I have twenty different hats, I wear dark glasses, I change my car every three or four months, I have even thought of a false beard or wig. Cloak and dagger stuff, you know!"

He gave Brodie a conspiratorial glance.

"I've heard people wonder whether your hair could be a wig," Brodie said tentatively.

"Oh, indeed? That is very funny. Is it not, Dominic?"

"How long have you been in this country?" Brodie asked, seeing he would get nothing from this cast.

"I feel as if I have been here for ever—as if I have come home," Harry said expansively. Pressed, he admitted that it might have been six months, maybe seven or eight. And, yes, some time he hoped to do a world tour, who knew when?

"Before you came here you were in France—for long?"

"For a short time only."

"Why did you not stay there—what made you decide to come here?"

Harry spread his hands. "Many things. But chiefly—there is no privacy in France. One is always in the public eye. Here, nobody knows anybody else; an Englishman may let years go by without speaking to his neighbour, even without recognising him. This I like. It is restful. In France I have some good friends, but the French as a race are too sociable."

"You knew Fresca Garroux, didn't you?"

For a moment Harry looked extremely startled.

"Who told you that?"

"Oddly enough, my grandmother," the ingenuous Mr. Brodie confessed. "Granny was once an opera singer, a friend of Madame Garroux. They used to correspond."

"Yes, I knew Fresca—a little," Harry admitted. "A wonderful personality—and a superb voice. The world has few such."

"She is a great loss," Mr. Brodie ventured.

"It was inevitable, however. When such an artist knows her powers are beginning to fail, better to go fast than to linger too long and become a laughingstock."

"She must have been a long way from that, surely?"

"She could not tolerate anything less than perfection. She took the quick way."

"It really was suicide then, not accident?"

"Oh, undoubtedly." Harry said, raising his eyebrows. "I was not in touch with her at that time, alas, but I should have thought that generally accepted."

"She was a very rich woman, wasn't she, Fresca Garroux? I wonder, did she leave—"

Harry glanced at his watch and said smoothly, "Now, my dear fellow, I am really afraid I must be on my way, but do not hesitate to ask me or Dominic if there is anything else you want to know. I am so *pleased* to have met you."

"Why did you lie to him?" Tree inquired with interest when the door had shut behind the young man.

"Lie?"

"About your flat—saying you lived out of a suitcase.

And all that stuff about the forest of Clun. You've never been there, have you?"

"No, but I shall go there now," Harry replied with perfect calm. "There *is* a forest, I suppose? You must find a suitable cottage for me, Dominic, with roses round the door."

"Oh, very well, but why? What's wrong with your flat —and the places you really frequent?"

"Just that I do not choose to have them thrown open to the public," Harry replied with sudden violence. "Why should all the readers of the Bridpool *Chronicle* have a view of my bedroom? Or the woods where I prefer to walk? It was the truth I spoke—I came to this country because I like to be private—I have had enough of communal living. You do not mind, do you, that I use your kitchen as a background for me frying the egg?"

"I suppose not. It just seems unnecessarily devious."

"Aha, my dear Dominic, you good, straightforward citizen! Never mind, you are my virtuous mentor, in time you will win me from my devious ways." Harry tucked his arm through that of Dominic and walked with him to the door of the hall. He thought with pleasure of Hilda, gay and decorative: she would be smoking a cigarette and doing the crossword while she waited for him in the upstairs bar of the Minerva Club.

The afternoon's recital audience, and the dark girl from the second row, had long since melted away.

A tiny square in the heart of the old town houses the Bridpool University Lady Graduates' Club in a beautifully proportioned but rather dark house built by John Dawes in 1780. It is to be supposed that today's female university graduates do sometimes find their way to this club and make use of its facilities, its large pleasant reception rooms, reasonably priced sleeping accommodation, and Beetonesque cuisine—but they are seldom seen doing so; the learned ladies found in its precincts are all elderly and look as if they took their degrees at a time when they would have been called blue-stockings. The club furniture is comfortable but uncompromisingly Victorian; the windows are veiled in thick lace curtains, the floors covered in Turkey carpet, and the walls somewhat gloomily adorned with photographs of classical statuary. The elderly maids (they are never called waitresses) have a uniform that contrives to suggest black ankle-length bombazine and white caps with long streamers.

Miss Hume, principal of the Cadwallader School for Girls, was a respected club member of long standing, entitled by unwritten law to a particular wing-armchair and small piecrust table by the fireplace in the big drawing room with its portrait of Jane Welsh Carlyle. Here Miss Hume sat, on the same afternoon that Hari Lupac gave his recital, entertaining her old friend the archaeologist Professor Lockhart, and learnedly twitting him about some of his recent discoveries which had not turned out according to plan.

Side view, Miss Hume's profile had a decided resemblance to that of the Duke of Wellington, and she looked a little forbidding, worthy of her name and the aristocratic traditions of the great school she ruled; but when viewed from the front this chiselled nose could be seen to have a pronounced twist to the left which, with her quick bright eyes, gave her a benevolent appearance more indicative of her real character. Nevertheless generations of schoolgirls had known Miss Hume as the Iron Duchess and the legend of her adamantine inflexibility was one she rather liked to foster. She wore her grey hair in a sort of pancake on top of her head, and her clothes were carefully chosen, but not for style.

"I hope that child is not going to be late," she observed now, looking at the watch on her lapel. "It would be unlike her behaviour at school; but then I haven't seen her since she came out of hospital. I really think, Gervase, that if she is better, she would be just the girl for you. I do trust—ah, here she is. Gervase, this is Mrs. Conroy—Professor Lockhart. Caroline, my dear, how delightful to see you."

The girl came forward shyly and Professor Lockhart, standing up, studied her with interest: a small, fine-boned creature with an air of fragility and strain about her. She seemed somewhat daunted at finding herself in the company of a distinguished elderly man as well as that of her dear head-mistress, and Miss Hume, when she had performed the introductions, pointed to a massive red woollen rope by the door, suitable, one would have thought, for tolling curfew bell, and said, "Gervase, as you are up, would you be so kind as to ring for tea?" When he was out of earshot she added, "Forgive me, my dear Caroline, for combining you with another old friend, but my trips to Bridpool are so brief that I have to do some dovetailing. However Gervase has to run away very soon to lecture to the Archaeological Society and then we can have a comfortable gossip together. How are you now?" She studied the girl with kindly, piercing eyes. "You look far too thin, my dear. Are your burns quite better?"

"Yes, much better, thank you," Caroline murmured. Unconsciously she pushed her arms deeper against the velvet sides of the armchair.

One of the elderly maids came to take Miss Hume's order.

"Oh, Matty, we should like muffins, please—this is the one place in England where you can still get real muffins, Gervase—and plum cake and *strong* China tea. Caroline, you look as if you were not eating enough."

When tea had been served it soon appeared that Miss Hume's arrangement in bringing her guests together had not been fortuitous.

"Now Caroline," she said, setting her cup down briskly, "Professor Lockhart and I have a plan for you. You are still living at home, are you not?" Caroline nodded, looking apprehensive. "Still seeing the doctor regularly?"

"No, Miss Hume," Caroline answered in a low voice. "He said I—" She swallowed and started again. "Today was my last visit."

"Excellent. Excellent. Then you'll be in need of some regular occupation. Your husband is still in the Middle East?"

"Yes—he had to stay. There was such a lot to do after the explosion. Repairs and—and—"

"Of course," Miss Hume said kindly. "But I am sure it is the very worst possible thing for you to be living at home without any job while you wait for him. So as Professor Lockhart is looking for an assistant, I at once thought of you."

"Oh, but I couldn't—I'm sure I can't—" Caroline began, looking terrified.

Professor Lockhart took a hand. "From all Miss Hume tells me about you I am sure you can," he said, giving Caroline a very friendly smile. "What I need is somebody to do a lot of research for me in museums—you can take your time over this, do it at your own convenience—and sometimes come and write a few notes for me. Then, next year, I shall be going out to do a series of excavations at Yezd—"

"You see how convenient that would be, only forty miles or so from where your husband is at Ras al-Abdan," Miss Hume pointed out. "Now, does not this seem a job made for you, Caroline? Both Gervase and I thought so."

Caroline twisted her handkerchief between her hands. She said miserably, "It's terribly kind of both of you to think of me and it does sound very interesting, but I can't. Truly I can't." The thought of having an excuse to escape whenever she wanted to the haven of museums and libraries was almost irresistibly tempting, but she spoke with conviction.

"Why not, my dear?" Miss Hume's voice held sympathy but a hint of sternness.

"Because I'm just not well enough yet," Caroline blurted desperately. "I shouldn't be good enough for the job, truly! I seem to lose things all the time and make muddles—I'm so forgetful—" she checked herself, overcome with shame at the recollection of that panic-stricken moment in Dr. Galbraith's office.

"If you ask me," Miss Hume said—reproof again—"a nice distracting job is just what you need to settle you. And I am sure you would find working for Professor

Lockhart most rewarding. As you know, Caroline, I was always sorry that with your interest in history you were not able to go on to the university. This job now—"

"Oh, come, Teresa," Professor Lockhart said laughing. "I hope you are not trying to suggest to poor Mrs. Conroy that collecting notes for me is equivalent to a university education. Why don't you think about it, anyway, Mrs. Conroy, and let me know how you feel in a day or two? No need to make a hasty decision. Here's my card —you could ring up or come and call, if you feel like undertaking the work. I hope very much that you *will* be inclined to help me—Miss Hume has told me so much about you that I feel we are friends already." He gave Caroline a reassuring smile and rose to take his leave.

"I will see you out, Gervase," announced Miss Hume, and did so.

In the lobby Professor Lockhart said quietly, "There is something badly wrong with that child, Teresa."

"She certainly does not appear to have picked up as I would have hoped," Miss Hume agreed, frowning. "It must be nearly six weeks since she came out of hospital. But if she is not under the doctor any longer I should have thought a job—"

"Well, perhaps. Let us hope she changes her mind."

"She had a very bad experience."

"She looks to me," said Professor Lockhart, "as if it is still going on. As if something were happening to her *now*."

"Nothing except having to live with that odious mother. She would certainly be better out of that setup."

"Well, Teresa," said the Professor, kissing Miss Hume's hand with antique gallantry, "at least she is extremely lucky to have you for a friend."

The heavy street door shut behind him.

"Now, Caroline." The headmistress returned briskly to her armchair. "Tell me, what are your plans?"

Caroline looked daunted. "To try and get well, I suppose."

"You won't do that by staying at home and feeling

sorry for yourself. Really," Miss Hume added in affectionate exasperation, "you had more notion of what was good for you when you wrote to me from hospital."

"I? Wrote to you?" Caroline looked thoroughly startled.

"Why yes. Don't you remember? Well, I'm not altogether surprised. You were a bit under the weather then. Jane Knollys, the matron—I think she left Cadwallader the year before you came—very intelligently gathered that the letter was meant for me and sent it on. It was a great piece of luck that when you had that unfortunate nervous collapse they got you into the Beaumont; you couldn't have gone to a better place."

Caroline squeezed her fingers together until the knuckles showed white. She asked, not too steadily, "Did it—did the letter make *sense*, Miss Hume?"

"Well, my dear—" Miss Hume said kindly, "I won't deny it was a bit chaotic. But you were under heavy sedation at the time. I was abroad then, unfortunately, but I thought I'd look you up when I came back." She did not add that she had been so deeply shocked by the pathetic scrawl that she had curtailed a long-awaited tour of educational centres in the U.S.A. in order to get back as soon as possible.

"What did I say?"

"You seemed very much afraid of the idea of going back to Woodhoe to convalesce. I was sorry I couldn't return in time to help you make other arrangements. But is it actually so bad?"

She thought of the letter: *I shall be turned to stone, I shall be trapped,* over and over again, to the foot of the page.

"Does your mother resent your coming back, is that it?"

Caroline picked nervously at the fringe on her chair. "In a way I suppose she does. She's always found me a bit of a nuisance. She used to say—her attitude was—she had sent me to a school where I would make good social contacts"—Misss Hume's lip curled in fine disdain at hearing her precious academy with its high educational standards thus traduced—"I think she hoped I'd marry somebody's brother. She was furious when I didn't make many friends. She used to send Hilda and me to Hunt Balls and we were in disgrace if we didn't have many partners; her one aim seemed to be to marry us off."

"Why? Did she want to be free to remarry herself?"

"I sometimes wondered—" Caroline confessed. "A few years after Father died there was a time when she—I couldn't be definite, she never took us into her confidence about anything. But I used to wonder if some man had let her down, someone that she'd expected—she's always been pretty sour about men, but around then she was really—really savage. She behaved as if she could hardly bear to see us about. I can remember Hilda coming home from dances and crying because Mother went on at her so—about her lameness, too, which was unfair. And yet Hilda was her favourite. When I did marry—when I married Tim—she wasn't really pleased. We'd kept our—our friendship secret for a long time, you see. Maybe I imagined it, but it seemed to me they both held it against me—Hilda too, because she wasn't married."

"You still feel that?"

Caroline hesitated, then brought out, "Now Mother's always accusing Tim of meanness. You see, although his family's quite well off—"

"Oil, isn't it?"

"Oil and lots of other interests. But Tim will only draw a junior executive salary while he learns all the different sides; it's a family tradition. They're very proud of it. So we really aren't rich. Not to give Mother the sort of help she seems to expect. She'd got some scheme for turning Woodhoe into a guesthouse—"

"You couldn't live with your mother-in-law for a while?" Miss Hume suggested.

"She sold her house when Tim's father died, and she's always travelling about. She does a lot of welfare work for the firm—they have offices in Rome and Athens, you know, as well as London."

"You can't go back to your husband yet?"

"He thinks it would be unwise while he's still out there. *Everyone* thinks so," Caroline said desperately.

"You haven't quarrelled?"

"Oh, *no!* If only I could be with him—" She stopped, fighting for control.

"Yes, I see. Well, my dear child, I still feel that job with Gervase Lockhart might be the answer to your problem: he's a dear man and the work would distract you and he'd pay you enough to leave home and take a room in Bridpool."

"Yes," Caroline agreed hopelessly. "But I just know I couldn't do it."

"I'm not sure about that. But I won't nag at you now, child; I can see you're tired still, and under strain. I shall be thinking about you, though, so keep in touch. And, as Gervase said, don't make your mind up right away."

The warmth of her smile was like a glimpse into a world where friendship and logic had not crumbled away, where kind actions could be disinterested, and detachment benevolent. It was like the last ray of the setting sun.

Caroline said goodbye and went out into the dark.

For a long time after the slight figure had left the room Miss Hume sat frowning. Then she roused herself, went briskly to a walnut escritoire under the portrait of Mme de Staël, opened a businesslike little portable typewriter which travelled with her everywhere, and sat down to write a letter to Timothy Conroy, Esq., c/o Conroy Natural Fuels Production Alliance, Ltd., Anticline House, London W.C.2: *My dear Mr. Conroy: We have never met, but I feel the circumstances are such as to justify my getting in touch with you* . . .

Please forward, she added, on the outside of the envelope. Then, being a methodical woman, she put the letter in her briefcase for reconsideration in the morning.

"Well!" Hilda said. "You were long enough. What have you been doing all this time?"

Hilda was looking exhilarated. Her eyes were very bright; obviously she had had several drinks. She had had her hair done a new way: swathed and swept and bent and lacquered until it looked like a carving in finely grained red pine. Notwithstanding her words, she did not seem to have been waiting in the car very long; there were no stubs in the ashtray. But Caroline apologised.

"Oh well, never mind." Hilda slid along the seat. "Other door, ducky. You're going to drive us home."

"Oh, Hilda, no!"

"Don't be tedious, sweetie, you've got to start again sometime. You can't hide your head in the sand for ever. And now's the moment, when the car's been serviced and is in good trim. They've put in the new brake unit today, too, if you should get into trouble, there'll be no problem about stopping. Come on—don't stand there and dither."

Caroline slipped in the driver's door and sat trembling. It was several moments before she could summon enough resolution to pull the starter. When she did so, and the engine burst into life, she seemed dazed by the noise, and paused irresolutely with her hand on the gear lever.

"Aren't you at all nervous?" she asked. "At being driven by me?"

"Nope." And it was the truth: Hilda leaned calmly back, lighting a second cigarette from the stub of the first. "I've nerves of iron, ducky," she said cheerfully. "Go ahead and run us into the parking meter if you must, maybe it's just what you need. Shock therapy."

Thus encouraged, Caroline levered the car cautiously into gear and they moved off in a series of jerks. One of these dislocated the horn control, which was insecurely clamped to the steering-column, and it suddenly began to bray deafeningly as they approached a pedestrian crossing. Caroline started and the car swerved.

"Watch it, sweetie!" Hilda removed her cigarette and grabbed the wheel, giving it a deft twist to the left. "Footbrake, girl!"

The new unit was certainly effective; when Caroline

touched the brake pedal the car came to a violent, shuddering halt, throwing both passengers forward in their seats. A smell of scorched rubber blew through the window.

"Well, you needn't have stalled us," Hilda said, putting the cigarette back. "There's no one on the crossing. Start her up again!"

"Hilda, I—"

"Hurry up, ducks. Mother'll be having kittens, wondering where we've got to."

They crept forward again. With irritated good nature Hilda piloted her younger sister through the network of the city centre and on to the Exeter road, sometimes grabbing the wheel, sometimes hastily jerking back the handbrake when disaster was particularly imminent. She seemed quite immune to fear; her eyes sparkled, she gave an impression of enjoying the ride and laughed at a male driver who turned and shook his fist at them as Caroline nosed the car apprehensively across a roundabout.

"Perhaps that'll teach him to give way to traffic coming from the right, the churlish swine!" she said. "I'm sorry we didn't scrape his wing off. Hey, jump to it, girl, we turn right here! Wait, though, dimwit, can't you see you're being overtaken?"

A roar, and a deafening blare of horn exploded past their right window, missing them, it seemed, by millimeters. Caroline stamped on the brake. Her own horn became dislodged again and brayed its protest. The car stalled. She dragged up the handbrake, thrust the gear lever grindingly into neutral, and slumped forward against the wheel, shaking all over. Tears began to course down her cheeks.

"I can't do it. I just damn well *can't* do it, Hilda."

"Okay, okay, sweetie. Keep your hair on. You'll be all right in a minute. But you'd better shift us. We can't sit in the middle of the A.38 all night, or we'll be flattened. Come on, now, get her going."

"No."

Caroline was completely expended. She opened her

door, climbed out, heedless of a passing Vespa which avoided her by a violent wiggle, and stood swaying beside the bonnet. Steadied a little by some gulps of fresh air she made her way to the side of the road, fatalistically ignoring the evening traffic, and sat on the grass verge.

Shrugging, Hilda put the cigarette back between her lips, slid into the driver's seat, and worked the car across to the kerb.

"Come on, then!" she called. "In you get. I'll take her the rest of the way if you can't face it. Just as well, maybe. It'll be dark soon."

Silent and obedient, Caroline got in. Hilda switched on the lights and started up. After she had driven—calm, swift, and skilful—for about twenty miles, Caroline said in a small voice,

"I'm sorry, Dee."

"*Don't* call me by that ghastly pet name, please. Oh well—" Hilda was quite unperturbed, "maybe you aren't quite ready for driving yet. What did old Galbers have to say?"

"He said I was better," Caroline answered dully. "I'm not to go back to him any more. He seemed to think I was making a fuss about nothing."

"Did he? Lorraine Duke did warn, when she recommended him, that he might seem a bit *unsympathetic*. But she said he was *good*. He was pretty shrewd about her mad old pa, she said. I wonder if she really knew what she was talking about? Probably half these psychiatrist boys are quacks if we did but know it. Oh well, we shall just have to see how you go on, shan't we? What did you do after you'd seen him?"

"I went to a recital at the Philharmonic Hall."

"*What—*"

The steering wheel kicked violently between Hilda's hands, the car slowed, and a rampart of grass bank suddenly rushed at them in the headlights. There was no other traffic about, luckily; they were now on a little-used minor road, well up on the moors. "Lord," Hilda said lightly, "they over-lubricated this steering a bit, didn't they? I'm a little less surprised, now, at the way you were sliding about in Bridpool." She straightened the car. "What were you saying?"

"I said I'd been to a lunch-hour recital at the Philharmonic Hall. A violinist called Lupac—you know, the one who escaped from somewhere in Eastern Europe, or was it Russia? You were watching him not long ago on television."

"Was I? Can't think why. I'd forgotten. Any good?"

"I suppose so. I wasn't in the right mood for it. And then I had tea with Miss Hume."

"Oh yes, your dear old head-ma'am. Well," Hilda said, steering neatly through a pair of far-from-perpendicular gateposts lacking a gate, "here we are, back on the ancestral acres. Huzza for the old squire. Christ, I wish the old squire, or somebody, had had enough money to dump a few tons of hardcore along this track, it's like the Cresta run."

Coming home by night was better, Caroline thought. You missed the distant, dolorous prospect of the house as you crept down the drive. Only at the last minute was there a view of its peeling façade in the headlights; then they swung round to the stable yard and left the car under a sagging archway. A chorus of yelps, barks, and whines greeted them from the stables. "Damn those brutes, I bet Hudson hasn't exercised them," Hilda remarked, stretching and yawning. "Wonder what sort of mood Ma's in. Not that one need wonder. Hers are always the same. You'd hardly get the impression she was fond of our company when we're in the house, but she seems to get properly cheesed when she's left alone with Cousin Flora. Oh well, to hell with it all."

She led the way through a back door. Caroline followed in silence, along a dimly lit stone passage which smelt of dry rot.

In the butler's pantry a stooped, white-headed figure, outlined against the feeble light of a small oil lamp, sat filling out football coupons.

"Oh, Hudson, could you put the car away," Hilda said. "Where's Mother, do you know?"

"Lady Trevis is in the drawing room, Miss Hilda."

The old man hardly bothered to turn his head; his voice was full of dislike. "She said to wait dinner till you and Miss Caroline returned."

"Oh, strewth. I hoped we'd be spared that. Can't be helped. Tell her we're back, sweetie, while I drop these things upstairs, will you?"

Hilda disappeared up the back way with her rapid, slightly rocking walk.

Lady Trevis was watching a quiz programme on television, sitting in the dusk, lividly illuminated by the dim blue glare. Caroline switched on the light. The TV set was the only modern article in the shabby room; nobody had troubled to buy new furniture or curtains since the days of Grandfather Trevis, who, like the Prince Consort, had had a lot of taste and all of it bad.

Without troubling to turn down the volume, Lady Trevis snapped, "Don't worry about me, will you? Stay in town till all hours; I can fret myself stiff thinking you've had a smash, but neither of you cares a hoot. You might at least have phoned to say you'd be late. Why didn't you take in a show while you were about it? Why didn't you stay the night?"

"Sorry, Mother," Caroline said mechanically.

"Sorry! A lot of use that is! God knows you make it plain enough you don't enjoy being back at home but since you *are* here, the least you can do is be a bit of company. Where's Hilda? What's she *doing?* And where's Flora? Eating ginger biscuits up in her room I suppose. I'm nearly starved to death waiting for you." A blizzard of cheers and laughter vibrated the television set; "God, why do I watch this trollop," said Lady Trevis irritably, but she did not turn it off.

No worse than usual, anyway, thought Caroline watching her mother.

Lady Trevis had aged a good deal in the last four years. At first sight, her face gave the impression of having slipped a little, sideways, as a mask might: a bright orange mouth had been carelessly painted on, missing the lips; black lines inaccurately straddled the natural arch of her plucked brows. No false lashes today; her

eyelids wore their own fringe of sandy stubble. The pale
eyes she turned on Caroline seemed unfocused, sightless,
like those of a cat in a bright light. Her determinedly
blonde hair was becalmed in the rigid ripples of thirty
years back. She wore slacks and slippers and no girdle
and her shirt was not very clean.

"Well?" she went on, automatically raising her husky
voice above the clamour of the TV. "What did Galbraith
have to say?"

"He says I'm better."

"Then he's crazy himself. Of course you're not better. You don't look it, anyway. You look terrible, like a
washed-out rag. Where the *hell's* Hilda got to?"

"Here she comes."

"Thank God."

"Dinner is served," Hudson announced glumly.

"Thank God for that too."

Cousin Flora appeared from upstairs with lightning
promptitude as Hudson banged the gong.

"Well?" she inquired chirpily of the girls. "Had a good
day? Did you bring me some paperbacks, Hilda, like a
kind girl?"

"Galvanising, thanks." Hilda's tone was lackadaisical,
but her eyes were still very bright. "Hudson, bring me
some coffee, will you, I couldn't eat a thing, I had a sau-
sage at the club. Paperbacks in the hall, Cousin Flora,
hope they're okay."

Caroline could not eat either. She sat pushing food
about her plate, while Cousin Flora demolished a businesslike proportion of her nine weekly guineas' worth,
her eyes flicking neatly round the table to see how the
others did. From time to time she let fall a chatty remark; she was the only one of the four who bothered to
talk. Lady Trevis ate voraciously, shovelling down her
food like a hungry dog. When she had reached the second course and slowed down a little she said,

"Well? Why don't you tell me about town? What's
new?"

"Nothing to tell," Hilda said concisely. "Shopped,
had my hair done, had a drink with Esmee and Brenda,

picked up Caroline—who, it seems, went in for culture in a big way, concert at the Philharmonic—"

"What*ever* for? Thought you were supposed to be meeting Miss Hume?" Lady Trevis was instantly suspicious, hostile.

"I did meet Miss Hume. The concert was just to fill in time."

"Well, go on. Where did you meet her?"

"At her club, the Lady Graduates'."

"Oh, that hole," Lady Trevis said scornfully. "Hardly a gay choice. Full of old frumps, I suppose. The Hume's a frump too; she always managed to put me in my place because I didn't wear a hat like a cowpat and wasn't out of the top drawer. God what a waste of money it was sending you to that school. Wish I'd got that cash now. Well, what did the revered Miss Hume summon you for?"

"She wanted me to take a job."

"A *job?*" Lady Trevis gave a shrill and mirthless laugh. "That's a good one. What sort of job could you do in your state? Quite apart from the fact that you've never had a job in your life."

She rang the bell and Hudson came in to clear. As he skirted the table, crabwise, he could be heard muttering to himself, "A thousand, thousand slimy things liv'd on; and so did I." Nobody paid any attention.

"Take a job?" Hilda said. "Old Hume's a bit of an optimist, isn't she?"

"But dearies, why shouldn't Caro take a little job? Such a sensible idea! There must be lots of simple, routine things she could turn her hand to."

Nobody took any notice of Cousin Flora's plaintive suggestion.

"Miss Hume had a friend there—a professor who wanted some historical research done." Caroline's voice became more and more colourless. She bent her head over her coffee cup.

"You couldn't do it," Hilda said flatly. "Research? You wouldn't know where to start. Be your age! You'd get lost, make mistakes, we'd have the police asking us to come and fetch you from the Bridpool Library because you'd forgotten who you were, and we'd be blamed for letting you do it. Rest and quiet is what you're supposed to be having, remember, sweetie?—that is, if you ever want to get back to that handsome husband of yours."

She gave Caroline a quick, inimical smile; her cheek flickered in a tiny muscular spasm.

"Yes, perhaps research would be a *tiny* bit beyond Caro's powers just at the moment. We must walk before we can run, dearie, mustn't we? *I* had thought something like helping with the school meals or knitting for the blind—"

"What did you say to Miss Hume?" Lady Trevis asked Caroline, moving into the drawing room.

"I said I'd see. I don't suppose I'll do it. But the professor gave me his card and asked me to think it over."

"Card? Let's see?" Hilda stretched out a hand. Caroline found the card in her bag. "Gervase Lockhart, M.A., F.S.A., Inst. of Arch. Studies, Prof. Lond. School of Arch., Hon this that and the other. Dig the fancy degrees! Not quite your cuppa, sweetie, honestly, I'd have thought?" She balanced the card on the mantel.

"Phone, Hilda," said Lady Trevis, as a bell began ringing.

"Why can't Hudson answer it for once?"

"Phone, dearies!" carolled Cousin Flora superfluously from a closet where she kept wool for her perennial occupation of knitting for the blind. "I'd go but there's not the slightest chance it would be for poor old me!"

"You know Hudson's too deaf, he never hears."

Hilda mooched off, yawning, and came back to announce in a tone of slight surprise,

"It's for you, Caroline."

"For *me*? Are you sure? Who?"

"Didn't say. A man."

"A man?" Brilliant hope lit in Caroline's eyes. "Not *Tim*?" She flew from the room. Hilda and Lady Trevis exchanged glances. Cousin Flora gave an indulgent smile, selecting a skein of violent arsenical green which it was as well the recipients would never see.

But after a few moments Caroline came back dejectedly. Three pairs of eyes fixed on her.

"Well? Who was it?"

"I don't know. Whoever it was had rung off: there was only the dialling tone."

"Well, you did take rather a long time getting there, sweetie. Never mind; perhaps he'll ring back."

After half an hour Caroline said, "I've rather a headache; I think I'll go to bed. You will let me know if there's another call, won't you?"

"Of *course,* sweetie."

As Caroline dragged herself up the stairs, walking as if she ached not only in her head but all over, Hilda thoughtfully picked up Professor Lockhart's card, tore it in half, and dropped the bits into the smoldering fire. To Cousin Flora's raised eyebrows she remarked,

"Much better get rid of it. She'll never do anything more about him anyway, and to have it sitting there will only upset her and make her feel guilty."

Lady Trevis nodded, shrugging; she switched on the TV and became engrossed in a programme called *Treble Your Luck.*

Cousin Flora remarked, "Well, I'm for beddy-byes too. I wonder if Hudson remembered to fill my bottle?" She picked up the pile of luridly jacketed paperbacks Hilda had brought her, and departed to see.

Half an hour or so went by. Hilda played patience, slapping one card irritably on top of another. Once she remarked,

"I tried letting her drive this afternoon."

"How was it?"

"Hopeless. She was all over the road."

"Well, what did you expect?"

"Just that, I suppose. Maybe she takes after you—you never learnt the knack, did you?" Hilda blew a cloud of smoke and through it glanced maliciously at her mother. Suddenly from upstairs came a thud, and a scream.

"Oh God," Lady Trevis said resignedly. "Now what?"

"Sit still. I'll go."

Hilda balanced her cigarette on an ashtray and went quickly upstairs to a square, dark, windowless hall decorated with crossed pairs of corroded oriental weapons.

Caroline was there, in an old blue woollen robe, leaning against the banisters. She was deathly pale and clutched Hilda's arm.

"There's a snake in the bathroom!"

"Are you sure?" Hilda said, raising her eyebrows. "You know—"

"Positive! It moved!"

"Where?"

"In the bath."

"Oh well. Here goes." Hilda calmly selected a Malayan kris off the wall.

"Aren't you going to fetch Hudson?"

"What use would *he* be?" Hilda said with scorn, and went into the bathroom. After a moment she came out again, her face expressionless, carrying a damp cleaning-cloth. "Here's your snake," she said. "This must have been what you saw. Gladys must have left it in the bath after cleaning."

"It can't have been that! It was a black snake, shiny, with a white V on its head! I saw it distinctly."

"And it vanished out of the bath? Down the plug-hole perhaps? I'm tired, so we won't argue about it now." Hilda said, piloting Caroline back to her bedroom. "Have you got some sleeping pills still? Well come on, for God's sake swallow one and let's all get a bit of rest." Ignoring Caroline's protests she administered the pill, switched off the light, and ran downstairs again.

Her cigarette had smouldered to a long column of ash and Lady Trevis, flapping a hand, said disgustedly, "This room stinks of burnt paper. Open the window. Well, what was all that about?"

"Snakes, yet."

"Christmas. It'll be pink elephants next. That super marvellous head shrinker doesn't seem to have done her much good for all the fees the Conroys have been paying out. God knows why they bothered wasting their money —if they had all that cash to spare why couldn't they let me have a loan to turn this place into a guesthouse."

"For Pete's sake, who'd want to come here? I can't say I blame the Conroys for being cagey about that." Hilda glanced disparagingly round the dismal room. "A Home for the Blind would be the only appropriate thing. Pity Cousin Flora's so tight with the purse strings, or you could touch *her* for a loan—since the blind seem so dear to her heart."

"Flora? Don't be silly," Lady Trevis said carelessly. "Flora hasn't any capital to lend."

"How do you mean? What about Aunt Prue's nest egg?"

"Flora turned it all into an annuity—no, she didn't tell me, she's far too secretive, old Hatherleigh did when I was asking him about my unit trust dividends—he thought I knew, of course. Flora hasn't anything else. Why," said Lady Trevis, darting a shrewd look at Hilda who for once appeared thoroughly taken aback, "were you counting on a nice little legacy? You can put that right out of your head, ducky." She laughed sourly.

Hilda made no reply but for some minutes two red spots burnt on her cheekbones and she fanned out the patience cards with even more than her usual inattention. After a while she remarked inconsequently, "Well, if it's therapeutic for Caroline to work she'd better make a start by helping with the dogs."

Lady Trevis looked sceptical.

"D'you think that's wise? She'd probably poison them."

"Hell, Mother, I badly need some help, you don't give me much, Hudson's utterly past it, and there are plenty of things Caroline can do. If I teach her now she can do it when I go away in October."

"Oh? First I knew you were going away in October?" Lady Trevis inquired disagreeably.

"You know now. I'll start showing Caroline the ropes tomorrow. Well, I'm going to have a bath," Hilda said, and went.

Lady Trevis switched to a programme called *Chance Your Arm* and sat watching it till she fell asleep in her chair; presently she roused herself, grimacing with boredom, and staggered like a somnambulist to bed.

Two

Friday, August 20—Saturday, August 21.

"Here's Lorraine Duke," Hilda said, glancing out of the rain-streaked drawing-room window. "Wonder what brings her down this neck of the woods on a wet afternoon. Not love of our company, I bet. Let her in, would you, sweetie. Hudson's out exercising the chows and my hands are all sticky with trying to get Oegycin into this damn pooch's ear."

The poodle on her knees struggled and whined asthmatically.

Caroline was pale and listless; there were black circles under her eyes. Without replying she went to the front door and let in Lorraine, a big, bouncing, pink-cheeked girl with a mop of black fuzzy hair, who exclaimed in a penetrating voice,

"He*llo*, Carey, you still here? Making out all right among us rustics? Finding it a bit slow after abroad?"

She did not wait for Caroline to answer but strode on into the drawing room. Caroline followed, depressed by the feeling, which Lorraine usually contrived to give her, that she did not quite exist. Lorraine's loud, frequent laugh, her ringing public-school tones, her slightly thick-skinned exuberance and failure to listen had this effect fairly often on her more diffident acquaintances.

"Can you do something for me, Hilda?" she was asking. "I've got to give up some of my jobs temporarily—

my dear, I simply haven't *time* for them while I'm help-ing my brother. Guides, Red Cross, Meals on Wheels, W.V.S., Theatre Group—normally I can fit everything in but at the moment it just can't be done or my social life simply dwindles away. Believe it or not, I hardly see a soul!" She rolled her bulging plum-black eyes upward.

"You make me weep," Hilda said drily. "Well? What is it you want me to do? If it's Guides I can tell you straight away the answer's no. I'm not much for the social service lark, you know. We don't have these tradi-tions in our family."

"No, not Guides. My dear, *could* you take over the vil-lage library for me? It's not much of a chore. You only have to sit in the Parish hut dealing out the reading mat-ter for an hour twice a week, Wednesday and Friday eve-nings. You wouldn't mind, would you? All you do is write the name in a book and remind the old dears if they get overdue; hardly anyone comes in now, they all much prefer to watch telly."

Hilda looked far from enthusiastic. "I often go to Bridpool on Friday nights. Can't you find someone else? How about Caroline? *Yes,*" she added, kindling as the advantages of this idea dawned on her, "Caroline will do it for me, won't you, sweetie? It's just what you need, you were wanting a job of some kind weren't you?"

"Caroline? I thought she'd be leaving again any min-ute?" Lorraine turned and stared at Caroline doubtfully as if such an idea would never have occurred to her, but Hilda went on in a persuasive tone,

"This will be a nice starter, just to get you mixing with people again. All you have to do is sit quietly in the Parish hut, you know where it is, by the harbour wall; you can gossip away with the old girls and hear all their troubles, couldn't be better."

"I'm not really—Caroline began, but she was firmly talked down by the other two, who both, for different rea-sons, thought the plan an excellent one.

"How are the arms getting on, Caroline?" Lorraine recollected herself to ask presently. "You ought to go swimming more. I'll come and take you down one of these days. Imagine who I saw swimming off Pennose Head the other day, you'll never guess——"

"Who?" Hilda was plainly not interested. "Very likely I shan't know——I haven't your extensive acquaintance with the locals."

"Oh, nobody from around here. No, that violinist, Loopack, Loopatch, or however he pronounces his name? The one who scarpered from Czechoslovakia or Hungary or somewhere."

"Lupac?" Caroline said involuntarily. "I heard him play yesterday. Are you sure it was him, Lorraine? It seems so unlikely he'd be down this way."

"Dunno why. I suppose violinists go swimming sometimes, like normal people. Pennose is quite a famous bit of coast, after all, if it is rather inaccessible."

"I suppose it *could* have been him," said Hilda, who appeared to pull herself out of silence with an effort.

"Possible? I tell you it was Lupac. When there's only one other person on the bench you can't help noticing them. And I couldn't mistake his face, it's been so much in the news lately. Didn't speak, of course, that type's not much in my line——besides he made tracks when he saw me. D'you suppose he's really a Commie agent? Daddy's sure of it."

"Shouldn't think so," Hilda said indifferently. "After all, why should he bother? He's obviously going to make his fortune in the West, everybody says he's a genius. I expect the Reds are thoroughly fed up at losing him."

"Ah, but they might have some secret hold on him!" Lorraine exclaimed in thrilling tones.

"Don't you believe it!"

"Why?" Lorraine said. "What makes you so positive?"

"Oh——nothing. Only his face. He looks a pretty tough character. I can't imagine him letting himself be blackmailed. You must have got that impression if you saw him close to?"

"Ye-es. Not tough, exactly, but sort of cold and ruthless——he gave me the shivers. That's why *I* think he looks like a spy."

Losing her faint interest in this subject, Caroline walked quietly out of the room. "Hey, where are you off to?" Hilda called. No reply came back. A moment later Caroline's rain-coated figure could be seen passing the window, diminishing along the leafy path by the Tebburn river.

"Damn that girl!" Hilda said. "At least half a dozen dogs need exercising and I'd several things I wanted doing in the village. She loathes going there, that's the trouble."

"I expect seeing the children upsets her," Lorraine suggested, a shade of what appeared to be unwilling concern momentarily reflected on her healthy face. "They're bound to remind her . . . How's she getting on, really? She looks pretty mouldy still. Is she going back to that place, wherever it was—"

"The hospital?"

"No, where Tim is, the island in the Red Sea."

"Ras al-Abdan—"

"—or will Tim get a job in England?" Lorraine put this question with the most casual air in the world, but under Hilda's sharp eyes she slowly turned a dusky, unbecoming pink.

"No use hoping Tim will come back to England yet, sweetie, they can't do without him out there, it seems. So don't get too many hopes up. Your best plan would be to wangle yourself a job there. Because I *very* much doubt if Caroline will ever be up to facing that climate again."

"Hilda, you can be an absolute *beast* sometimes." Losing her casual air entirely, Lorraine began to stamer. "As if—I mean, you know p-perfectly well that I wouldn't—"

"Wouldn't you? I would, in your shoes," Hilda said flatly. "You always wanted Tim, didn't you, God knows why. Well you won't get him by staying here riding in gymkhanas and winning the West Country Ladies' Lawn Tennis Challenge Shield, I can tell you that."

Sourly amused, she watched Lorraine's discomfited departure.

When Caroline, several hours later, came in and began slowly taking off her wet rain-things, she could hear Hilda's voice from the little telephone annexe in the front hall.

"You mean tomorrow's date's off? Rather short notice, don't you think? Supposing you hadn't been able to get hold of me, what would you have done? Good heavens, *no,* I'm not complaining. I know professional contacts must come first. I'm only suggesting you might give a bit more warning . . . Of *course* not, sweetie, your career is sacred, I quite appreciate that . . . I hope she's pretty too. No, no! Good God, I was joking; our famous island sense of humour, you know. When shall we meet, then? Right. Right. Just as you say. Fine. Okay. Be hearing from you. 'Bye." There was a longish pause, then Caroline heard her viciously dialling another number.

"Cecilia? Oh, Siss, is that you? How's the horn-blowing going? Bazooka still in good order? Listen, sweetie, can you do me a favour, I wonder?"

Lady Trevis was in the drawing room watching a programme called *Chance in a Million.* "Where the dickens have *you* been?" she asked irritably.

"Up in the woods, for a walk," Caroline said.

"You might have said you were going out, you could have taken the pekes. And I wanted some more cigarettes. Fix me another drink before you sit down will you?"

"What is it?"

"Gin and Coca-Cola." Lady Trevis had to repeat herself to be heard above the roar of the studio audience.

"Cripes, what a combination. Haven't we any tonic?" Hilda had come in and poked about the mahogany tantalus. She looked both annoyed and triumphant. As she prized the cap off the bottle her hands shook a little. "Turn down the volume, Mother, for God's sake. Didn't you order the drinks, Caroline?"

"No, was I supposed to?"

"You know I asked you to, sweetie. I gave you the list and said ring them at ten, in time for the delivery round."

"List? You never gave me a list."

Hilda sighed. "You put it in your pocket," she said. "I gave it to you, you said, 'I'll do it when I've washed my stockings,' and then you put it in your pocket."

With good-natured sisterly roughness she thrust a hand into Caroline's pocket and brought out a piece of paper.

"There!"

Caroline stared at it, lips compressed. "I— I'd *swear* I'd never seen that before. Are you sure?"

"How else could it have got there?"

"I did wash some stockings—but I don't remember—"

"Oh, do stop arguing you two," Lady Trevis snapped. "How I bear this life I don't know. Two women in a house is bad enough, but four— Go and ring Mackenzies now, Caroline, can't you?"

"They'll be shut."

"Give the order to Gladys, then, she can stick it through their letter box when she goes home this evening."

"Has Caroline told you about her job?" Hilda said as they waited for the maid.

"Job, what job? I thought she was going to help you with the dogs?"

"This is as well—only in the village," Hilda said soothingly, blowing a smoke ring. "Our hockey-playing friend wanted someone to take over the library. Caroline ought to be able to manage that."

"If she doesn't muddle up all the books and mislay the tickets. I wondered what Lorraine had come for— knew she wouldn't call in just for the pleasure of our company . . . Oh, there you are, Gladys. Take the drinks order, will you, and stick it through Mackenzies' door when you go home."

Gladys was dumpy, with stout calves bulging in black stockings; her rather flat face, which must have had a pale ethereal prettiness in her early teens, had settled into the pasty stolidity of its final cast, and what might have been an expression of simple good nature was heavily disguised by wax-pale lipstick and vampirelike loads of eyeshadow. Her blonde hair was built into a huge beehive.

"Thanks ever so much for the clothes, Miss Caro," she said earnestly, as Caroline handed the list to her, after giving it a last troubled glance.

"Clothes?"

"You remember, Caroline," Lady Trevis broke in. "I suggested it would be a good thing to give the case full of—the boy's things to Gladys."

"It was ever so kind," Gladys repeated awkwardly. "The little T shirts are beautiful. I wouldn't want you to think I didn't appreciate them, Miss Caro. My Garry thinks they're ever so with it."

"Yes, well, all right, Gladys," Lady Trevis cut her short. "You'd better run along or you'll be working overtime. And that wouldn't do, would it? Come on, Caroline, pull yourself together!" she added sharply as the door closed behind Gladys. "There was absolutely no point in keeping the clothes, was there? Don't start working yourself up over them, we aren't living in some morbid nineteenth-century novel where people wear wedding dresses for the rest of their lives. You've got to snap out of it."

Caroline nodded, knitting her fingers together. She was very white.

"Hey," Hilda said, looking at her watch. "You'd better be bundling down to the village, sweetie: library night, don't forget. Lorraine left the key of the Parish hut; here it is. By the way, I could see she thought it was rather odd the way you just walked out in the middle of her call—not very civil, was it? She asked me to say good-bye to you and said she'd come and take you swimming one of these days."

"Thanks," Caroline said mechanically.

"Jump to it now, girl, or the old things will be queueing up in the rain and getting their books wet. You remember where the hut is? By the foot bridge, just beyond the school, on the harbour wall. Here, you'll need a torch—don't stand there looking moonfaced now—get going!"

Caroline found herself out in the wet night, crunching along the rutted drive, past the dark ramparts of rhodo-

dendrons. And the darker, higher ramparts hidden behind them of wooded valley sides, where the disused railway creeps like an old, empty rat run. And down the
narrow path where the river's voice drowns all other
sounds. It is dark now, too dark to see the brown water
creaming to greenish-white over the rocks, but the smell of
water is everywhere; small stone and plank bridges at
intervals along the path span midget cataracts, hurling
down to join the main stream below.

Woodmouth council skimped on street lighting. Why
not, when all the villagers were indoors by seven? Two
dim standards flickered, one at the near end of the
street, where the moor road, having come down a one-
in-three gradient, joined the river, and the valley widened
just enough to accommodate them both beside a double
row of houses with back gardens running up at an angle
of forty-five degrees. The other street lamp stood on the
harbour wall, at the far end of the tiny street. Beside
it, boxed between granite walls, the mingled waters of the
Tare and the Tebburn flung themselves roaring into the
Atlantic.

Caroline picked her way over the shingle, which summer gales had dumped on the pavement, to a smallish
wooden hut, built where the harbour wall ran off into an
abbreviated, cliff-encircled beach. Once, the hut had
hopefully offered Teas, but this venture failing through
lack of tourists, it had been taken over by the council
for mixed parochial use.

The village was quiet behind her, and overhead the
wooded cliffs carved off half the night sky.

As she approached the hut, a dark figure stepped out
of the deeper blackness in its litte porch.

Caroline gave an involuntary cry and dropped her
flashlight.

"Here, hold up, girl! No need to go historical on me."

The creaking voice was so familiar that for a moment
she was quite unable to identify it. Then, weak with relief,
she exclaimed,

"Hudson! Goodness, you frightened me. Whatever
are you doing here?"

"Come to change my library book, what d'you think?" the butler said peevishly. However he picked up the torch and shone it for her while she unlocked the door.

The hall smelt cold and dusty and salty. Sand gritted on the board floor. Hudson found the bank of light switches and turned them on, illuminating the place, which was cheerless: an oblong brown room, straight wooden chairs all round the walls, a stage at one end with hessain curtains, another door leading to a little greenroom-cum-kitchen with a sink and tap.

"The books are in those boxes," Hudson instructed. "You put them out on the table."

"There aren't very many; is this all they have?" Caroline said, doing so.

"A van comes round with a new lot every three months," Hudson said. He helped her, wheezing asthmatically. She looked with curiosity at his pale, secretive, hairless face.

"I didn't know you were fond of reading, Hudson."

"O' course I read. What else can you do in a place like this? It passes the time, dunnit?"

"I suppose so . . ." Caroline glanced uneasily round the sombre little hall. "They have lectures here sometimes, don't they? Do you think we should draw these curtains, it feels awfully exposed. Anyone could look in."

"Draw 'em if you like, but there's nobody to look. Only the school on the one side and the beach on the other."

She stared out into darkness and caught a gleam of white where the sea, at low ebb, muttered along the shingle-bank.

"And on the bay the moonlight lay, And the shadow of the moon," Hudson's voice said close behind her.

"Goodness, Hudson, I wish you wouldn't keep making me jump!" She rattled the curtains across and returned to the table.

"Arr, you can't beat poetry for getting to the marrow of a thing," Hudson grunted, rummaging among the books. He held Caroline with his glittering eye, and declaimed, "Fear at my heart, as at a cup, My life-blood seemed to sip! That's expressive, ennit? Makes your hair prickle, eh? And I could quote lots more."

"I'd just as soon you wouldn't," she said, shivering, and busied herself with setting out the books in categories.

"Miss Caroline." All of a sudden Hudson's creaking whisper had become charged, meaningful, urgent.

"Yes, Hudson? What?"

He glanced behind him and sank his voice conspiratorially even lower. "I came down here on purpose tonight, when I heard Miss Hilda say you was to take over from Miss Duke."

"Why, Hudson?" Caroline said stupidly. "Why did you come?"

"To warn you, o'course. Some folks are born gormless, if you ask me."

"To warn me? How do you mean?" She too had sunk her voice, as if fearful of the silence, only broken by the sea's murmur.

"Woodhoe House isn't a right place for you. You didn't ought to stay here. There's ill will about—don't you feel it, like a sickness in the air?"

She stammered, "I—I don't understand, I'm not sure. What do you mean?"

"It's always been bad down here," he said. "Too shut in. Too dark, things go sour and queer. Special so if you're young. When young things is shut in, then they can't grow straight, all the life in 'em turns to malice. Oh, I've seen it happen here. That's why you didn't ought to stop. There's somebody here wishes you ill, can't you feel it?"

"How do you know? Who wishes me ill?"

"That's not for me to say, Miss Caroline." His pale cheeks wrinkled into a series of parallel creases for a moment, as if something secretly amused him, though the watery eyes were still fixed on her, unblinking. "But there's someone down here hates you, I can say and I will. Hates you enough to"—he glanced about and moved nearer still—"*harm* you. Don't you know who it is? Can't you guess?"

"No," she whispered, pressing her fingers to her forehead. "How can I guess who it is? It's true I've felt—something—I thought it was just my own—*who is it,* Hudson?"

But he had moved away from her again and was saying in a louder, casual voice, "Miss Duke keeps the tickets in this biscuit tin, miss, and the names she writes down in the red book here; two weeks you're allowed for a book and after that it's a penny a week fine."

The door opened and a dumpy, familiar figure walked in.

"Why, Miss Caro! I didn't know it was you running the library now. What a nice surprise!"

"Hullo, Gladys," Caroline said dully, taking the two books held out to her.

Towards the end of the two-hour period Cousin Flora trotted in; mist had come up and she wore a hooded, buttoned, belted raincoat in shiny floral plastic that contrived to be both neat and gaudy.

"All going well, dearie?" she chirruped. "That's the ticket! Just come to change me whodunnits. Must have something to get me off to sleep at night!" and she laid down an armful of books whose wrappers were a dazzle of blood splashes, fingerprints, guns, and knotted rope. "Now what? Now what?" she hummed, casting over the selection on the table. "This silly old rheumatism in my knees makes the nights seem so long, without plenty of thrillers and a flask of tea I really don't know how I'd manage. Gracious knows how many cuppas I drink while you're all in the Land of Nod. Now, are you finished? Then I'll help you lock up and walk home with you; I'll be glad of an arm and an extra torch."

"Can you manage the walk with your rheumatism, Cousin Flora?"

"Just about, dearie, just about; poor old me! Kind Mr. Pearce the vet gave me a lift down. But I must confess I miss my grand old hikes sadly, when I used to be able to do five or ten miles. Oh me, to see the sun set from Baggy Tor just once more! But it's naughty to grumble."

"Wouldn't you be better somewhere less damp?" Caroline remarked vaguely as they left the village and set off arm in arm along the narrow river path. But Cousin Flora seemed quite affronted by such a suggestion and briskly refuted the idea that the air of Woodhoe could be damp.

"*Sea* air is *never* damp, dearie—not the sort of damp that does harm. And with all that glorious moorland up behind us the ground is bound to be well drained—drainage is the ticket, you know—"

Her voice rattled on in the darkness. Not sufficiently interested to pursue the argument—let Cousin Flora stay and be a martyr to rheumatism if that was what she enjoyed—Caroline let her mind revert to Hudson's mysterious communication. Had he been serious? Hudson was such an oddity that at the time she had been half inclined to believe he was doing it for the fun of scaring her. But out here among the trees, with the sound of the unseen river coming loud and insistent from the gulley below, she knew better.

She could feel it, the ill will, the malice, like a sickness in the air.

The Chumley's cocktail party at the Nabob had begun at seven but arrivals were sparse for the first half hour. Now, however, at a quarter to eight, guests were pouring into the suite of rooms, which were linked in a square so that it was possible to make a complete circuit without retracing one's steps.

Sir Horace Chumley was a small bald man with an expression of unvarying sadness and a lividly pale complexion; the strange thing was that he should combine so much dynamism with this deathlike appearance. He seemed like an exceptionally lively corpse as he darted round and round the suite of rooms, pursuing one female guest after another.

"He's a powerful conductor, I know," said the Dutch pianist who was talking to Dominic Tree, "but he's a bit of an old goat, isn't he? Something out of Hieronymus Bosch. No wonder he gets orchestras to do what he wants;

it must be like being conducted by Old Horny in person. I should think Night on the Bare Mountain would be his specialty. His daughter's very different, isn't she?"

"Takes after her mother," said Dominic, who knew everything about everybody. He glanced approvingly towards the corner where Fernanda Chumley, shy and serious in a white dress, was talking to Harry Lupac. Harry was so much taller that he had to lean over her in a gallantly attentive attitude to catch what she said; the party was warming up now, and the hum of talk rose shriller and shriller, like gnat buzzings infinitely amplified.

"What happened to the mother?"

"Killed in an air crash; a blessed release for Sir Horace."

"Fernanda's a pretty girl; looks a bit out of her depth here; still, your latest lion seems to be looking after her nicely."

"I ought to make him circulate," Dominic said, but in fact he was quite content to leave Harry to his tête-à-tête which seemed to be proceeding most satisfactorily; Fernanda's eyes were bright and her pallor had acquired a tinge of pink; she was laughing at Harry's jokes. I wonder what possessed him to be so co-operative? Dominic asked himself; the other day I wouldn't have given two pins for his intentions of coming to the party. I know it meant his cancelling some other date, and he hates any hint of coercion. Should think he could be an ugly customer if he was really crossed over anything; obstinate certainly. But he's one for charming the girls, all right.

He gave another look at Harry's long, smiling jaw, and the conscious gesture with which he tossed back the flopping lock of hair; a momentary twinge of compunction touched Dominic for Fernanda Chumley's vulnerability, but he put this aside; after all it was Sir Horace's job to watch out for his daughter.

The party drew on. Guests were now jammed elbow to elbow; Dominic had a number of short, useful conversations with different acquaintances. Presently a young tenor sang a group of *lieder*, which Dominic thought a mistake;

nearly everybody there was connected with music in some way but they had come for Sir Horace's excellent drinks and the cachet it gave to be seen at his party, not to listen to an indifferent parlour performance. Talk faltered to a halt, or was conducted in embarrassed mutters under cover of the accompaniment. Dominic noticed that Harry had not left Fernanda's side; he was now perched on the arm of her chair contriving to look deferential and adoring, like the hero of a nineteenth-century novel. Hope he doesn't overdo it and ask her for a lock of hair, or send her books about the Language of Flowers, just out of cussedness, Dominic thought. Sir Horace is a fly old boy, he'd soon see through that.

"Who's the girl Sir Horace has got hold of now?" asked his neighbour.

"I don't know her name," Dominic was obliged to admit. "I saw her come in with some people from the Western Counties College of Music so I suppose she's connected with that. She's got something, hasn't she?"

"She's certainly got Sir Horace quite steamed up."

"That's not difficult," Dominic said drily.

The girl now with Sir Horace was not pretty but her face on top of its rather long neck was so animated that the features could not easily be judged; they were never still. She laughed a great deal, twisting her neck about; she smoked incessantly, she gestured with her hands. Her suit of dead plain cut in brown-and-white tiger-striped material led the eye upward to the elaborately coiled swathe of her bright brown hair, in which she wore a large green sparkling stone.

Sir Horace was pointing to this ornament and saying something; from his funereal expression nothing of the purport could be gathered but it seemed to be a piece of gallantry for the brown-haired girl let out a peal of laughter, audible all over the emptying room, and exclaimed,

"*Woolworth's,* Sir Horace! I get all my jewellery there, I can't afford anything better."

Harry looked up sharply from his conversation with

Fernanda; his eyes narrowed as he stared across the room. What's surprised him? Dominic wondered.

Enough guests had now filtered away so that Sir Horace, counting heads with a glazed but still-shrewd eye, evidently reckoned that he could start rounding-up for his dinner party.

"You can stay and have a bite can't you, Tree?" he said, noddingly lugubriously to Dominic. "Only sardines on toast, y'know, snack sort of thing, too poor for anything else—have to get used to that, midear," he said to the girl with him, giving her arm, which was tucked through his, a shake, "people will tell you I'm wealthy but it ain't so! Tourist accommodation and bread-and-cheese—that's all you'll get if we elope!"

"Why, Sir Horace, I thought we were going to live in a log hut and cook over a camp fire. Tourist accommodation is luxury to me!"

"Used to roughing it, eh?" Sir Horace disengaged his arm long enough to smack her familiarly on the bottom. "This beautiful gal is Hilda Trevis, a charmin' new acquaintance of mine," he told Dominic. "She and I are going to elope together to Australia, aren't we, midear?"

"Oh, now, Sir Horace, you told me the Solomon Islands!" The girl gave him a gay, flirtatious look. "I couldn't *stand* Australia, I'm afraid."

"Oh, very well, very well—any place where there's a bit of sun and the girls wear grass skirts," the conductor said, steering her with a hand on her thigh and calling over his shoulder, "Come along, come along, Fernanda and you others; I'm starving for a bit of food. Moved to these parts recently, have you?" Dominic heard him saying to the girl as they proceeded downstairs. "Good heavens, no, Sir Horace," she said in her high, carrying voice, "I've lived at Woodmouth ever since I was born, we do all our shopping in Bridpool."

"Have you, midear? How comes it that I've never seen you before, then?"

Dominic followed to the private dining room with Harry, Fernanda, and a group of half a dozen other people; he had not been mentioned in the original supper invitation and was rather annoyed at this casual, last-minute inclusion; for a moment he had had half a mind to plead another engagement, but something about Harry's expression made him curious, and a little apprehensive; he decided to swallow pride in the interests of professional research.

Sir Horace waved his guests vaguely to the table without troubling as to who sat where, and continued to devote his entire attention to the brown-haired girl. He was now asking her what she did for a living.

"I breed dogs, Sir Horace."

"Dogs! Good God!"

"I *know!* Isn't it *terrible!*" she agreed with another peal of laughter. "But it's the only thing I can do! I don't know any useful trade, I never had a proper education. And if we're going to elope, Sir Horace, I think it's only fair to warn you that I'm a perfect ignoramus—I don't know one note of music from another!"

"Well, I don't know anything about dogs, so that makes two of us." Sir Horace gave her his corpselike grin. "What's more, I don't want to. Nasty dangerous brutes. Don't you ever get bitten!"

"Oh, gracious yes, all the time, I'm covered with dog bites all *over!* But I'm used to it. Dog bites can be dangerous, though, if you don't take proper precautions. Don't you agree, Mr. Lupac?" She laughed provocatively across the table at Harry, who was sitting opposite her; Dominic observed that he had suspended his conversation with Fernanda to listen to this exchange.

But he gave the girl a cool, dismissing glance and only said, "Can they? I do not know anything about dogs either, I am afraid," before turning his head back to Fernanda.

Something odd there, Dominic said to himself, eating Sir Horace's delicious cold food with absent-minded approval while he continued to monitor the conversation of the two couples. That girl's needling Harry. Has she met him before? How can she have?

His neighbours became gayer and gayer. Sir Horace, looking more than ever like the death's head at the feast, was telling Hilda scandalous tales of orchestral tours in South America, at which she laughed loudly and uninhibitedly; Harry was entertaining Fernanda with descriptions of life in Paris. But Fernanda was very quiet, answering in monosyllables; she seemed embarrassed by her father's macabre hilarity.

"You and I are the quiet ones, Miss Chumley," Dominic murmured to her, in a moment when Sir Horace was appealing to Harry about some musical date—"Was it in '58 or '59, Harry, that the Warsaw Philharmonia fathered eighteen Maltese crosses?"

Fernanda Chumley turned her large, rather piteous dark eyes on him.

"You know what I feel like?" she said in a low voice. "Like an understudy who has forgotten her lines . . . Isn't that a silly thing to say?"

"A very charming understudy," Dominic answered inanely. She had hit the nail on the head, poor Fernanda, he thought; in some indefinable way she did not belong there at all, she was only a stand-in. But for whom? For two small, darkhaired girls abandoned somewhere in Eastern Europe?

Now Harry was playing the clown, mimicking a whole series of well-known operatic stars. Plainly these fireworks were not aimed at Fernanda any longer. All of a sudden it struck the listening Dominic that the three of them, Harry, Sir Horace, and the brown-haired girl, were like three birds competing in some courtship ritual, preening and displaying themselves—but who was courting whom? For whose benefit was it all put on? Harry's impersonations were startlingly clever and cruel, and most unsuitable; Dominic longed to kick him under the table. This party, he thought, was getting out of hand, not going according to plan at all, and the sooner he could extricate Harry the better it would be.

"This Harry's a clever boy, isn't he, Hilda?" Sir Horace was saying. "We'll have to arrange a series of concerts for him, yes, I think so. I'd better fix it before he starts his own comedy programme on telly, eh, Harry? Didn't know you had such a lot of hidden talent, me boy!"

"I'm sure he's quite brilliant," Hilda said with her side-long, flirtatious look at Harry, "but one opera singer is the same as another to me, I'm so dumb! Who was that last one supposed to be, Fresca Garroux? Oh no, she's the one who died, isn't she? Didn't you know her, though, Mr. Lupac? Now if only I were my sister I'd be able to appreciate you better. She's quite a musical girl —only fancy, Mr. Lupac, she was at a concert of yours on Thursday at the Philharmonic, isn't that a coincidence?"

"I should hardly have thought so. People do attend my concerts, I believe." Harry raised his brows. An odd silence fell.

"Harry—" Dominic glanced at his watch. "I hate to drag you away but remember you're playing in Bournemouth tomorrow afternoon—I think really—"

"This Dominic looks after me like one of your English nannies." Harry lamented to Fernanda. "And the worst of it is that he is always right! But I hope that we do not part for long—can we please meet again soon?"

"Of course," she murmured shyly.

"Goodbye, my boy. I'll be in touch about that series of concerts," Sir Horace gave Harry his graveyard leer. "Unless of course I decide to flit off to Papua with my charmin' neighbour here—" and he dug Hilda in the ribs. She squealed delightedly.

"What a man-eater," Dominic said as they went down in the lift. "I should think old Horace Chumley had met his match for once."

"Oh, I doubt it." Harry's tone was indifferent. "He really hardly tells one female from another. So soon as he picks up an orchestral score he will forget her existence again."

Dominic surprised himself by his next remark. "I thought there was something dangerous about her." Like a blade, he thought, like a sharp, bright razor blade that might fall into the wrong hands.

They reached the street in a silence which Harry ended by saying lightly, "So you led me away to protect your investment from her evil influence? Well, I am grateful to you, Dominic, for all your care. Now I am going to leave you to take a walk. We shall meet at two tomorrow at the Bournemouth Pavilion? Correct? Goodnight, then."

He strode off, his footsteps echoing hollowly in the empty streets. Dominic had an impulse to call after him, then checked himself; Harry, who seemed to need the barest minimum of sleep, was fascinated by Bridpool at night and often walked for miles through the docks. He would turn up in time for the concert tomorrow; professionally he was perfectly reliable.

Dominic shook himself impatiently and went round to the car-park, wondering why his own last words, spoken out of pure instinct, seemed to be lingering in his mind with such a dismal, prophetic ring.

Something dangerous about her.

Sunlight in these woods seemed a rarity and, when it came, strange and beautiful as a dream. Trees were close and thickset in the Woodhoe valley; the original oak forest had been allowed to remain on the lower slopes which belonged to the National Trust, but all the upper land, bordering on the moor, had been sold years ago to a thrifty company which had planted the slopes with a stand of chestnuts for fence-poles, and quick-growing conifers. The young chestnuts were about fifteen feet high now, bushy from cutting back, growing close together. Every half mile a long ride, or firebreak, gave a vista down the steep slope and a glimpse of the narrow road, painfully cut out of the hillside, which led down the side of the valley, ending at Woodmouth. Even into these artificial rides the sun filtered only on rare occasions, the leaves were so dense overhead; they made green, silent tunnels, carpeted with grass and last year's chestnut prickles, where the only sound was the dreamy roucouling of woodpigeons, the occasional squawk of a pheasant. Caroline preferred this part of the wood to the conifers; although so thick it was not dark because the trees were short; when, as now, the sun did shine, the warmth could be felt overhead even through the roof of leaves.

Head bent, hands in her pockets, she went along the slope with her quick fawnlike step, striking across from one ride to the next.

She had managed to escape once more without taking any of the dogs; there would be a scene when Hilda found out. Hilda seemed to have a current of electricity running through her these days; the slightest touch drew a jagged, tearing spark.

She had gone off to some party last night—Hilda never discussed her friends at home or talked of where she had been unless information was dragged from her by Lady Trevis—but she had dressed for this occasion with extreme care and when she came back, very late, was in a strange mood, angry, triumphant, feverishly gay, ready to lash out at trifles. The mood had lasted overnight and into today, Sunday. Even Cousin Flora's usual chirpiness was somewhat quenched by it; a good many of Hilda's barbed remarks seemed aimed in her direction. Caroline, strung to unbearable tension, had slipped out after lunch to get away into a few hours' peace and freedom; the charged atmosphere had given her a violent headache.

Late afternoon sunshine, brilliant gold, shot with dust motes, slanted between the chestnuts and bathed the road at the bottom of the tunnel, striking sparks from flecks of mica in the metalled surface. In the village, two miles down the valley, a church bell donged faintly for evensong, but no cars passed; the valley road was little used because of its final precipitously steep drop into Woodmouth. The main Bridpool highway, bulldozed into easier gradients, curved in an arc south of the village and rejoined this minor road ten miles away on the moor.

These woods were safe; no troubling memories haunted them. But above, on Caroline's left, the old railway ran out of the hill and the signalman's cottage lay hidden behind a thicket of young ash saplings, grown tall since four years ago. Not for any consideration would she climb up there; at the very thought of the place, her heart was compressed by anguish and shame, by a hopeless longing to push time back and let her life take a different course no matter how humble, unhappy, or shadowed. She dared not remember the celestial happiness of those far-off days; it had been bought at too high a price.

In an effort to outdistance these thoughts she unconsciously quickened her pace, then froze, hearing footsteps and a shrill tuneless whistling ahead of her. Somebody was running down the next ride, approaching Caroline's course at right angles. In a moment she saw him.

"Oh, God, no!" whispered Caroline.

A small boy in jeans, in a red T shirt with a large blue anchor on it; for a moment the illusion was complete, and Caroline, in utter terror, thought, It can't be, how can it be? What is happening to me? It *is*—before the boy swung round, revealing a totally unknown face, and saw her.

The shirt, of course. It's just the shirt. Her mind began freewheeling. Gladys's Garry—he's bigger, the shirt is really too small for him, she thought. It's Gladys Vernon's Garry. Surely he's wandering rather a long way from home for such a little boy—he can't be much over five. Older—a couple of years older than—but he must be small for his age.

Even in the brief face-to-face glimpse they had, something of the shock and dread in Caroline's face must have communicated itself to the boy. Throwing back a startled glance he fled on down the hill even faster, making for the sunlit circle of roadway at the foot of the tunnel. He carried a crudely made bow and a handful of arrows—Hereward? or Robin Hood? Perhaps he was playing outlaws and Normans; perhaps he thought she was the owner of the woods and might punish him.

"It's all right, I won't hurt you," called Caroline. "Wait—"

But he dashed on unheeding. Neither of them had noticed the car coming down from the moor, its sound muffled by the twisting of the upper valley. Now it turned a last bend, entered the long, straight tempting stretch of road directly below, and accelerated.

Caroline, reaching the ride, looked down and saw the little red-and-blue figure recede at headlong speed, then flash out into the circle of sunlight. She saw the quick dazzle of a windscreen, heard the scream of brakes, the bite of metal on rubber, rubber on tarmac. A voice shouted. A car door slammed.

She began to run, on legs that felt curiously weak. As she ran she was sobbing, dry sobs from a constricted throat. Oh, please not. Please not. Oh, please.

When she was two-thirds of the way down, the scene below her drew into focus like the circle of light at the end of a telescope: the rear end of a white sports car slewed diagonally across the road, a man in a white shirt stooping over something that lay on the ground—a crumpled heap of red and blue. The man straightened up; he flung some object from him with a violent look of revulsion and walked quickly out of the circle. He was not aware of Caroline, yards above him in the ride's sloping shaft of dimness. A moment later there came the loud double roar of the car's exhaust, its rear end swung round out of view, and a flash of white passed a gap in the trees further away.

The red-and-blue bundle lay motionless.

Caroline took another faltering step. Her legs felt like wool. The green roof above, upheld by its lancelike chestnut columns, began to revolve and swirl in a dizzy kaleidoscope of light and shade, which narrowed to a deep green pit, open to swallow her. She fell into it, down and down. She lay where she had fallen, hidden from the road, behind a thick screen of low-growing secondary growth.

She did not hear the other car that slowed and stopped, an hour later, or the footsteps, or the shocked exclamations. By the time she came back to consciousness the sun had set, and the road was empty, and no sound broke the twilight hush. A thin rain had begun to fall.

I must have dreamed it, she said to herself. I fell asleep in the wood and had a dreadful dream. No worse than the ones I've been getting at night but I've never had one in daytime before. And she thought again, what is happening to me? Why does Dr. Galbraith say that I'm better? Oh, Tim, Tim, what shall I do?

She pulled herself up weakly and started for home on a slanting course, diagonally down the side of the valley, cutting across the rides on stiff legs that still trembled from the deep aftermath of shock. The evening's chill seemed to have settled under her skin.

"*There* you are," Hilda said irritably when she entered the house with its depressing smell of damp and dogs. "What *have* you been doing? Walking to Mars? A man's rung up twice for you—wouldn't leave a message."

"Who was it?" Caroline put a hand against the dark panelling to steady herself; her eyes were dazed, overbright. "Not—not Tim?"

"Lord, no. *I* don't know. He wouldn't say. Of course not Tim—have a bit of sense! I daresay he'll ring again. Why the dickens can't you take some of the dogs when you go out; you might make a *slight* effort to be useful."

"You know they'd get away from me," Caroline said. "I couldn't hold them."

She went exhaustedly up the stairs and lay on her bed; she knew she ought to change her damp clothes but felt too weak. Presently the telephone rang.

"Caroline!" Hilda's voice called. "It's for you."

Galvanised, she somehow pulled herself up and ran downstairs.

"Where do you get to?" Hilda said with precariously controlled exasperation.

"I was in my room."

"You took long enough to answer."

Caroline walked past her into the annexe and picked up the receiver, which lay on the shelf by the telephone. It buzzed at her faintly.

"Hullo?" she said into it. "Hullo?"

After a pause a voice snapped, "Number, please? What number did you want?"

"Somebody rang me up—somebody wanted this number."

"They must have rung off—there's nobody on the line now."

"Could you trace where the call came from?"

"Sorry, can't do that."

"I see. Thank you." Slowly, Caroline replaced the receiver in its cradle.

Three

The gong, dented brass, large as a young coffee table, hung among cobwebs and shadows in the downstairs hall.

Of all Hudson's tasks, the only one he truly appeared to enjoy was banging on it before breakfast; this he did with the vindictive pleasure of a Chinese torturer in an early film. Everything in the hall vibrated: the antlers, the warped billiards' cues, the crossed weapons. Several dogs always set up a dismayed barking.

One day, thought Caroline, perhaps the whole house will topple down, in a mess of crumbling stone and powdered, rotten wood, when Hudson hammers on the gong. She shivered as she came slowly downstairs; outside, rain fell steadily, flattening the murmur of the river; indoors, the brazen clangour seemed to penetrate her bones and shake loose memories of last night's troubled dreams; she had slept badly with recurring nightmares.

Hudson's blanked-out expression hardly changed when she said good morning; it was as if they had never held that strange little conversation the other night. Today he seemed even more tremulous than usual and his watery eyes were red-rimmed.

Lady Trevis, who suffered from insomnia, was always awake by seven and longing for human company, even that of her daughters or her cousin. Seldom dressed before noon, she trailed about the house in a random assortment of nightwear, and with the hollow look of somebody who has been thrown on their own resources for longer than is bearable.

This morning she was already in the dining room, ignoring the conversational essays of Cousin Flora, shredding savagely through a pile of mail that consisted entirely of bills and advertisements. Hilda, having sorted through the mail when it came, extracted and read two letters—who wrote to Hilda? nobody knew—and dropped them into the sulky fire, was staring out of the window with a morose, preoccupied air. Her feverish mood of the previous day seemed to have gone, leaving her with an emotional hangover; she ignored the others in the room.

"Bills, bills, bills! Anybody would think the bloody dogs lived on caviare and salmon," Lady Trevis said, riffling through the heap of buttery, crumby envelopes round her plate. "Hudson, this toast's foul—burnt at the edges and soggy in the middle. Bring some more, will you?"

"Sorry, m'lady." Hudson took the toast rack and gave her a hating look out of his filmy eyes. "Mrs. Hudson's upset, as is only to be expected. I'll tell her you didn't like the toast." He shuffled away.

"What a shame!" sympathised Cousin Flora brightly. "Burnt toast *is* so nasty, isn't it? Such a pity you don't eat these Slimyum Toastiebisks—are you sure you won't have one while you wait? They're ever so good for you!"

"For God's sake, no, Flora!"

Flora subsided, looking hurt, and applied herself to reading the medical brochures which she sent for and received in large numbers, and the reviews of detective fiction in yesterday's Sunday papers.

"You were supposed to inquire," Hilda said, coming out of her abstraction and speaking to her mother.

"Inquire what?"

"Why Mrs. Hudson's upset, of course."

"Oh, tell me now! If something's the matter, then why don't they say so? I'm not psychic! I can't stand being hinted at."

Hilda shrugged and turned back to the window.

Since Hudson was demonstrating his independence

by being as slow as possible with the toast, Lady Trevis turned on the silent Caroline.

"That husband of yours doesn't write very often does he?"

"I expect he's busy," Caroline said defensively.

"Busy or not, you'd think he'd find time to drop a line. It would be only civil to write to me, sometimes—after all, who's putting you up and looking after you? Not that precious mother of his who's always flying off to Syria. And while we're on the subject of Tim, Caroline, I really do think that after all the time we've had you here the least he could do—"

"Oh, Mother—"

"What do you mean, oh Mother?" demanded Lady Trevis.

"If you're going to say he ought to invest in the dogs or start a guesthouse—"

"Of course he ought!" said Lady Trevis indignantly. "There are the Conroys, stinking with money, here we are practically starving on our feet, and what do you do to help us? Invest all Aunt Prue's legacy in that firm. What does Tim do? Fine sort of son-in-law he is!"

"I've told you, all he draws from the firm is the salary of a junior executive. And anyway," said Caroline rashly, "why should he? He's not likely to get much return on it."

Lady Trevis opened her mouth to reply, but Hudson returned at this moment and thumped down the large tarnished silver toast rack angrily in front of her. One of Lady Trevis's post-wedding extravagances had been a glass table with elaborate wrought-iron legs; it stood out, incongruous and forlorn among the late-Victorian dining-room furniture. Hudson always clanged dishes down on it as if he hoped that one day a fine long crack would appear on its rippled surface.

"Gladys won't be coming today," he announced with gloomy relish. "*As* is to be expected in the circumstances."

"Do take care, Hudson!" Lady Trevis snapped. "*What* circumstances? Why is it to be expected?"

"Hadn't you heard, then?"

"Heard what? Of course we haven't heard anything."

"Gladys lost her little boy."

Caroline put down her cup with a clatter; the colour slowly ebbed from her cheeks.

"Lost him? How do you mean lost him? You mean he wandered off? I've told her before that she should keep a better eye on him, or leave him in charge of somebody. I've seen him right up in the woods before now."

"Not wandered off—*killed*." Hudson stared at her, trembling but truculent.

"Killed?"

He held his audience now; they were all watching him as if hypnotised.

"By one o' them hit-and-run motorists," he said. "I told her time and agen how it would be if she chose to come up here, leaving him to run wild, just account of she wanted to earn a few bob extra. They make out all right on Joe's salary as police constable, they don't need more. But these gals are all the same nowadays, anything to get money for perms and never-never payments and let their kids go to pot."

"But when did it happen?"

"Yesterday art'noon, time she was up here washing the dinner dishes. Parson found him up to Woodhoe Bottom, 'bout ha'past six. 'Course he was done for."

Oh my God, thought Caroline, it wasn't a dream then. *I* did that. If he hadn't been wearing that shirt—if he hadn't seen me and been startled—I know I should have burned those clothes, I should never have let Mother give them away. I was too cowardly to deal with them myself and now the black influence that's on me has touched somebody else . . .

She stumbled to her feet, knocking against the table.

"Dearie, what's the matter? Take care!"

"Caroline, do look out. You've spilt coffee all over my mail."

Hilda raised her brows and Hudson turned his old tortoise's head in vague perturbation, but Caroline, without speaking, hurried blindly from the room.

"Now I suppose we'll have a relapse and highstrikes all over the place again," Lady Trevis said irritably.

Hilda shrugged and drank some more coffee and went on staring out over the rain-pocked river.

On the roof of Tim Conroy's bungalow in Ras al-Abdan the sun struck with pitiless strength. The faulty air conditioning had gone wrong again, but he was used to that. He sat with a wet towel round his head and neck, trying to work. There was a sort of desperation in his young, ugly, intelligent face; the lines on either side of the wide mouth deepened and his eyes darkened as he took out and read for the fourth time a little scribbled letter on airmail paper:

Darling Tim—Oh I wish, I wish I was with you. I'm sure I'm strong enough, whatever Mother says. The trouble is that I still can't remember what happened but Dr. Galbraith says I will in time—but it wasn't all my fault, was it? Please say it wasn't. I'm sure it isn't because it was my fault that I can't remember. Darling, they say you'll never want me again but please come and get me. I truly am well enough to come back and I do hate it so here, I'm so frightened and lonely and unhappy. Please don't forget me, please come for me soon. . . .

It was blotted and unevenly written, the paper had a soiled appearance as if it had been hidden in a pocket and furtively taken out to post. Tim compared it with another letter, efficiently typed, which said:

Dear Tim, I do hope you are not worrying about Caroline. As you know, she is still in a highly neurotic state, which is not to be wondered at, but her physical condition is definitely improving. Dr. Galbraith does think, though, that it will be a long time, if ever, before she is fit enough to go out to Ras al-Abdan and face the hot weather—and inevitable unhappy memories—again. In the circumstances,

*though it seems hard, we do feel it would be better
if you didn't encourage her to false hopes by writing
too often or making any promises that might be
hard to keep, as she gets overbalanced and upset
at the slightest thing. Of course Mother and I are
taking the greatest care of her.*

Affectionately,

Hilda

His eye went back to the first letter. Please, please
don't forget me, please come for me soon—

Today there was another envelope with an English
stamp and unfamiliar handwriting. He had left it till last
and now picked it up without much interest because of
the depressed mood that English mail always aroused in
him.

The room where he sat was unnaturally neat and
quiet; sometimes he felt tempted to strew newspapers
and gramophone records, leave drawers and books
open, drop his clothes on the floor, just for a bit of com-
panionable mess, but he found this too unnatural, he was
scrupulously neat by nature. And yet he had not been
worried by Caroline's untidiness; he had been touched
and amused by it, feeling that to be untidy liberated
something in her.

"This looks like a *real* bedroom," he used to say,
sniffing spilt powder with relish, admiring the fine hotch-
potch of tossed-down filmy garments and cosmetics—
not that Caroline used a great deal of make-up, or
needed to, he thought affectionately—and sandals and
sketchbooks and volumes of poetry. "You can see that
people really live here. A tidy house means that nobody's living properly—they just spend their lives tidying
up." "Oh darling, I do love you," Caroline said hug-
ging him, "I will reform a bit, presently, about putting
things away, but living out here with you is such a pleasure, there are so many wonderful things to do, that tidying
always seems to come at the bottom of the list."

Caroline had loved the life at Ras al-Abdan. Unlike
some of the company wives, she had never been bored.

And there had been toys strewn about, too. . . .

With a strong, deliberate effort, Tim put that thought out of his mind and opened his last letter. It was in a black, flamboyant handwriting; in bulk on the page it became vaguely familiar from a long time back.

Dear old Tim, I expect you will be thunderstruck at getting a letter from your ancient tennis and sword-dance partner (do you still remember those terrible dancing classes when Monsieur Bolitoff used to come to our house and you were so furious because you were made to wear a kilt?). Well, while you've been gadding about seeing the world I've been an old stay-at-home helping Brother Marcus school his hunters—quite amusing up to a point but it's beginning to pall and I'm looking round for fresh pastures!! I'd never have thought of getting in touch with you if something Hilda said hadn't put it into my head. So I'm taking me courage in both hands to write and ask if there's any chance of a job out there for me with your firm?!!! I've got secretarial qualifications (believe it or not) as I've been doing Mark's accounts and correspondence, and my French isn't bad because of all those years at Vevey. Am I very forward to write like this? Anyway you can always slap me down!

I saw Caroline the other day. She still looks a bit peaky, can't seem to cheer up. Are you sure that Woodhoe House is the best place for her? There isn't much going on down here. You'll probably say it's none of my business but I should have thought a nice cheerful convalescent home would be a better bet. But then I've never been exactly crazy about Lady T and Hilda as you may remember.

Forgive me for writing such reams when you're probably up to your neck in work.

All the best,
Lorraine

(still Miss Duke in case you didn't know)

Lorraine! Of course now he remembered. A big hearty girl with golliwog hair, seen at all the local dances and tennis matches, brash, loud-voiced, and cheerful, with hardly two ideas to rub together. What on earth had suddenly possessed her to write to him for a job? Weren't there any employment agencies? He read the letter again. This time he noticed the phrase "something Hilda said." Hilda had always despised Lorraine, what could have persuaded her to turn helpful and make suggestions? It was not in Hilda's character. Perhaps Lorraine had taken up a casual remark of Hilda's and magnified its importance. Or had her letter a hidden motive? Frowning, he read the last paragraph a third time. Was Lorraine hinting that Caroline needed help? Were the words intended to be taken like that? Or could she—possibly—be trying to break it to him that Caroline was now so much worse that a mental home would be the only solution?

He summoned up the image of Lorraine: big plummy eyes and cushiony cheeks, that rather braying laugh. She had always seemed a straightforward enough creature, a little thick-skinned but harmless and good-natured. Not the kind to drop obscure hints, he would have said, or write the sort of lines that needed to be read between. He decided to take the letter at its face value. In any case there were no jobs for her out here. He would write politely in a few days and tell her so.

But all the same he was left vaguely troubled by her remarks about Woodhoe House.

The rain persisted for the rest of the day, like a sullen protest against yesterday's unaccustomed fine weather. There was a brief brightening in the afternoon, then the sky sank and thickened, closing down like a dripping grey lid. The trees in the valley hunched their shoulders against the downpour and kept away what light there was from Woodhoe House.

By five the disused nursery on the second floor was almost dark. Its bare, rubbed floor palely reflected the dismal sky, but the two people who had come there to talk undisturbed were almost invisible to each other, since there was no bulb in the light socket. Not for years had the room held toys or children, and its air of frigid abeyance had affected the present occupants, who spoke conspiratorially, in undertones.

"But I tell you I recognised him—I knew his face. I couldn't possibly mistake it. Why, I saw him so recently. And in any case, with all there's been about him in the papers for the last few months he's as familiar as—as one of the Beatles."

"All right. All right. You recognised the face. You think you did. But honey, just think for a minute"—the other voice was weary, had been over this several times —"are you sure you didn't just dream the whole thing? In your present state an upsetting bit of news like that could so easily trigger off something of the kind. You know you've been—well, imagining a lot of things lately that haven't actually happened. All those times you thought you heard the phone ringing in the night. And the lights you thought you saw in the garden, and that business of the snake in the bath—"

"*Don't.* I know I saw this, I know I did." The first voice was agonised, trembling. "The—the blood. It was horrible. I couldn't have imagined it."

"And you've been sleepwalking, too, ducky, and losing things and forgetting things. You see—if we went to the police as you suggest—well, everyone round here knows you, and of course we all *love* you, but, frankly, sweetie, just the way things are at present, I doubt if they'd believe your story for one moment. They know you've been— well, ill, you see, and they all sympathise like mad, but—"

"I've got to make them believe. You'll help me, Dee, won't you?"

"Please *don't* call me Dee."

"I'm sorry—I forget. But please help me. Because in a way it was my fault."

"Your *fault?* What do you mean?"

"He—you see when I saw Garry, I thought—he was wearing one of the shirts."

"One of the shirts? What shirts?"

"The—the clothes that were given to Gladys. And when I saw Garry wearing it, for a moment I thought—"

"All right, Ducky, take it easy. You saw him wearing the shirt and you were upset, that's natural. But after all there wasn't a *hoodoo* on the shirt, let's be practical."

"No," doubtfully, "but it was such a shock to *me* that I frightened *him*. He went rushing down the hill and out into the road—"

"Oh, rubbish, ducky, young Garry was always charging about. It probably had nothing to do with you."

"And then I had to go and faint—if I'd helped him right away—"

"Look, you've got to stop thinking in this morbid way," the second voice said with a touch of irritation. "What good does it do?"

"But I can't just keep quiet if I knew who ran him over, can I? And then just calmly drove on and left him lying there in the road. . . ."

"You really must make an effort to put all this out of your mind. Who are you trying to punish? Think of yourself. Think of Tim. You'll only make yourself worse again. And Tim wouldn't want you to be mixed up with some nasty sordid case, giving evidence in court, would he? Don't you *want* to get well enough to go back to him? And then you see," the second voice ran on persuasively without a pause, "it's a frightfully tricky legal position. Someone as well known as that would get the best lawyers, you can be sure, and the next thing would be that you found yourself hit by a slander action, let in for huge damages. Tim would simply hate that, wouldn't he? Honestly, ducky, I'd leave it alone. Forget the whole thing. Much better. You see, it isn't as if you have a shred of proof, have you?"

"But I have. I have! I saw his white sports car and the number—CC 5000."

"Ah."

The silence about them changed its quality and became suddenly dynamic. There was a pause.

"Look." Hilda's voice was quite different. Kindly, patient, disbelieving reasonableness had gone. Something hard, purposeful, and reserved had taken its place. "Leave it to me. Don't do a thing; don't say a word to anyone. They'll only think you're nuts if you do, and you don't want that, do you? When you do see Galbraith again you want him to say you're well enough to go back to Tim, don't you? Well, then, ducky, don't get all steamed up, *I'll* take care of this. I'm going to town this evening to a play with Esmee and Brenda; I'll stop over and see a lawyer tomorrow and tell him the whole story. A day won't make any difference. Okay?"

"Okay." It was the faintest sigh, hardly more than a whisper, and it was suddenly, raucously drowned by the violent shrilling of a bell somewhere nearby which exploded the silence. "Hilda! What was that?"

"What was what, sweetie?"

"That—that noise. That bell."

"Bell? There hasn't been any bell. There hasn't been any noise at all."

"You must have heard it, Hilda! It was deafening."

"Ducky, you know you're still pretty mouldy and overwrought. This business has got you all shaken up again, I'm afraid—"

"Do—do you think I'd better go and see Galbraith about it? He could hardly say that I'd made *this* up."

"I'd not bother him at the moment, sweetie. After all, it's only five days since he gave you the push, isn't it —I mean, said you were better. Rather bad if you hustle back so fast. D'you think he'd be *pleased?*"

"N-no, but I'd feel happier if I could talk to him—"

"I wouldn't, if I were you. No, I think he'd definitely call it a bad sign if you run yipping to him at the first trifle. He told you, didn't he, to try and stand on your own feet? I should leave it a while. You just concentrate on getting well enough to go back to Tim. Come along, we'd better go downstairs. We don't want to be found here, do we?"

The auditorium of the Philharmonic Hall was packed for Harry's Festival Week concert; until the final bell, people continued to pour and pour up the wide, airy,

polished stairs. Dozens of optimists, queueing in hopes
of a cancelled seat, were disappointed and had to con-
sole themselves as best they might with a view of Bridpool by night from the roof garden, garlands of lights
climbing the encircling hills. Dominic, craning round to
survey the hall, noted the ranks of internationally famous
faces with satisfaction. This was Harry's first major concert and all seemed set for success.

The confused drone and mutter of tuning died away
as Sir Horace came in, nodded to the scatter of applause, and led the orchestra briskly into the Sicilian Ves-
pers overture (he said he had chosen it because it always reminded him of his honeymoon, but Dominic felt
more inclined to believe that he enjoyed the thought of a
good massacre).

Harry was to play the Sibelius D minor violin concerto
and, in the second half of the concert, to conduct himself and the orchestra in a Mozart violin concerto. Dominic hoped this programme would not put too much of
a strain on him; for the last day or two he had seemed
faintly distrait, not exactly worried, but as if the thought
of some forgotten task were fidgeting at his mind. Whatever this might be, it did not seem to affect his playing,
however; Sir Horace had been enthusiastic, after his
usual funereal fashion, at the morning's rehearsal.

"Really, it's a remarkable talent," he confided to Dominic. "The astonishing thing is that he didn't pop across
the fence to liberty and the pursuit of happiness long ago,
considering how the Reds must have kept him under a
bushel; you can't tell *me* that fiddlers of his calibre are
two a penny over there. And he's only, what, thirty-one—
years of professional life before him still. Hope we
don't lose him to the Yanks, that's all."

"He seems happy enough here," Dominic said, ob-
serving with interest that Harry had taken advantage of
the rehearsal break to work his way round to Fernanda
and chat with her over a cup of coffee.

"Have to keep him happy, shan't we?" Sir Horace
said, following Dominic's eye with a lugubrious grin.

*　　*　　*

Where was Fernanda tonight? Dominic wondered. He glanced about while the orchestra was being redisposed, and found her sitting not very far away. She wore grey, with white ruffles, which did not make the best of her pale colouring, and she looked tense and nervous, leaning forward, twisting her gloves. Dominic smiled at her reassuringly, and received a faint smile in return. Well, a bit of anxiety did her credit and was natural enough; after all Harry was quite a protégé of her father's and this was his first appearance before an audience containing Royalty.

The little man seated beside Fernanda seemed to be asking her numerous questions and Dominic studied him curiously; who could this total stranger be and how had he acquired a seat? Round, plump, and spectacled, he looked about him with unblushing curiosity as if he had never been in a concert hall before. Fernanda answered his questions kindly and he nodded, sitting back and studying the door through which Harry would appear.

Harry came in; there was a wash of applause, which he acknowledged briefly. He looked, as always in public, preoccupied, stern, and quite unconcerned by the size of his audience. Ignoring the mass of faces, he kept his attention fixed on Sir Horace.

It's all right, Dominic thought after a few minutes. I needn't have worried. He's never played better. It was ridiculous to have doubts; if there's anything that one can be sure of with Lupac it's stability. So-called artistic temperament is quite lacking from his make-up; he's completely cold-blooded. His playing isn't cold-blooded, though, Dominic conceded; it's . . . triumphant. Sir Horace was right to choose the Sibelius. Leaning back, surrendering professional responsibility for a minute, he allowed the music to pour over and through him like a great wind.

Harry had made it known that he wished to be left alone in the interval, so after the waves of thunderous clapping had died, Dominic went to talk to Fernanda. The little man next to her had gone out, to get a drink or look at the roof garden; Dominic slipped into his empty seat.

"Who's your friend?" he asked with his usual direct curiosity.

"Which?"

"The man with glasses who looks like an insurance salesman."

"I don't know."

"I saw him talking to you, I thought—"

"No, he was just asking questions about the orchestra. And if Harry—Mr. Lupac—had come in yet. He's playing well, isn't he?"

"Very well. Your father ought to be pleased."

"Oh, he is, you can see. Look, he's left the Earl and Countess; he's up there talking to that girl, Miss Trevis."

Dominic looked up, startled, and saw that Sir Horace was perched on the edge of one of the drawerlike tiers of boxes, looking like an animated gargoyle, and talking vigorously to the occupant of the box, who was laughing a great deal.

"I didn't know she was here," Dominic said rather discontentedly. "Did your father get her the box?"

"I suppose so. Here's my neighbour coming back."

Dominic stood up to make way for the plump man.

"Shall I be seeing you after the performance?" he asked Fernanda politely. "Are you joining your father's party?"

"Perhaps—I'll see." She gave him another anxious smile and he went back to his seat.

Bother that Trevis girl, he thought, not attending to the Passacaglia which began the second half of the programme. Why do I have the feeling that she's a kind of Jonah? It isn't like me to have premonitions. But I hope she turns out to be one of Sir Horace's more passing fancies. He glanced uneasily towards Hilda's box where she was sitting erect and composed, with a remote, thoughtful expression. I wonder if Harry knows she's here? Dominic wondered.

Harry evidently did not, and just as evidently noticed her when he came on to conduct the Mozart. Sir Horace had reappeared in her box and gave Harry the leer that was his version of a friendly encouraging smile. Harry's recovery was instantaneous; he raised his brows and glanced briefly over the rest of the boxes; Dominic thought that an amused gleam came into the Trevis girl's eye.

Her presence certainly did not affect Harry's performance or conducting. Standing with his back to the orchestra, he shepherded them with an occasional admonishing glance over his shoulder; the Mozart was sheer bravura, a dazzling display from beginning to end. Harry finally relaxed his stern demeanour enough to give the audience one confiding schoolboy grin which was rapturously acclaimed. His lock of hair had fallen forward again and his tie had worked loose with the energy of his playing. He rode the sea of applause like a cork.

"Fireworks, fireworks," Sir Horace muttered in Dominic's ear afterwards. "They like it, though."

Everybody was exhilarated; Sir Horace came down and patted Harry on the back, the audience cheered and roared; later, in his dressing room, Harry was friendly to the press, and when they all left, Dominic had the comfortable expectation of some excellent notices in tomorrow's papers. Even Fernanda's cheeks were faintly pink.

"Well, well, shall we all go and have a drink somewhere?" said Sir Horace, bustling in when he had said civil goodnights to the Highnesses. He brought Hilda with him; she seemed gay and combative; her eyes had the tempered glitter of Scandinavian steel. "How about popping along to the Hoopoe and listening to some jazz for a change, that suit you, Harry?"

"I am so sorry," Harry said smoothly, "but I promised Fernanda that I would take her somewhere quiet; I do not think she will feel like jazz and I too am a little tired. Another time I should love to come to the Hoopoe. We will think of you listening to your jazz, will we not, Fernanda? Goodnight everybody, goodnight, dear Dominic."

His glance roved past Hilda without interest. Neatly and expeditiously he whisked Fernanda away before anybody had time to make a counterproposal.

"Aha," Sir Horace said, not at all put out. "Plans of

his own, eh, the cunning young dog! Well, youth will to youth. What about you, eh, Tree, won't you come along with us?"

Dominic excused himself on the grounds of a full and elaborate schedule next day; he left Sir Horace and Hilda making hilarious plans for the evening's entertainment and wondered if he had imagined a momentary flash of pure cold rage in her eye when Harry left without speaking to her.

It was after one when Harry returned home, silent, sober, and alone.

He had found a flat on the top floor of an old building near the docks, high up and isolated among warehouses and shipping offices; hardly any of his associates knew about it, apart from Dominic. At night and at week ends he had no neighbours—except caretakers and nightwatchmen—and could practise for hours together if he chose without complaints from disturbed sleepers. On all sides of him barred doors, locked gates, empty counters, covered typewriters brooded in a labyrinth of silence.

One of the flat's disadvantages was the lack of a lift, but this did not disturb Harry; he ran easily up the stairs, whistling a Mozart cadenza, fresh and businesslike as if it had been brisk morning instead of the dead hour of night.

At the top of the stairs he paused, frowning slightly; a narrow streak of light showed under his front door. He knew the light had not been switched on when he left, in daylight. Nobody else had access to his flat.

He opened the door and went in.

The place was only half furnished; some rooms were quite empty and he had not bothered to decorate the lobby. Its paint was peeling and blistered and the old, thick oak floorboards were grey with age. He stepped quickly and quietly across them and looked through the door beyond into a good-sized room with a fireplace oddly sited in one corner and sloping attic ceilings. The walls had been newly distempered in cream, and dark blue curtains hid the windows, but beyond this there was no attempt at decoration. It was a bony, masculine room; the chairs, acquired secondhand, were office furniture, tubular metal and canvas; a large leather-covered table, much stained, was smothered in manuscript music. A grand piano stood in one corner, a divan in another; there were two heavy, wide, leather-covered armchairs, which had plainly been clawed by generations of cats. Hilda Trevis was sitting in one of them, smoking. She gave Harry a brilliant smile.

"Hullo, darling! What late hours you keep! How was the quiet spot? Did you have a nice time?"

Harry had checked at sight of her; he bit back an exclamation in his own language and then said slowly, without much expression,

"Hilda. How did you get in?"

He was both relieved and annoyed.

"Wouldn't you like to know?" Hilda said gaily. "Shall I keep it a secret?"

He crossed the room and stood by her armchair. She lay back, indolent, smiling, looking up at him.

"You had better tell me," he said.

"That sounds terribly ominous, sweetie! What will you do if I don't? Bamboo slivers under the fingernails, or one of those horrid techniques you had to learn in your military training? I expect you're quite capable of it."

"It is just," he said with patient reasonableness, "that if there is an unauthorized means of entry into my flat I would wish to know and do something about it. One of my fiddles is a Stradivarius, which is quite valuable, you know."

He glanced about the room as if checking its contents. All seemed as he had left it. The floor was thick with cigarette ash and newspapers. Half unrolled on the piano top was a Philharmonic Hall poster, printed in black and red: Harry's face staring remotely at the ceiling over the single word LUPAC and tonight's programme. Drawers and cupboards were shut.

"You keep everything locked, anyway," Hilda remarked, following his eyes. "Secretive bastard, aren't you? Naturally I hoped to rummage for your old love letters from other women, but no such luck. I really pity the poor burglar that gets in here."

"You have not told me yet how *you* got in."

"Simple, darling." She blew a smoke ring expertly. "Let it be a lesson to you not to send your girl friends on errands. Remember on Thursday when you thought it would be nice if I went out for cigarettes? That shady little man, Vosper, who has a stall in the Corn Market, cuts keys while you wait."

"Give it to me," he said calmly, holding out his hand.

"But sweetie, why? What's wrong with my having a key?"

"Just that I do not choose to allow anybody but myself the freedom of this flat."

She looked as if she were meditating resistance, but his eyes held hers coldly; after a moment or two she shrugged, opened her bag, and handed over the key.

He inspected it, tried it in the door to make sure that it was the correct one, and then put it in his pocket.

"How do you know," Hilda said, "that I haven't two more at home?"

Harry turned and stared at her; he had been taking cans of beer out of a cupboard. After a moment he said, "I do not believe you, but if you have, you are a very silly girl. It means only that I shall have to change the lock. Did you leave your car outside?"

"No, no, relax! It's in the public car-park as usual."

"I am glad to hear it. Do you want some beer?"

"Please."

When he handed her the glass she put up a hand and lazily stroked his cheek.

"Don't be such an old sourpuss! You know you're really quite pleased to see me. You had a devilish tiring evening with that drippy girl—come on, confess!"

"Not a bit. It was very pleasant," he said, throwing himself back in the other armchair. "You, of course, had a riotous time with Sir Horace?"

"Oh, I needed to slap him down a few times," she said cheerfully, "but he's not bad."

"Tell me why you are chasing him?"

"Sweetie! To get a sight of you, naturally."

She beamed at him so brilliantly that he gave her a reluctant smile.

"You spider-woman! Weaving your webs—you won't catch me unless I choose."

"We shall see," Hilda said. "Anyway you rather like to be woven for, don't you? And I'm a lot better company than Fernanda Chumley, come now, amn't I?" She got up and slid into his chair beside him working an arm under his neck. "I know your tastes; I know you don't like sad, inhibited, dark girls." She wriggled herself more comfortably against him, resting her chin on his head, brushing her breast against his cheek.

"How have you been lately? Working yourself to death? I keep reading about your concerts in the papers. Wasn't it odd that my sister should drop in at your afternoon recital on Thursday?"

"It was lucky she didn't see us together," he said. "What was she doing there?"

"Her psychiatrist lives just up the hill from there; she'd been seeing him."

"Is she getting any better?" he asked, beginning, with an absorbed, preoccupied expression, to stroke her breast with one finger.

"Caroline? I suppose a little." Hilda's voice held a faint note of surprise at his interest. "She was offered a job in Bridpool. But I soon put a stop to that idea. I've found her something much more suitable—voluntary work in Woodmouth, sitting in the Parish hut on Wednesday and Friday nights, doling out books to the villagers." She laughed quietly to herself.

Harry said lazily, "You intend that she shall be tied down by these local commitments, little by little, until she is paralysed, is that it?"

"Perhaps.—Harry," Hilda said.

"What is it?"

"Why all this elaborate secrecy about you and me?

Why should it matter if Caroline saw us together? Why do I get the brush-off at Sir Horace's party?"

"Why?"

"Yes, why?" she insisted. "You're a free agent—who the hell cares if we do know each other?"

"Because"—he smiled at her caressingly, his eyes half shut—"simply because—and you know this very well, I think—I have this mania for privacy. I do not like my personal life exposed to the world. I do not like the newspapers to say 'Mr. Lupac the noted violinist tells us he is just very good friends with Miss Hilda Trevis the well-known West Country beauty!'" He ran his hand lingerlingly down her lame leg. She flinched a little. "I like it that our connection is a secret—that not a single soul in the whole world knows we are together. Do not you? Is there not something fascinating about such a relationship?"

"Perhaps," she said slowly.

"I think there is." He twisted himself round and moved her head forward, with a hand on her long neck, so that he could kiss her, which he did with a thoughtful, faraway expression.

"Perhaps," said Hilda again. Then added, "But not as a permanency."

His eyes flew open. "Who mentioned a permanency?"

Hilda made no answer. The silence drew out. Harry's expression remained remote; but presently he sighed a little, and said as if recalled from some absorbing field of thought:

"Yes, well, all right; to bed then."

Hilda gave him a derisive little grin and said, "Sure you've time?" Then, pushing herself briskly out of the chair, she began to undress.

A couple of hours later Hilda said,

"I'm hungry."

"Scramble some eggs, if you wish."

She reflected and said, "I don't think I'm as hungry as that."

Harry was silent. She knelt up in bed and leaned over him to look at his averted face.

"Are you asleep? Well don't be. I've something to tell you."

"I am not interested," he said, yawning, but waking up nevertheless. He never slept for long at a time.

"You will be. It's about a girl—one of those thin, dark girls, the type you don't care for."

"You mean Fernanda?"

"No, not her. A girl who lives in our village. Never mind her name."

"It sounds like the beginning of a fairy story," Harry said indifferently, getting up and wrapping himself in a terry robe. "Well and so—what about her?"

"Only this: she saw you run over little Garry Vernon."

There was a moment's silence while his hands finished tying the belt and then he said,

"What is this nonsense?"

"Just what I say. She saw you run over little Garry Vernon. You thought you were all alone in the middle of the country. Well—somebody was watching you."

"I do not know what you are talking about. Who is this Vernon? I have never heard the name, even."

He strolled into the room beyond, a kitchen, and Hilda heard the pop of gas; soon a smell of coffee stole out. Feeling at a disadvantage, she put on some clothes.

"Maybe you hadn't heard his name," she said presently, starting to comb her hair into its bright-brown swathes, "but he was the little boy you ran over. Do you want to hear about it?"

"Go on," he said indulgently, returning and picking up a pile of sheet music which he proceeded to sort. "Rid yourself of this fantasy if you must."

Hilda considered, looking down at the hairpins she held in her hands. "It was on Sunday, on the long straight stretch of the road that leads down from the moors to Woodmouth. I expect you were driving back to Whistle Cottage after the Bournemouth afternoon concert; you might have told me that you were going to be there." She paused a minute looking at him interrogatively, but he made no response and she went on, "I don't suppose you were driving very fast—a moderate seventy. Quite reasonable on that straight stretch of road—practically nobody uses it. Little Garry Vernon must have been playing in the woods and he suddenly ran out into the road, right under your wheels."

Having put the music in order, Harry shook it neatly together and slid it into a plastic folder; he did not look up.

"It must have been nasty for you. I shouldn't have liked it myself. Of course this person who was watching said that you seemed to be going *rather* fast but we don't know that's true, do we? You stopped and got out. He was lying in the road, bleeding, not moving. So you panicked, jumped back into the car, and drove off in a hurry. It's lucky there wasn't blood on the wheels or any mark on the car. And the rain began soon after, didn't it? That must have been a help. Really, getting away quickly seemed the most sensible thing to do. You couldn't help the child and, without a single witness, how could you prove that you hadn't been negligent, that you couldn't have braked or avoided him? It wouldn't look very nice, would it, for Hari Lupac, that rising young musician of international repute, to have run over a child and killed him? What about those sensitive interpretations of cradle songs and lullabies? I daresay the Soviet press would really go to town and some of it might stick this time. Oh, no, it was much better to get clear away. Only it was a pity that someone happened to be watching."

He snapped shut the folder. "Very well," he said. "Who was this watcher? You?"

His voice had not altered in the least and it was now queerly plain how lacking in emotional colour it was, how parched and bloodless; his speech, except when he had one of his rare moods of elation as at Sir Horace's party, emerged as though from a filter.

"No, not me," said Hilda, "But someone I know well."

"It was you," he said again. She shook her head.

"Is that coffee you've made? I'd love some. No, my sweet. Unluckily for you. I should probably keep quiet;

after all, what's the use of saying anything now? The child's dead. But *she* has a conscience and she recognised you, quite by chance—wasn't that another piece of bad luck?—so she came to me and asked my advice."

"Knowing about you and me?" Harry brought a pot of coffee and sat down at the table but forgot to pour any out; he was sweating lightly now, he ran a finger cautiously along his forehead, glanced at it, and then laid his hand with care on the table.

"No, darling." Hilda laughed and poured herself a cup. She stood in front of a wall mirror and applied lipstick to her mouth with vigorous care. "Owing to your secretive instincts, nobody knows about you and me. But this person thought I would know the right authorities to contact—whether she should go to the police, you know, or the Royal Council for Music and the Arts. It was a fearful shock to her, poor thing—like seeing Mr. Gladstone knock somebody down."

"And so, what did you say?"

"I said"—Hilda brushed on some eyeshadow, frowning in concentration—"I said it would be best not to breathe a word till I'd seen a lawyer and asked his advice. I said I had a friend who was a lawyer. Because, I said, you might be able to sue for defamation unless she was very sure of her facts."

"Of course," he said, breathing a little more easily. "Of course, that is so. How sensible of you, Hilda. Only tell me, my darling, who is this person? I have guessed, it is the hysterical sister Caroline, isn't it? The one who saw me at the concert?"

"No," said Hilda lightly, "it's not her."

"Your old cousin then."

"No. I shan't tell you who it is at present. What was that useful maxim, another of the things those Reds taught you in your military training. Never let out more than one piece of information at a time? I've given you one piece and that must satisfy you."

Harry began to say something but was interrupted by the doorbell which rang suddenly, a short, brisk peal. They both looked towards the lobby in astonishment.

"Odd hours people choose for calling on you?" Hilda said, raising an eyebrow. "Or do you always receive guests at four a.m.?"

"I do not know who it can be." Harry frowned. "Unless the nightwatchman sees my light and wishes to know it is not a burglar."

"Maybe the building's on fire," she suggested cheerfully. "Or you left your car somewhere you shouldn't."

"Keep out of sight," he said.

Hilda shrugged. As soon as he had gone to answer the door, she put on her coat and picked up handbag and scarf, glancing about deliberately to make sure she had left nothing else. She gave herself a last critical scrutiny in the glass.

Voices came from the lobby.

"Mr. Lupac, I believe?"

"Yes, I am Lupac," Harry said coldly. "You choose a rather unorthodox time to call."

"Not for you, surely? I understand you keep late hours. And I could be sure of finding you in."

Smiling a little, Hilda moved into the lobby, disregarding Harry's annoyed expression. The man who stood there with him seemed slightly startled at seeing her.

"Oh, I don't wish to intrude—" he began.

"It's quite all right, *pray* don't worry," Hilda said graciously. "I was just leaving in any case. Goodnight, Harry, dear. See you again very soon."

She gave a radiant smile at Harry and another at the man with him. He was, she noticed, a small, stout, balding man, with pebble-coloured eyes behind rimless glasses. She felt she might have seen him somewhere before.

As she stepped through the doorway Hilda heard him say,

"May I introduce myself? My name is Basil Todd. Perhaps you may have passed my bookshop at one time or another? It's a secondhand one, in the Corn Market."

"Well, come in," Harry said shortly to Mr. Todd. "As it happens you are just in time for a cup of coffee."

"No thanks." Mr. Todd followed him in and sat down.

"Never touch the stuff. Gives me indigestion. I have gastric trouble—have to be very careful about my diet. If you could spare a glass of milk, now—" He glanced round the room and remarked, "Surprisingly big rooms you often find at the tops of these old buildings, don't you? And I don't suppose you have to pay all that amount of rent, do you? How much would it be, if you don't mind my asking?"

Irritably, Harry told him, and he nodded as if pleased to have a theory confirmed.

"I was saying to the wife only the other day that if we could find a residence in Bridpool it would probably be a big saving. I live out at Barlock, you know; not a cheap district by any means and when you add to that the trouble and expense of getting in and out to business. Mind you, I'd miss the garden and the better air, I'm not saying I wouldn't."

"While I am greatly interested in the details of your life," Harry said, "I do not suppose that it was to discuss the cost of living that you called on me. Would you be so obliging as to come to the point?"

"Oh," Mr. Todd said, "I should have thought you'd have guessed that. I've been sent by your friends—well, our mutual friends, should I say?"

He sat back in the chair, which fitted snugly round his solid form, clasped his hands on his stomach, and inspected his short, clean fingernails. He looked the epitome of the small businessman with vaguely cultural interests; dozens of replicas would be found at any booksellers' conference or antique dealers' fair.

"I see." Harry poured himself a cup of coffee; his movements were slow and calm. He added, "And you keep a bookshop yourself, I think you said?"

"That's right. Secondhand, paperback and hardcover. You must come and see it some time. Nice little business."

"I am sure it must be. How would it be if you were to mind it, and leave me to mind mine?"

"Oh, I couldn't do that." Mr. Todd looked at him reproachfully. "You know really, Mr. Lupac, if you don't

mind my saying so, you've behaved downright ungrate-
fully. Doesn't it ever upset you to think of that? All the
special training you received—let alone your musical education which must have run into thousands upon thousands of pounds—"

"Well," Harry said smiling, "that was their risk,
wasn't it? I didn't ask them to spend the money."

Mr. Todd looked scandalised at this unethical attitude.

"If I choose to forfeit my deposit," Harry went on,
"they must be prepared to do the same."

"Now, my dear young fellow, if you don't mind my
saying so, that's most irresponsible behaviour, you'd
never do well in business with ideas like that. And I may
say that your friends are very disappointed in you, very
shocked and grieved."

"I am so sorry to hear that," Harry said politely. "I
hope they will soon recover from their disappointment,
since there is so little they can do about it." He glanced
at his watch. "Now, if you will excuse me—"

"Well," Mr. Todd said, "there are some things they can
do."

"Oh, really? What would you suggest?"

"Well, for a start," Mr. Todd said, inspecting his fingernails again, "they could arrange to have you collected
and returned to factory as defective goods. For renova-
tion and servicing, as it were."

"They could, I daresay," agreed Harry, "but don't
you think this would make rather an unfortunate impression on the Western world?"

"Oh, hardly. Your statement would be published in
Moscow to the effect that you had been utterly disillu-
sioned and disappointed by your experience of so-called
capitalist freedom."

"Yes, well," said Harry, "that would hardly agree with
the very full, long statement that I have deposited at my
bank, to be opened and published in the event of my
death or disappearance. It goes into quite considerable
detail about arrangements, you know, and quite a few
names are mentioned; I think this would be an embar-
rassment to them."

Mr. Todd nodded his head, blinking his pale, bristly lashes as if he had expected something of the kind. "It would," he agreed, "but in the circumstances, and for disciplinary reasons, they might consider it worthwhile. However," he cleared his throat, "naturally they would much prefer that you stay here and begin to cooperate in the way originally planned. That would suit their purpose much better. The slight initial delay would then be obviated; would be an asset if anything." He recrossed his legs.

"I daresay. But why should I change my mind? The life I am leading suits me very well."

"No doubt," Mr. Todd said, "but we must think of others in this life as well as ourselves, mustn't we? That's what I was always taught at Sunday school. Your life may suit you very well just now, but it's possible, too, that it might presently become open to misconstruction in some quarters. Our friends will be paying *very* close attention to all you do from now on; it would be most unfortunate, would it not, if you became discredited in any way? The British like their public figures to be virtuous, you know, as well as talented; history has shown that recently; one slip from the straight and narrow might be disastrous for you, and would quite destroy your putative value to our friends."

"I really cannot imagine what sort of thing you have in mind," Harry said. "If your friends had me discredited, I shouldn't be able to start co-operating, would I? There is an English idiom, cutting off your nose to spite your face, which seems to apply very well here. And now—forgive me but it is getting rather late—"

"Just a friendly warning, my dear boy." Mr. Todd got up briskly. "As I say—think it over. Your friends will be very interested in your decision. We mustn't waste our talents, must we, and yours, if I may say so, are exceptional."

"I know," said Harry politely.

"I was at your concert this evening—yesterday evening, rather—and I am bound to admit, my dear boy, that I was impressed; quite impressed. I don't often listen to music, I'm a football fan myself, and it takes quite a lot to impress me. I said to the wife afterwards (she didn't come to the concert, she prefers the pictures, but we met for a cup of tea when it was over), I said, Minnie, it was really impressive. That young fellow's certainly got something, *must* have. All that applause! And you enjoyed it, didn't you? Oh yes, it's a heart-warming feeling to stir a big audience like that—very. Funny, isn't it, how some people enjoy one thing and some another. As I often say to the wife, Minnie, it's a good thing we're all made different or it would be a dull old world. Well, I've enjoyed our little chat. Don't bother to see me out. I'll say au revoir then."

He was gone: a stocky, plump figure walking briskly down the stairs.

Four

Tuesday, August 24.

There was a little shed-office out by the new oil rig; just a hut with a fan which did no more than circulate the thick, dusty air. The whole place was in constant vibration from the roar of the machinery.

Tim Conroy was there looking at some core samples when Nicolson, his relief, arrived in the Landrover.

"What are we doing now?" Nicolson asked.

"About ten feet an hour; another two weeks of this should see us down to the anticline if nothing goes wrong."

The two men walked outside and climbed up on to the derrick platform. The steel plates had been masked with sacking, otherwise they would have been too hot to stand on. The evening sun beat down stupefyingly through a brown haze of smoke and sand.

"Oh," Nicolson said. "Nearly forgot. Brought out a letter for you, forwarded from head office." He handed it over. It had a typed address and a London postmark superimposed over a Bridpool one.

"Who the devil that I know in Bridpool owns a typewriter?" Tim said.

"Probably a sherry advertisement; just what you need out here, a nice bottle of sweet, dark, liverish Oloroso. Or a pot of rum butter. God, wouldn't it be wonderful, though, to be out in a real fog on the moor with the wet soaking through your trousers and a fire to come home to."

Tim opened his envelope and began reading the typed letter.

My dear Mr. Conroy: We have never met but I feel the circumstances are such as to justify my getting in touch with you. I have just seen your wife who, as you know, was a very dear pupil of mine, and I am not at all happy about her.

Although physically she appears to have recovered fairly well from the accident and breakdown, it seemed to me that there was something extremely unsatisfactory about her mental state. Please do not run away with the idea that I found her in any way unbalanced—I am sure that, basically, Caroline is one of the sanest people you could come across. But I received most powerfully the impression that some element in her present environment is putting an almost intolerable strain on her. This impression was confirmed by my friend Professor Gervase Lockhart, the archaeologist, to whom I introduced Caroline in the hope that she might do some research for him. I am afraid it seems unlikely that she will be persuaded to agree to this although it might be of the greatest benefit: she appears to have lost confidence in herself to a dangerous extent.

I gathered from Caroline that you are yourself under severe pressure of work still, following the distressing affair. I know it may be extremely difficult to delegate your responsibilities, or to put them aside, but I believe it is of paramount importance that you should return and see Caroline if this can by any means be managed. I cannot overemphasise the strength of my feeling. (This sentence was heavily underlined twice.) *You must still be in great personal grief for your loss, for which I hope you will accept my sincere sympathy, but I am sure it would be a consolation to you to feel that by prompt action you had averted what might otherwise turn out to be another tragedy.*

Your sincere friend,
Teresa Hume.

Nicolson was asking something. Tim realised that he hadn't heard.

"Sorry, what did you say?"

"I was asking if you'd stay on at the rig till they get the new length of pipe in?"

Slowly the dark, tree-clad slopes of Woodhoe Valley receded; barren desert lay round them, flat and shimmering. The fuel pipeline stretched north, veering away from the track like a minute hand set at five to twelve.

"What time is it?" said Tim. "No, I'd better get back to base, I think. I may have a lot of quick organising to do."

"Really, Caroline," Lady Trevis said, "I wish you'd have a little more consideration. There's a lot of work this morning, you simply cannot go slipping off in your usual way. Hilda won't be back till after lunch, and then she'll probably have hell's own hangover if she's been to one of those all-night parties that Esmee and Brenda seem to specialise in. Anyway, feed the chows, will you, sweetie, and exercise the poodles and pekes. I've arranged for a boy to come from the village and take out the big ones; if he doesn't turn up, which is *more* than probable, you'll have to do it after tea. You can manage that, can't you?"

"Lorraine's coming to take me swimming then."

"Oh damn, well, perhaps Hilda will have come back by then. Is it wise to go swimming? I must say, you look terrible today—great black bags under your eyes again—but then you've done that for the last few days. Did you remember to ask Hilda to get you a tonic when she was in Bridpool? Oh, before you feed the chows, just help me check the stores, will you? Flora's gone in to Bridpool on the bus; anyway, it's no use asking her to help, she wouldn't lift a finger to pick me up if I was dying on the floor. And this is a good moment while Hudson's out with the deerhounds; I'm not at all sure that he hasn't been pinching puppy biscuit to sell in the village."

"Mother," Caroline protested, "how can you? Why, Hudson wouldn't think of doing such a thing—he's been with us ever since I was born."

"What difference does that make? He only stays because he knows he's past getting a job anywhere else. All these people would do you down as soon as look at you. And Hudson's always loathed me—he invariably took your father's side. Oh, never *said* anything, but you could see it in his eye. He hates the whole pack of us. Now, get up those steps and count the sacks, will you; I'm too old for clambering up and down."

It was icy cold in the old tumbledown coach house where the stores were kept; a damp wind whistled through the cracks from one side to the other.

"Might be November," Lady Trevis said, turning up the collar of the moth-eaten fur jacket she had slung over her shoulders. "Get a move on, sweetie, will you?"

Caroline found it almost impossible to count the piles of sacks because her mother would persist in talking all the time, asking questions and interrupting. "For heaven's sake, hurry up," she kept repeating. *"That* can't be right," she said incredulously when Caroline produced a total. "You'll have to do it again." Caroline's second total was no more acceptable then her first, and Lady Trevis irritably removed her jacket, stuck her cigarette in a corner of her mouth, and began counting herself. She looked strangely incongruous, perched up there, in bell-bottomed navy jersey trousers and a mauve cardigan sagging off her thin frame. In the middle, Hudson returned unexpectedly.

Lady Trevis stormed at Hudson and Caroline, declaring that it was impossible to get anything done decently in a place where people were fools and incapable of obeying orders; Caroline, shivering, offered to count again, Lady Trevis gave her a furious look and snapped,

"No, leave it. *Leave* it! What's the good? What's the good of anything? Hudson, bring me a pot of coffee, will you? And, Caroline, you'd better get on with the chows, since any effort in the mental lines seems too much for you."

The Corn Market was a triangular piece of ground in the Old Town, paved with sandstone flags, surrounded by ancient office buildings, and approached by a narrow alley at either end. No cars were allowed through, only pedestrians, and here, on Tuesdays, a cheerfully raffish assemblage of stalls and barrows did a brisk trade, selling to tourists and the more gullible of the locals food and household goods which they could have purchased just as cheaply if not so pleasurably at the nearby chainstores. It was a well-known place of interest for sightseers, and this afternoon Miss Flora Tidbury's small, jaunty figure, clad in crocodile's-tooth check tweed, moved in rapt appreciation past the various stands. She loved the market as free entertainment though she never bought anything there; in fact she spent very little money at all since the household at Woodhoe supplied all her daily needs and the vast wardrobe of expensive and durable clothes bequeathed her by Aunt Prudence would undoubtedly outlast her lifetime.

Cousin Flora's one weakness was for paperback thrillers, and to minimise expenditure on these she had, as with much else in her life, developed a highly practical routine. Whenever Hilda went into Bridpool, Flora would ask her to bring back one or two paperbacks from Smith's; Hilda generally obliged—since the request was made in a plaintive left-behind-again-and-after-all-I-don't-ask-you-to-do-much-for-me manner—and generally forgot to claim back the money she had spent, as it seemed petty to niggle over a few shillings. Cousin Flora, after reading the books, made a modest profit by selling them secondhand. This arrangement, so tidy, frugal, and productive, gave her a small perennial glow of satisfaction.

Having pottered among the stalls, now, and admired

the machine-cut glass, nylons printed with the faces of pop singers, silk head-squares, flowers, farm produce, and pieces of junk appearing hopefully under the label of antiques, she made a purposeful line for the bookshop which occupied a ground floor and cellar in one of the sixteenth-century houses at the back of the market.

"Good afternoon, Mr. Todd!" she sang out happily. "And how is your ulcer keeping?"

"Quiescent, thank you, Miss Tidbury, quiescent at the moment." The propietor, who had been dusting the trolley of sixpenny titles outside his door, followed her into the shop. "Provided I lead a carefully regulated life and stick to a bland diet—" *"Plenty* of milk and steamed fish," agreed Flora, nodding with vigour so that her white curls bounced "—I find it gives me very little trouble, very little trouble indeed. Except for the occasional sharp attack. And you? I hope I see you well? How is the rheumatism?"

She supplied him with her symptoms in loving detail— nobody at Woodhoe ever bothered to ask about them— and, fair exchange, listened to a description of a bad three days his ulcer had given him last month.

"My gall bladder was tied in knots, Miss Tidbury, I assure you. Of course I believe it's all due to nerves—I suffer very intensely indeed from my nerves."

"Oh I understand that so *well,* Mr. Todd; on some days I can feel the nerves in my knees opening and shutting like castanets."

"It's all this radioactive fall-out in the air if you ask me," he said gloomily.

"Oh no, Mr. Todd, I'm certain all our troubles stem from insecticides and exhaust fumes. If only we could learn to live without the petrol engine—"

But here Mr. Todd could not agree; insecticides, yes, but he himself had a motor scooter and found it of inestimable value for business and pleasure. He did not know how he would do without it, indeed; he had been saying to his wife Minnie that very morning—

At the end of ten minutes' agreeable chat Cousin Flora deprecatingly laid on his desk the dozen thrillers she had brought along, tied into a neat bundle with string. Mr. Todd scanned them expertly.

"Fleming, Christie, Creasey, Gardner—all nice, fast-selling titles, Miss Tidbury. And all in good condition, I can see."

"Good as new," she assured him blithely.

"Shall we say sixpence each?"

This was ritual; he always gave her sixpence for each book, and she always proceeded to plough back her profits immediately by spending the money in his shop. Accordingly she moved past him, her eyes bright with happy anticipation, into the inner room, where a number of long, narrow, rather dark aisles, shelved to ceiling height, looked as if they contained all the paperbacks that had ever been printed.

It generally took her some time to make a choice; she prided herself that she could remember every thriller she had ever read, but often she needed to skim through a chapter or so to make certain; meanwhile customers came and went. The shop was surprisingly busy, as Miss Tidbury had noticed on former occasions; from the fact that his clients tended to be sailors, arrived singly at regularly spaced intervals, held low-voiced conversations, and often handed over or were given wrapped packages, she deduced that Mr. Todd was connected with some illicit business, probably smuggling; but this, far from shocking her, rather enhanced his interest in her eyes. After all, smuggling was not exactly wicked; merely illegal; a hundred years ago it had been quite a gentlemanly pastime, indulged in by many of the upper classes. Miss Tidbury, therefore, tactfully turned a blind eye and a deaf ear to the transactions in the front of the shop. As Mr. Todd did not seem disturbed by her presence during these interviews, she concluded that, classing her as either too innocent or too foolish to constitute a source of anxiety, he probably felt she lent a useful touch of verisimilitude and respectability to his premises.

Having acquired an excellent bag of thrillers—including an early Ngaio Marsh that she had never read—Miss Tidbury was about to pay for them and take her leave when a voice from the front of the shop made her stop dead, and then move instinctively to the very back of the darkest aisle.

"Good afternoon!" Hilda said gaily, entering the shop with her slightly uneven, rocking walk. She looked round in curiosity at the books and then at Mr. Todd, who returned her look with a small professional smile. "Would you have such a thing as a guide to the orchestra or an elementary handbook on music?"

"A guide to the orchestra? That's a bit out of my line. I'm not sure now," Mr. Todd said doubtfully, but moving to his front tier of shelves. "I did have something of the sort a while back—"

"You see I feel such a fool when I'm with my musical friends, having to admit that I don't know a harp from an oboe," confided Hilda. There was an armchair in front of Mr. Todd's desk, for favoured customers; she sat in it, and gave him a simple, ingenuous glance which deepened, by nicely graded stages, into one of recognition; then she exclaimed, "*I* know where I've seen you before! Of *course* you were at the concert! You're Harry's friend who called at his flat, aren't you?"

"I'd hardly presume to call myself a friend of Mr. Lupac," Mr. Todd said, looking down demurely. "More of a business contact, shall we say?"

"Oh, I'm disappointed!" She flashed her three-cornered, flirtatious smile. "Darling Harry's such a dark horse, I hoped you were a lifelong bosom buddy of his who could give me the lowdown on him. *All* the background! Of course I *adore* him, but he's so enigmatic; I find it quite tiring, sometimes, talking to him. Don't you feel that? And nobody seems to know a thing about him, really. You're the first person I've met who knows him at all, outside of music circles."

Still hidden, at the back of the shop, Cousin Flora was in agony. There, in full view on Mr. Todd's desk, was the pile of paperbacks that Hilda herself had bought; suppose she were to recognise this evidence of ingratitude and sordid profiteering on the part of her cousin? If only Mr. Todd had put them on the floor! And why, in the name of goodness, had Hilda chosen to leave her usual shopping grounds and come here?

"What sort of thing did you wish to learn?" Mr. Todd inquired cautiously.

"Oh, *you* know—who his friends are, what he did when he was in France, *anything* about his past life—I'm always dying to know every last thing about my friends, aren't you?" She beamed at him, turning round in the chair to watch as he methodically scanned the rows of titles.

Miss Tidbury began to creep forward, still hidden from Hilda by a rampart of shelves. She was wondering madly if she dared reach out an arm and snatch the incriminating pile of thrillers from view; but she heard Hilda move, and shrank back again.

"Oh, I'm afraid I could tell you very little that would interest you," Mr. Todd was saying. "My connection with him was solely over the repayment of a loan; somebody he did a kindness to in France, a hard-up young musician. Mr. Lupac is very philanthropic, you know."

"Is he? You surprise me, rather."

"Oh, yes, very; in a quiet way. And he hates to be repaid; in fact he flatly refused to accept this money, which puts me in rather an awkward position, as the man concerned is a deck-hand, on a tramp freighter; I shan't be able to get in touch with him for months."

"Well, this is a new light on Harry—one he certainly keeps under a bushel! Lending money to young musicians —how benevolent! Why did the man come to you?"

"I know a lot of sailors," Mr. Todd said primly, "I act as a sort of unofficial agent and clearing-house for them. So, as this man didn't know Lupac's address, he consulted me, and I said I'd deliver the money. But now I'm rather at a loss as to what to do."

"Can't you just pay the money into Harry's bank?"

"Why yes," Mr. Todd pondered, as if such an idea had not occurred to him, "I suppose I *could* do that if I knew where he banked."

"Western Counties," said Hilda. "The Cabot Street

branch. I happened to be with him once when he had to cash a cheque."

"Really? That's most useful, I'm very much obliged to you. *Quid pro quo*," said Mr. Todd affably. "I give you some information about our friend, you give me some! But I'm very much afraid I can't do much for you in my professional capacity. I don't seem to have a guide to the orchestra. Of course I could get you one, if you cared to leave your address?"

"Would you?" she said. "That's very sweet of you. I'll write it down."

She turned to the desk, just in time to catch a glimpse of an arm in a familiar tweed, which had been stretched out but was hastily withdrawn. Rather startled, Hilda walked forward and looked round into the inner room.

"*Cousin Flora!* I didn't know anybody else was in here, let alone you! In fact, I'd no idea that you were even coming in to Bridpool today."

"Why, Hilda dear! What a surprise!" Cousin Flora emerged blinking and slightly flushed with confusion. "Have you been here long? I never even heard you come into the shop—I became so absorbed, browsing through the shelves, that I'm quite lost to the world! Yes, I had seized the chance of a lift to the bus stop with the kind man who came to mend the television—hoping, of course, when I was in Bridpool, to be able to catch you at Esmee and Brenda's and drive home with you. But, alas, when I rang them I learned that you were not there, and I had just resigned myself to the long, slow bus ride home again. So is not this a fortunate coincidence?"

By now she had almost recovered her aplomb, though it was an effort to keep her eyes from slipping sideways to the pile of books.

"Well, well, well," Hilda said lightly and not altogether pleasantly; there was an echo of Lady Trevis in her tone. "You certainly struck lucky; I was just about to start for home."

She finished scribbling down her address and handed the paper to Mr. Todd.

"How long do you suppose it will take you to get the book, Mr. Todd?"

"A couple of days, perhaps."

"I'm coming in to Bridpool again on Thursday; I might call in and inquire. I've so much enjoyed our little chat."

"Why fancy," he said, studying the address, "isn't that nice now, that you two ladies from Woodmouth should run into one another like this? Quite providential, as you might say."

"Quite." Hilda's tone was dry. Flora still could not be certain whether or not she had noticed the books.

"Woodmouth," said Mr. Todd meditatively. "That's a beautiful part, I understand. Very picturesque, aren't I right? I really must get on my scooter and go out there, perhaps with the wife, one of these days—we're very keen on visiting beauty spots. Especially if we know anyone who lives there—it makes the trip so much more interesting, doesn't it? Yes, indeed, I must do that."

With great courtesy he ushered his lady customers out of the shop, and stood on the threshold smiling until they had left the Corn Market; then he went back to his desk, still smiling, and re-read the address that Hilda had given him. His cheerfulness remained unimpaired even when he realised that he had let Miss Tidbury get away without paying for her thrillers.

Hilda's return from Bridpool synchronised with the arrival of Lorraine to take Caroline swimming.

"Hallo, dears!" Cousin Flora beamed, bouncing into the drawing room with her books. "How's all at home?"

"Nice party?" Caroline asked Hilda, who yawned.

"Didn't break up till five. Here you are, I got your tonic." She handed Caroline a little bottle of red-and-black capsules.

"My dear Hilda, what a round of dissipation!" Lorraine exclaimed in her throaty contralto. "Parties, parties—no wonder you haven't any time for good works. Coming, Carey?"

But at this moment Lady Trevis, hearing voices, slip-slopped downstairs and insisted on everybody staying to have a cup of tea and tell her something new. Caroline would have liked a moment alone with Hilda to ask the result of her errand but there seemed no chance of this at present; she fixed her eyes questioningly on Hilda, who was pouring tea; all the response she got was a slight nod. Hilda was pale and her eyes were very bright; she seemed, Caroline thought, pleased, secretly amused about something.

"For the Lord's sake, take one of those Vitogen pills right away, Caroline," Lady Trevis said. "I'm fed up with your looking like something that's crawled from under a stone. You can't start too soon."

Obediently, Caroline swallowed one of the capsules with her tea; Lorraine, who was dying for her swim, then dragged her away.

"Old Hilda's going it a bit, isn't she?" Lorraine said, when they were crawling up the drive in the Dukes' big Vauxhall. "Madge Curtis from the choral society told me she went to a terribly grand party given by the Chumleys last week, and Hilda was there hobnobbing away with Sir Horace like one o'clock."

"Was she? I didn't know," Caroline said vaguely. "She doesn't say much about where she goes or Mother would want to know every last detail."

"Old Hilda's a dark horse, if you ask me." Lorraine suddenly rolled her black-currant eyes sideways and asked, "How's it going, Carey—can you bear being back at home? Must be a trifle odd after running a house of your own—bit of a comedown?"

Odd? Caroline considered. Not odd, she thought, all too familiar. Running my own house was odd; I wasn't very good at it. I enjoyed housekeeping, though; I was learning how; Tim was helping me.

"Bit dismal, surely, after living abroad," she heard Lorraine say with pity—or was it scorn?—in her voice.

"I'm not really particular about where I live." It's the people, she thought.

"I should think Tim is fairly particular? After that terribly perfect establishment of his mother's. The Conroys used to give such marvellous parties when they lived down here."

"Tim didn't seem to mind my housekeeping."

"Of course old Tim's such a sporting, outdoor boy, isn't he? That sort aren't generally too fussy."

"Is he?"

"But, my dear! He's *always* been *crazy* about golf and sailing and tennis! Don't tell me you hadn't noticed?"

"We didn't do those sorts of things together," Caroline said defensively.

"Good Lord, anyone would think we were talking about two different people. I can't think what you and Tim see in one another. You've always loathed sport, haven't you?"

"I suppose so. I loathed those fearful P.T. sessions your mother used to organise at your house before Monsieur Bolitoff's dancing classes."

But that's where I met Tim, equally bored, she thought, one afternoon when I twisted my ankle, and he took me home and we talked about books. That was a golden day. I can still remember waking up next morning and knowing that I had found a friend. I was thirteen.

"Heard from Tim lately?" Lorraine asked. There was a shade of eagerness in her voice every time she mentioned his name. Caroline suddenly thought, Poor Lorraine, out of the depths of her own darkness.

"Not very lately." Her hands curled protectively around a folded letter in her pocket. Tim's letters, precious as gold coins. This one was a fortnight old, she carried it everywhere like a talisman. How soon could he be expected to write again?

"Here we are, then," Lorraine said presently.

The big Vauxhall swung through a gate in a drystone wall and bumped its way up across a field to a well-worn patch on the cliff top.

"Looks beastly cold, doesn't it?" Lorraine remarked, surveying the immense expanse of dark-blue silky sea, capped here and there with curling white. Caroline shivered. She did not really feel enthusiastic about swimming. "Never mind, I'm sure it will do us good," Lorraine went on. "The cliff path's over there to the left. Coming?"

"Mother?" Tim said into the receiver. "Is that you? Thank God I've caught you."

"Tim, my darling! Wonderful to hear you! But what at all are you doing, ringing me up, you extravagant creature? Let alone at this hour—it must be past midnight where you are."

"It is." He looked out of the window at the stars, which dissected by a grid of mosquito-gauze, spread their tropic brightness into strange geometric shapes.

"What's the matter, Tim?" Mrs. Conroy said quickly and anxiously. "You're all right?"

"Yes, yes," he reassured her. "I'm fine. I've been working rather hard for the last twenty-four hours, that's all. It's just—have you seen anything of Caroline lately?"

"Oh, darling, I haven't!" Mrs. Conroy sounded remorseful. "Bridpool's such a long way from London and indeed I've not had a minute, careering back and forth to Athens with the world at my heels. You're not the only busy one in the family, I'd have you know! This week is the first time I've had three nights on my own pillow in the last three months."

"I know, love! I know you're busy."

"Is there something ailing Caroline, then? Are you worried about her, my dearest?"

"Yes, I am, a bit. No, that's not true," Tim said, "I'm a helluva lot worried about her. I've had a letter—two letters—"

"From Caroline?"

"No, from her headmistress—and from a neighbour —remember Lorraine Duke? Well, for that matter I've heard from Caroline too. I'm beginning to think there's something badly wrong at Woodhoe House."

"Well, if you're worried you must drop everything and come home. How could you do anything else? Get on a plane tomorrow. In fact," said Mrs. Conroy, "I don't know could it have come at a better time; faith, you might have been inspired to ring up. There's this oil-producers' conference in London on Friday and your Un-

cle Sean in hospital with a slipped disc. So just whip
on the first plane, let you, and it'll do my heart good to
set eyes on you. Will I go down and see Caroline tomorrow, now? I'm up to my eyes but I can put it all
off at the drop of a hat—"

"Oh no, don't you do that, love." An immense
weight of worry had lifted from Tim's heart. "I can't get
away tomorrow but I can make the night plane on
Thursday. And go down on Friday to Woodmouth, as
soon as the meeting's over. A day won't make
all that difference. I'll ring Caroline tomorrow and
tell her."

"That's so, indeed. A day won't hurt. And it's you
she'll be aching to see. Well, bless you, my darling. A
safe journey now."

"Goodnight, Mother."

"Well! What antic will you think up next?" Lady Trevis said acidly to Caroline. "Hilda, Lorraine looks as if
she could do with something to pull her together. What'll
you have, Lorraine?"

"Oh, thanks awfully, Lady Trevis, but I really ought
to be getting home." Lorraine looked white, shaken, and
thoroughly uncomfortable; patently she wished herself
a thousand miles off. "Marcus will be wondering where
I've got to."

"Good heavens, you can stay five minutes, can't you,
after saving Caroline's life?" Lady Trevis exclaimed,
irritability coming through stronger than goodwill.

"Oh well, just for a minute then. Gin and lime, a tiny
one, please Hilda."

"*You'd* better not have one after a bump on the
head," Cousin Flora told Caroline who lay on the sofa
leaning wearily against a cushion.

"I told Hudson to make some hot sweet tea," Lady Trevis said with an impatient glance towards the door.
"That's right for shock, isn't it? Ring again, Hilda."

"Don't bother, please," Caroline said faintly. "Truly
I'd rather go straight to bed."

"Nonsense, you'll be all right in a little. Thanks for bringing her home, Lorraine."

"Least I could do," Lorraine replied awkwardly. "Actually I was pretty scared."

"What exactly happened? I wasn't in the room when you told it," Hilda said.

"We went out to swim at Pennose Head. Tide was in, so we thought we'd dive off the rocks; I happened to turn round just before I dived to make sure Carey was all right; lucky thing I did because there she was, green as a cucumber, sort of swaying about; before I could get back to her she just fell, slap into the sea. Bumped her head on a rock and she went down and pretty well knocked herself out hitting the water."

"Goodness, gracious me, it's a mercy Lorraine was there," Cousin Flora said.

Glancing at Hilda, Caroline wondered vaguely why she had gone so white. When she spoke it was in a voice half stifled with passion.

"Do you mean to say—of all the bloody stupid lunatic capers! What on earth possessed you to go swimming there, of all places, Caroline? I'd have thought even you would have the sense to realise it was dangerous in your state? Why didn't anyone stop you? If I'd known *that* was where you were going—you might have been killed!"

Her angry glance swept over Lorraine and Lady Trevis.

"It's no use *my* saying anything to Caroline, you know perfectly well," Lady Trevis complained. "I might as well give advice to the barn door."

"Well, good heavens, I'm sorry, of course!" Lorraine exclaimed, looking at Hilda with some astonishment. "But how was I to know she was going to keel over so suddenly—she was perfectly all right when we started. I don't see you've any call to tick me off, Hilda." Affronted, and rather red-faced, she swallowed her drink and stood up.

"Please don't be cross, Lorraine," Caroline said weakly. "Of course it wasn't your fault—it was very kind of you to invite me. And I'll never forget how you saved my life. I ought to have known, myself, that I wasn't fit to swim yet—but I came over giddy so unexpectedly—"

Her eyes filled with tears; she dropped her head helplessly against the cushion.

Hudson brought in a tray of tea and set it by her.

"V.I.P. treatment," Hilda said. "You wouldn't bring me a tray of tea if I broke my neck, would you, Hudson? All right, go on, say I wouldn't need tea if I'd broken my neck."

Hudson said nothing. He waited, while Caroline shakily poured herself a cup of tea, making a desperate effort at self-control. "What I wondered was"—she brought out in a thread of a voice"—I've never felt giddy like this before, I wondered if it could have been the effect of that pill?"

"Your tonic? The Vitogen? Oh, grow up, sweetie!"

"The giddiness came on after I took it," Caroline persisted.

Hilda and her mother exchanged glances; Hilda shrugged and Lady Trevis laughed huskily until the laugh changed to a cough.

"Oh dear, Caroline, you're really too absurd. D'you think someone's trying to poison you? Talk about persecution mania! Why, we've all been swallowing down Vitogen pills for years, you've taken them yourself before now."

"Yes, but they've changed. They used to be orange, these are black and red."

"They've altered the formula, that's all—put in more calcium or something. No, you're just accident-prone, still, sweetie," Hilda said, shaking her head. "Sorry and all that, Lorraine, didn't mean to fly out at you. It's just that—well, I don't know *what* Tim would say if instead of looking after Caroline we had to write and tell him that we'd let her drown herself. We can't stop her seeing snakes in the bath but we can keep her *alive*." She directed a chilly smile at Lorraine, who said,

"That's okay, Hilda—we were all a bit shaken up." But she still looked puzzled. She gave Caroline's shoulder a clumsy pat. "Take it easy now, Carey. Don't you think you ought to have a doctor look at her, Lady Trevis?"

"Oh, I don't think there'll be any need for that. We'll see in the morning. You are tiresome, Caroline, giving everyone a fright like this."

"I really must fly now," Lorraine said. "Hope you're all right tomorrow, Carey, I'll ring and inquire. Thanks for the drink, Lady Trevis."

She walked out quickly and they heard the Vauxhall going up the drive.

"That girl's got absolutely no manners," remarked Lady Trevis, almost before the door had shut behind Lorraine.

"Oh, have a heart, Mother, she did save Caroline's life."

"Well, so I should hope! She's done Girl Guides and Red Cross and St. John and all those things for long enough, she ought to know how. Good practice for her. But it wouldn't have killed her to stay and chat for ten minutes longer, instead of racing off as if this place was a plague house. Nothing but trees to look at and water to listen to—I wonder I don't turn *into* a bloody tree. Well, what did you do in Bridpool, you haven't told me yet?"

"Nothing much," Hilda said carelessly. "Went to the dentist, had a shampoo and set. Cousin Flora bought some books, didn't you, Cousin Flora?"

"Books!" Lady Trevis said discontentedly. She stubbed out her cigarette and trailed upstairs.

"Oh, dear me! I'm afraid Gloria finds *our* conversation inadequate." Cousin Flora gave a little injured laugh, but she seemed unusually subdued and kept her eyes averted from Hilda. "Eh well, I must bestir meself and write some letters."

As she tripped off upstairs, Hudson, who had shown Lorraine out, came back and began collecting the glasses.

"That was a lovely cup of tea, thank you, Hudson," Caroline murmured.

As he took the tray his rheumy eyes met hers; he stared at her with curious intensity as if trying to convey a warning.

"Did you take out the chows, Hudson?"

"No, Miss Hilda."

"Oh God. Have you time to do it now? Otherwise I'll have to and I'm just about whacked."

Hudson stumped from the room without replying directly; to himself he muttered: "Her lips were red, her looks were free, her locks were yellow as gold . . . the nightmare Life-in-Death was she, who thicks men's blood with cold."

"Foul old man," Hilda said. "Lord, how I long to get out of this place."

"Hilda."

"Yes, what?"

"Did you see that man—you know, the one you—"

"Ssh!" Hilda gestured meaningly towards the door. "No names, no pack-drill! Yes, I did."

"What did he—?"

"He's going to consult somebody else—take advice, they say, don't they. I'm going to see him again on Thursday."

"Thursday? Not till then? But that will mean it's five days since it happened."

"Oh, don't worry your head about that. Time doesn't make any difference with these legal big shots—they're always slow-moving, you know—"

"I want to get it off my mind," Caroline said miserably. "I expect that's what's making me feel queer really."

"Now just don't fuss, sweetie! Don't be so egotistical —think of something else besides yourself. Better go and rest now, hadn't you?"

Caroline got up off the sofa and climbed the stairs stiffly. Her eyes, nose, and throat still stung from the salt water; there was a remote, threatening ache at the back of her head. Reaching her room she flung herself down on the white counterpane, which felt cool and sticky from the perpetual damp in the atmosphere. She closed her eyes. At once her body set up a violent, uncontrollable shivering.

Oh Tim, help me. Help me or I shall be lost. . . .

Downstairs the telephone rang but nobody answered it. Cousin Flora was having an orgy of vicarious crime in her bedroom; Hilda had taken out the dogs; and Lady Trevis, spellbound before the blue, flickering screen, was watching a programme called *Make Mine a Million.*

Five

"You don't need to see the doctor, do you?" Lady Trevis said at breakfast next morning. "Old Campbell would be furious if we fetched him out just because you had bumped your head. I suppose you could go to his evening surgery . . ."

Caroline thought of the dreary waiting room, the rows of dejected, mutely expectant patients, and old Dr. Campbell, the bad-tempered local G.P., impatiently twirling from side to side in his worn swivel chair. Dr. Campbell suffered from chronic arthritis, was in constant pain, would never go out on night calls. He was not profuse in sympathy for minor ills.

"What's the matter with ye, got a bang on the head? Well, why the devil d'ye come worrying me with a trifle like that? Put some arnica on it, or a cold vinegar compress."

"No, I don't see any point in going to Dr. Campbell," she said, and surreptitiously swallowed a couple of aspirins with her coffee.

"Where's your tonic?" Lady Trevis asked sharply.

"I don't know . . . I thought I left the bottle in here."

Extensive search failed to produce it.

"I'm sure I didn't take it out of this room—but I'll hunt upstairs," Caroline said helplessly.

Lady Trevis and Hilda looked at each other resignedly when she had gone.

140

"Threw them away, I suppose, because she imagined they'd poison her," Hilda said. "I'd better get some more next time I'm in Bridpool."

Caroline, rummaging fruitlessly in her bedroom thought of telephoning Dr. Galbraith. But what could she tell him? Nothing of importance. Only that she lost things, felt giddy, had a headache. On the subject that really festered in her mind she must keep silent. So what would he say? Only what she had heard already at home: accident-proneness and persecution mania; *much more of this, I heard mother say to Hilda, and she'll be right round the bend. What do we do then?*

What indeed? Pack her off to hospital, for an indefinite stay, this time. Suggest to Tim that a divorce would be the kindest and simplest step, eliminating a long, drawn-out period of slowly diminishing hope. . . .

All day Caroline felt tired and out of sorts. The suppressed headache smouldered at the back of her skull and yet she kept shivering; she could not get warm. Perhaps it was the uneasy weather. There had been a persistent mutter of thunder since noon, circling round the valley, never coming any closer.

"When you go down to the library this evening," Hilda said, "find something about music or musicians for me, will you, if they have anything."

"Oh, heavens, the library. Is it tonight? Do I have to go?"

"Of *course* you do, sweetie! You can't drop it just for any old thing." Hilda's voice was reproving. "All you have to do is sit at a table and cross names off in a book, that won't kill you. I'd do it, but it's Mother's bridge night—of course if you'd rather stand in for me here, I'll go to the library."

"Heavens, no." Caroline shuddered at the thought of an evening's bridge with Lady Trevis and two old pals from Bridpool repertory days. "Mother would kill me after a couple of revokes."

"Yes, she probably would," Hilda agreed. "Let's face it, bridge is not your strong suit."

"You don't think Cousin Flora—"

"Oh, you know how disobliging she is—she'd never put herself out for anybody. No, you run along, the fresh air will do you good. Better take a mac, though."

Fresh air was a misnomer, Caroline thought, walking down the river path. It was more like pushing one's way through a tank of lukewarm steam. Clouds of midges hung under the heavy trees. She turned to look at the house which, even from so short a distance, seemed insubstantial, its greyness turned to haze in the damp, sweltering twilight. A defeated, mournful, hideous house, and yet in a sort of way I love it; Tim has been there. It has memories of Tim.

She hurried on. The river's voice was hushed in the dense air; even the gulls had fallen silent at the harbour mouth and the sea fretted softly far off across the beach.

She went along the harbour wall and into the Parish hut.

The thunder growled nearer; with the approach of dusk it had gathered strength and momentum, was moving north down the valley. A flicker of sheet-lightning outlined the tree-hung cliffs above; Caroline made haste to shut the door. Switch on the lights. Draw the curtains. Take out the books and stack them on the table—display a few bright jackets. Find the record book and the cashbox. Wait for customers.

A louder peal cracked about five miles off; the rain began, pattering purposefully on the tarred roof.

Suddenly the door bumped open and Hudson came in. He was strangely wrapped up in a voluminous grey plastic garment that made him resemble a monk; below it his skinny old legs protruded like stalks, the black trousers tightly wrapped round them and secured with cycle clips.

"Miss Caroline you didn't ought to be here," he said earnestly; he seemed much agitated. "I could see you wasn't well all day. You oughta be at home laying down in your bed. Miss Hilda shouldn't a made you do it. Soon's I heard you was down here I ast Miss Tidbury to come along and take over and she said she was agreeable."

"Cousin Flora?" Caroline was considerably surprised. "She said she would?"

"Ah, she's frit of me, Miss Tidbury is," Hudson gave his eldritch chuckle. "Acos she knows I see through her fine lady ways and won't stand no nonsense. She agreed quick enough."

"But, how on earth will she get here? You know she can't walk both ways."

"I rung my cousin Tom Pescod; he'll pick her up on's way down to British Legion and bring her home, arter."

"Oh, Hudson, you are kind. I honestly do feel rather strange, so thirsty and shivery."

"Sickening for a cold, shouldn't wonder. Go along with you now. I'll stay till Miss Tidbury gets here. You can take my bike if you like."

"I'd probably fall off it, thanks all the same," she said, remembering the high spidery contraption. "I'll be better walking."

So she made her way home through the slow heavy rain. And the thunder muttered behind her like a beast of prey, still a good way off but coming closer.

When she had gone, Hudson, after first looking round to make sure he was not observed, walked to the harbour wall, took from his pocket a small bottle of red-and-black capsules, and emptied them into the racing water, tossing the bottle after to splinter on a rock.

Then he turned and hobbled rapidly back to the Parish hut.

Tim had all his windows open to derive full benefit from the evening wind. A pile of letters slipped and fluttered from his desk to the floor as he strode about, methodically packing clothes and papers into a canvas hold-all, checking passport and money, keeping an eye on the clock. He'd be in Cairo by nine; if he could pick up a cancelled booking on a night flight there would be a chance of reaching London in time for breakfast. His mind boggled at the familiar, fantastic thought that one could watch the sun set on this parched gridiron of sand

and oil, and by next morning be driving through the green and muddy suburbs of West London. He picked up the fallen papers and rammed them into his pocket-book.

Moving into the bathroom he collected razor and tooth-brush, hesitated a moment, and then took from the frame of the shaving mirror a snapshot of Caroline laughing with her baby in her arms, and slipped it into his pocket. He gave a final glance round the bare room and, satisfied, hoisted his bag, locked up the bungalow, and walked over to the company airstrip. A distant roar in the sky was steadily coming nearer.

"Got everything you need?" said Nicolson. Tim nodded.

"When d'you reckon you'll be back?"

"Hard to say. Sure you feel all right about holding the fort?"

Nicolson nodded, anxious but valiant.

"Don't worry about a thing. We'll be fine. We damn well ought to be, considering what you've managed to get done in the last two days."

"If anything should bother you, you can always yell for help to Cardew at the Aden Panol Office. He'd come like a shot; we've done him plenty of good turns."

"Oh, I wouldn't want to do that. No sense advertising our troubles to Panol." He looked at Tim devotedly. "I won't make a mess of it!"

"I'm sure you won't," Tim said. "I'll cable as soon as I know my plans. Friday night, most likely."

"Have fun. I suppose you'll be seeing your wife. Lucky devil! I—I hope she's quite better now? Remember me to her, won't you? Will she be coming back soon?"

The noise of the plane was now deafening and spared Tim the need for reply. He waved his hand amiably at Nicolson and moved towards the runway, his face taking on at once a bleak, preoccupied expression.

As the landing strip began to fall away behind them, and the island became a tiny speck in the dusk, Nicolson's final question kept repeating itself in a vision of Caroline's face with desperate, pleading eyes.

The racket of the little charter plane was almost too loud for Tim to be able to think collectedly, but he could not escape from that question. Caroline's last letter, received yesterday, was folded inside his pocketbook; he almost knew it by heart:

> Things are getting worse at home. Something terrible has happened, but I'm not allowed to tell anybody about it. Oh Tim, please come, please come soon.

Well: he was coming, as fast as he could make it. But what on earth could she mean?

"Good God," Lady Trevis muttered. "Not Lorraine Duke again? At nine in the morning? What have we done to deserve this honour? I'm going up to my room, that brassy voice of hers cuts through my head like a siren. You can talk to her, Caroline; I daresay she's come to ask after your bumped head. And ring for Hudson, will you, and tell him to take a tray up to Flora; she hasn't been down to breakfast so I suppose she's decided to have another one of her migraines."

Caroline moved unenthusiastically towards the front door as her mother started upstairs. Lorraine, however, forestalled them both, bursting in at top speed.

"My dears! I'm most terribly sorry! What a ghastly thing to happen!"

"What's happened?" Lady Trevis said testily, pausing on the stairs. "What are you talking about?"

Lorraine's mouth dropped open.

"Don't you *know*? Haven't the police rung?"

"The phone's out of order—*as* usual after a storm. Anyway, what is all this? Why should the police have rung?"

"Not something about Tim?" Caroline, already pale, became paler still.

"This is the police now, I expect." Lorraine glanced

through the open door as a black Jaguar crept carefully down the drive, which was even more hazardous than usual this morning, ploughed into a watercourse and littered with storm-broken boughs. Two police officers climbed out and approached Lady Trevis, who received them rather blankly.

"Where's Hilda?" Lorraine asked Caroline in a low voice.

"Left about ten minutes ago to go to Bridpool."

"*Again?*"

"Lorraine, what *has* happened?"

"Your cousin—Miss Tidbury's been found drowned. Didn't anyone notice she hadn't come home last night?"

"What?" Caroline whispered through white lips. "You mean—dead?"

Lorraine nodded. Though she was managing to preserve a proper solemnity and decorum, her eyes sparkled at being the bearer of such a plummy bit of news; anyway it was not as if boring old Miss Tidbury were likely to be very deeply mourned, even by her cousins.

"And you weren't aware that Miss Tidbury had not returned?" the police sergeant was asking Lady Trevis.

"Of course not," she returned peevishly. "I had friends in last night. When I went to bed, a good deal later than my usual time, she was nowhere about downstairs, so I presumed she'd gone up to bed already. She often turned in early and read in bed for hours. Where was she found?"

"Among the rocks at the river mouth, Lady Trevis. It's thought she must have fallen off the harbour wall in the dark yesterday evening—at least there are injuries suggesting that."

"She didn't drown, then?"

"Probably not. The post mortem will show—I'm afraid there will be one. She had a broken neck and a fractured skull, as well as various abrasions which may have occurred after death. The night tide will have washed her body about among the rocks a good deal and then carried it down; there's a very strong current at the river mouth. But we found her handbag caught under a rock by the handle at about the point where she must have fallen."

"How revolting," said Lady Trevis. "Poor old Flora. What was she doing there at that time of the evening? And how on earth do you suppose she came to tumble off the harbour wall? It's well enough lit, isn't it?"

"Unfortunately," said the sergeant, "if you recall, there was a three-hour power cut in the village, due to the storm, from about eight-thirty to eleven-thirty. The front was very dark then. Miss Tidbury presumably closed up the library when the lights failed, assuming nobody would come for books in such weather. The door had been locked and we found the key in her handbag. Mr. Pescod, who had promised to drive her home, found the place locked up at half-past nine and took it she'd left early and walked back. He told us this when her body was found this morning."

"Who found it?"

"Some children, out early after driftwood."

"First *I* heard Flora was looking after the library," Lady Trevis said. "Did she offer to do it for you Caroline? Wonders will never cease."

Finding the ghost of a voice, Caroline said, "Hudson suggested it to her because I was feeling so qu-queer. It's all on account of me. Oh, God——" She covered her face with her hands, thinking of Cousin Flora, harmless and chirpy, pleased with so little in life: a roof over her head, a good address, her tea, her knitting, her eternal thrillers.

"For heaven's sake," snapped Lady Trevis, "why must *you* cry, Caroline? You're as bad as Mrs. Gummidge! Why must *you* have the privilege of feeling everything more than other people—you never seemed particularly fond of Flora when she was alive. And what the devil had it to do with Hudson, anyway? I call it very officious of him."

"Poor Carey," said Lorraine. "Were you feeling rotten yesterday? I'd have done the library for you, but Marcus wanted me to take two of his hunters to be shod. Only think, though, it might have been you! That's twice in the last three days that you've missed being gathered to your fathers. I call it a jolly providential swap over, really—after all, no one can say old Flora Tidbury's any great loss."

"Lorraine, really!" exclaimed Lady Trevis.

The police sergeant shuffled his feet in a scandalised manner.

"Well, it's the truth, isn't it? Anyway it wasn't *your* fault, Carey—there's no need to look so stricken."

But it was Lady Trevis who suddenly looked stricken; open-mouthed with horror she had just realised that Cousin Flora's death would deprive her of nine guineas a week.

Harry was in his flat, sitting with his legs flung over the arm of a chair, examining the strings of a violin, softly plucking, tuning, and listening.

Outside, Bridpool was growing dark, and the square of blue sky pressing on the window became deeper and more mysterious every moment. Sounds of industry from the docks had long since ceased. The clamour of starlings on nearby roofs and cornices was working up to a climax as if the birds were trying to keep the dark at bay with their racket.

Harry rejected the A string, removed it, and with rapid precision replaced it by a new one. He was back at his previous tuning and listening when the doorbell rang.

He considered a moment, frowning; looked at his watch; finally opened the door.

"Hilda? So soon again?" His voice held a dry surprise and no particular pleasure, but she came in gaily, dropped an armful of parcels on the table and, when he had carefully shut the door, walked across and stood close to him with her hands behind her back, smiling up at him.

"No key, you see—virtue! Amn't I a good girl?"

She had been running up the stairs and was warm; he could see her quick breathing under the dark-blue poplin and, as it were absently, without making any other gesture to greet her, he laid the back of his hand against her breast and felt the living heat move against his bony wrist.

"Well! Aren't you going to kiss me?"

Still smiling, and with her hands still behind her back, she leaned up against him and pressed her closed lips to his; then, quickly, like a lizard, flung her hand round his neck, forcing his mouth down on to hers. Her lips parted and he felt her tongue dart against his teeth, inquisitively.

"I don't believe you've been out the whole day," she said, turning her head about on its long neck. "This place smells like the top deck of a bus."

"Fresh-air fiend! And I have, to buy the evening papers."

"Yes, I am a fresh-air fiend! Do I get anything to drink? I'm dying of thirst—been shopping all day long."

He made her a martini and set it beside her on the table. She had taken his armchair and was lying back, staring at the window. Rapidly, fastidiously, like someone who sees an undisciplined child at large, he moved the violin out of harm's way and put it in its case.

She said idly, "Is that the Strad that Fresca Garroux gave you?"

He made no answer.

"Aren't you having a drink?"

"I'm on the air in three-quarters of an hour."

"Oh," she sighed, "I'd forgotten your recital this evening."

"Are you planning to stay the night?"

As when he had let her in, his voice was dry and held no particular emotion, either pleasure or distaste; it was the voice of a host, reckoning up: enough coffee, half a pint of milk, clean towels just back from the laundry.

"No, I've got to get back because of the bloody dogs; this is Hudson's evening off. Caroline's supposed to be helping me—therapeutic activity—but she's not much use. She had a bang on the head the other day and she's still a bit queasy."

"Oh really?" he said, not very interested.

"In fact," Hilda went on, "I can't tell you what we've

been through with her in the last few days, she's properly getting Mother down. Ma never could stand her anyway; they were fighting like dogs at breakfast . . . Hullo," she remarked, her eye lighting on a headline in the evening papers which lay scattered on the floor. " 'Bank Damaged in Explosion! Western Counties Cabot Street Branch.' That's yours, isn't it? 'The strong room of the Western Counties Bank was almost completely destroyed when a gas main blew up in Cabot Street last night. No lives lost—fortunately the nightwatchman was upstairs at the time and escaped with injuries—but it is feared that many £1000s worth of securities have been destroyed. The manager, Mr. W. J. Conshotten, says . . .' Oh, well, I hope you didn't have all your fortune down there in bearer bonds and family diamonds, sweetie?"

"Not I." Harry seemed entertained at the thought. "No, nothing of any importance."

"So glad. It would have rather nullified the point of my errand. I've come to have a serious talk with you, my love."

"But sweetie"—his foreign pronunciation was sometimes noticeable on these long vowels—"sweetie, there's not a moment to talk now. I must be changing."

"Swee-eetie," she mocked him, "there's just got to be a moment. Go ahead and change if you must, but you'll have to listen to me carefully at the same time."

"Okay," he sighed, "but you must forgive me if you don't receive my full attention."

He was moving purposefully about the room, taking another violin from a cupboard, selecting a small pile of sheet music and sliding it into a zip case. Undoing his belt he walked into the bathroom. Hilda slewed round in the chair, eyeing him sharply.

"Come and dress in here," she called.

"A moment."

She lit a cigarette and idly picked up a large, heavy book which was lying on the floor among the papers, the *Oxford Companion to Music*. Flipping its pages she noticed that the flyleaf had been torn out, as if to dis-

pose of some undesirable inscription. Absently she
hefted it in her hand and then compared it with a
paperback guide to the orchestra which she had in her
handbag.

"So, what is it, this important thing you have to tell
me?" Harry was back in shirt tails, fastening a tie, his
tone one of weary patience.

"We still have to talk about your running over that
boy."

"Oh, do we? I thought that was all settled."

"Settled? How could it be? We were interrupted, if
you recall."

"You told this person—your sister without a shadow
of a doubt—that she would be engulfed in an action
for slander if she started making such wild accusations.
And that she had better leave well alone."

He strolled back into the bathroom and reappeared in
trousers, carrying an evening jacket over his arm. Laying
it on a chair he began combing his hair in long rasping
sweeps with a metal dog comb.

"Oh, that didn't settle it," Hilda said. "That was only
a temporary expedient."

"So how do you propose to settle it?"

"How do *I*? That's pretty cool, I must say."

"You are such a clever girl, my darling," Harry said
kindly. "You are sure to have some plan. You see, I
have such a great respect for you."

Hilda gave him another sharp look, and then appeared
to consider, turning her eyes down on to her hands. She
had picked up the rejected A string and twined it round
and round her finger.

"Well," she said, "and *I'm* extremely fond of *you*,
Harry—I should really be dreadfully upset if anything
happened to spoil your career."

The square of sky beyond the window was heavily
barred with cloud now, greyish-pink across deep blue,
and a last vivid streak of sunshine lay dustily over one
corner of the room. Beautiful, he thought absently, a sky
for the background of an Italian painting. In front, the

martyrdom, the arrows, the cruel faces, the baying dogs; and far behind, far back, the rain-washed green of heavy summer trees and wet grass picking up the dazzle of sunset after a storm. Beautiful.

He turned and smiled at Hilda. "What do you want?" he said gently. "It is always better to come directly to the point with me, don't you know that yet? What do you want? Money? Or do you want to drive me crazy? So you can perhaps make a scandal and have me tried for manslaughter. Will that make you happy, to wreck my career? Why must you come here and torment me just before a recital? I had thought you loved me."

"I do," she said softly. "I want to marry you."

"Eh?" He swung round, arms half into the sleeves of his jacket.

"I want to marry you."

"I marry nobody at gunpoint. That is out of the question," he said firmly and coldly.

"Not if it's the price of my keeping quiet, Harry. And the other person too, of course. I should be a good wife for you; you need a wife."

"This is foolishness," he exclaimed angrily. "You must be mad, out of your senses. To start, how do you know this other person will keep silent?"

"She will if I want her to," Hilda said confidently.

Harry, lighting a cigarette, gave her a long, narrow look between his fingers.

"It is blackmail, in fact?"

She nodded.

"I've had enough, you see, of being a sort of weekend amenity for you, living with Mother and the bloody dogs, so usefully at hand when you come down to Whistle Cottage. It's a gruesome life at home; I can't stand any more of it. And now's my moment to get away while Caroline's there; Mother loathes her, but she's someone to talk to, and take the dogs out, and see Hudson doesn't pinch the brandy."

"She will go back to her husband when she is better."

Hilda blew a puff of smoke. "I doubt it. Very much.

I'm going to get away this time. There's no reason why I should stay any longer—turns out Cousin Flora was leading me up the garden path all this time with her promises of a nice little nest egg. And I don't like rotting down there while you can go off to Rome, Paris, Milan. When you do your world tour I want to come with you. Besides, you need somebody like me around to keep you out of complications. Women fall for you, don't they, and it's often quite convenient; didn't Fresca Garroux leave you quite a lot of money when she jumped out of that window? And Fernanda Chumley's obviously head over ears, poor little thing; it's high time someone talked a bit of common sense to her and opened her eyes to reality. The point is, these affairs may be convenient at the time, but when they are over, snags can crop up—and you don't want any awkward rumours, do you?" She gave him a challenging look. "You could do a lot worse than marry me, ducky."

"And supposing I have a wife already—in Budapest or Minsk or Pinsk?"

"Then I go straight to the police with Ca—, with this nasty little story. I'm in earnest, Harry."

She glanced up at him sharply, but his look was so menacing that she almost faltered: his eyes were blazing oddly under the thick fair brows. He picked up the comb, was about to put it in his breast pocket and then paused, staring at it as if in concentration, and said,

"Is this an ultimatum?"

"Yes."

He slid the comb into the pocket. With one rapid stride he was behind her chair. As she half turned, his left hand thrust under her hair, pushing her head sideways, so that the upward blow with the edge of his hand caught her on the neck just below her ear. She had no time even for surprise. As he took his arm away she slumped over the arm of the chair. Harry looked down at her, breathing quickly.

"And that was another of the things they taught me in military training, my sweetheart," he said.

Hilda did not reply. And this was hardly surprising, for her neck was broken.

Harry's preparations for his broadcast were now complete. He ran downstairs to his car, which was parked outside, with Hilda's parcels and his violin and music, looked sharply this way and that to make sure that Hilda had not left her car incriminatingly parked nearby. Not a soul to be seen, the street was empty and shuttered, and it was beginning to spit with rain, so much the better. Nearly dark, too. Returning, he picked up Hilda's body with unexpected wiry strength and carried her down to the car, admonishing her in a gentle, cajoling voice as he did so: "Silly girl to come out if you were feeling ill. I shall tell your mother to take better care of you. How can I leave you here alone when I have to go off and give a recital? I must take you home first."

There was nobody within earshot to benefit by his monologue but he carried on just the same, with the relish of a good actor for his part. He put her in the back of the car, on the floor, doubled up and leaning against the rear door. Rug on top of her so that to the casual eye the car appeared empty; then upstairs again to remove any traces she might have left in the flat; but there were none.

He glanced at his watch. He had deliberately misled her about the time of his broadcast; not from any particular motive save that he was a habitual prevaricator; lying to him was as necessary as breathing or wrapping up against the cold—a defense against curiosity.

He still had forty minutes before the broadcast was due to begin. Driving south he crossed the river by the swing bridge, turned west, and threaded a maze of semi-slum streets until he came to the main arterial road running south to Exeter. At this hour of a wet evening it was deserted. Dusk had settled in early and the road surface shone black as glass under infrequent orange sodium lights, with huge pools of shadow in between. Suicide traps, Harry called the shadows; he had often noticed how obscure they were, how deceitful to motorists.

He stopped for a moment and twitched the rug off Hilda's body; then drove on half a mile or so accelerating slightly, but not too much, keeping a careful eye on the road before and behind. Empty and silent; he might have been the only living creature for miles. Steering with his left hand he reached behind him and eased open the right-hand rear door. The weight of Hilda's body forced the door wide and she fell out, deep into the shadow. The door swung back and Harry let it swing for a quarter-mile; then he slowed without pulling in to the side, shut it, and drove on. Rain was falling fast now; his tyre marks would probably be obscured already.

Fifteen minutes' moderate driving on a circular route brought him back to the swing bridge, and he arrived at the studios with ten minutes in hand, nodded to the commissionaire, who knew him well, and laid his violin and music case on the desk.

"Guard that with your life, Tyson," he said cheerfully. "I have to make a telephone call. I'll be back in one minute."

There were call-boxes round the corner and he went into one and dialled a Woodmouth number. He got through immediately, but though he heard the bell ringing, nobody answered it for a very long time and he was beginning to be anxious when at last a voice answered: a young, hesitant, breathless voice.

"Hullo?"

"Caroline?"

"Yes?"

So (as he had apprehended, a moment too late) it had not been Caroline last night. Never mind; better luck next time.

"Hilda here, sweetie."

It would have been odd, for a watcher, to hear Hilda's high, emphatic voice emerging from Harry's mouth; he made a grimacing grin at himself in the mirror. Imitating voices was one of the skills, one that he mostly kept to himself—with exceptions such as that unguarded display at Sir Horace's party. "Listen, ducky, tell Mother I won't be home tonight, will you? I've decided to stay in town."

"What about the dogs?"

"Oh, you and Mother can manage them between you, surely? And Caroline—about that other thing—are you listening?"

"Yes," said the faint voice. Was there a hint of fear?

"You know what I mean? About the accident? You haven't said a word to anybody?"

"No of course not, you told me not to. I was waiting—"

"Good. Well attend to me carefully. I'm coming down tomorrow with a lawyer who wants to talk it all over with you and get a sworn statement—an affidavit with your signature"—nonsense, but it sounded convincing enough. "Don't say anything to anybody, particularly not Mother, but come up to Whistle Cottage—you know the empty cottage up by the woods, by the old tunnel?—to-morrow evening. I'll be there with the lawyer and we can have a quiet, private talk without half Woodmouth wondering what's going on. He wants to collect some more evidence, too. Okay? Are you with me? Will you do that?"

"What time?"

"About six. Don't tell a soul—just say you're going for a walk. Right? Are you okay, sweetie?"

"Yes. Hilda—"

"What?"

"An awful thing's happened that you haven't heard. Cousin Flora was drowned last night."

"No! Really?" said Harry. He suppressed a mad desire to burst out laughing. "Poor old girl, what a do. Is Mother very upset? How did she—" But he felt his improvision running down and added, "Oh well, it comes to us all sometime I suppose. Goodbye, sweetie. I must ring off now, I'm going—going to the pictures with some people I bumped into. Old Marx Brothers film."

"Have a nice time," the faint voice said.

Harry rang off. Hundreds of people used these phone boxes; the call would never be traced. He came out and returned to the porter's desk to collect his violin.

"Gentleman left this note for you during the day," Tyson said. "Told the man on duty he understood you were coming in tonight and it could wait."

"Thanks, Tyson."

The note was short; he read it standing in the hallway. "Today's incident at the bank was just to remind you that we can be extremely thorough when it is necessary. You would be well advised to do some careful thinking."

Harry smiled, reading it; his smile widened to a grin and he tore the note into tiny pieces which fluttered down into a fire bucket.

He had done more careful thinking in the last two hours than in the whole of the previous six months, and he was entirely satisfied with the result. He picked up his violin and, walking into the soundproof studio, began tuning up, waiting for the red light to come on.

As he did so a sudden vague recollection came into his head. Wasn't Whistle Cottage the place where Caroline Trevis had once been caught with her lover—hadn't Hilda told him something of the sort? Would that be likely to affect the present issue in any way?

But no; he dismissed the notion as far-fetched and fanciful. Somewhat ironic, though, that the poor girl now had an appointment to die there.

Whistle Cottage was the perfect place for a murder, might have been planned for the purpose. Remote and unvisited up its long wandering track, it had suited Harry to perfection; he was only sorry that now it might be sensible to give up and find some other week-end sanctuary. But not for a month or two perhaps; not till the end of the summer.

It was dark when he drove down after his recital, the warm night air cut softly like unseen wings on either side of the car and Harry, humming the sonata theme again, tasted triumph like wine. Life spun in his hands with the wheel of the car, unfolded for him like the ribboning road. He was invincible.

He was sorry, of course, about Hilda, he regretted the

loss of her gay and ornamental presence, but as a companion she could easily be replaced. It might, now, be sensible to think seriously about harmless little Fernanda, who would be far more useful. And Hilda would have become troublesome—already the reef was beginning to show, the underlying rock beneath her enamelled attraction. He guessed where it came from, that hardness. But she had overreached herself with him.

As for Todd, with his vague threats, Harry found him merely laughable. It would be a long time yet before his masters gave up hope of their strayed lamb. Until then their hands were tied.

Calm and confident, he ran his white car into the shed by the cottage, and let himself into the house. He would sleep long and quietly, and then spend an agreeable day preparing for his visitor.

Mr. and Mrs. Todd lived in a bungalow which they had christened The Nook, at Barlock, and travelled daily to Bridpool where he ran the bookshop and she taught mathematics in a secondary modern school. They were in the habit of breakfasting early to allow ample time for the journey; on Friday their breakfast was even earlier than usual; they had, in fact, been up for several hours already, playing over a tape recording.

Minnie said, for the third time, "It's a pity you weren't able to get the microphone installed before Wednesday night."

She was a thin woman with a flat, expressionless face and a bun of light brown hair; her eyes, unlucent as grey mud, concealed a cold, assessing intelligence. The children she taught were given to making rude jokes behind her back about the dowdiness of the hand-woven, hand-knitted clothes she wore, but in her presence they were always subdued and anxiously polite.

"I told you," her husband said, "I only got the key on Monday night. It was a bit of luck getting it at all. Vosper had seen them together so when she asked him to cut it, he made a spare, on the chance. But Lupac was at home all Tuesday."

He played the tape over again: it was a recording of

Harry's conversation with Hilda on the previous evening.

"I don't know why you're grumbling, that's quite satisfactory," he said. "We could almost use it as it stands. Do you suppose he killed the girl?"

"Very possibly," she said in her dispassionate, toneless voice. "We shall know soon enough. In the meantime, until we do, you had better go out to this place and learn all you can about the death of the boy who was run over—I don't recall seeing it in the papers. Locate the cottage too. The more information we are armed with before we approach him again, the better it will be. It is to be hoped that he *has* killed the girl."

"Yes," he agreed. "And she would soon have been a nuisance to us, she was too inquisitive." He hesitated, then said timidly, "I suppose *you* wouldn't care to go to Woodmouth, Minnie? To tell you the truth, I'm feeling a bit mouldy this morning—touch of the trouble here." He patted his fat little paunch dolefully.

"Oh, don't be silly, Basil." She gave him an impatient look. "How can I possibly go? We're right in the middle of next term's timetables and it would look too odd if I took a day off without notice and roamed round Woodmouth asking questions. But you can do it perfectly well, say you're hunting for a week-end cottage. Drink your milk and take some Duodrox and stop making a fuss."

"What shall I do about my lunch?" he fretted. "I don't suppose there's a decent place in Woodmouth."

"Buy a pot of yoghurt at the dairy then. And be back by six—don't forget there's a meeting of the choral society."

He nodded and, grimacing, swallowed a handful of pills and several spoonsful of a thick white emulsion. His face was extra pale this morning and slightly glossy with moisture.

"You shouldn't have drunk that coffee last night," she said. "I told you so at the time. Are you ready?"

Without waiting for an answer she put on her coat and took up a large hand-woven bag full of corrected examination papers. Mr. Todd obediently wheeled out the scooter from its resting place, took Minnie on the pillion as far as her school, and then turned and headed for the second-class road which crossed the moors to Wood-mouth.

Six

Friday, August 27, morning-afternoon.

Caroline was brushing her hair as she listened to the morning weather forecast. An old habit, dating from four years back, when she had had long hair down to her waist. A hundred brushes, night and morning, and listen to the forecast to see if it will be fine. If it will be fine enough to go for a walk with Tim in the woods.

Now she listened to the forecast for company. Unless you counted Hudson, she heard no other male voice in the course of the day. And he had a pleasant, friendly voice, the announcer, with his businesslike chat about cold fronts and anticyclones. Caroline, sitting brush in hand beside the little old battery set, heard that it was going to be dry, for a wonder, and hot; the temperature would be above normal. She smiled a little at that; as if an English August day would ever come up to the heat that she had learned to know as normal.

"That is the end of the weather forecast," the announcer said, "and now there are two SOS messages. One for Tennant. Will Mrs. Joanne Tennant, believed to be touring Warwickshire in a Ford Vanguard, registration number DP 790, please go to Darley Hospital, Thornton Heath, where her mother, Mrs. Geraldine Cottrell, is dangerously ill. I will repeat that . . ."

Caroline's thoughts trailed away. If I were dangerously ill, she wondered, would they ask Tim to come? Would they broadcast a message? But no, of course not, why should they broadcast? They know where Tim is. I am here and he is there; if I were dangerous'y ill, all they would have to do would be to send a cable. But who would send it? Mother never would. And when I *was* ill—no, best not to start thinking of that. Better to listen to what the announcer says next.

"Now a police message," he was saying. "A woman was knocked down and killed last n'ght in Bridpool, near the junction of Grenville Road and Bath Crescent, by a motorist who failed to stop. Will anybody who saw the accident or can give any information about it please communicate with . . ."

Caroline sat rigid, her knuckles white on the handle of the hairbrush, her eyes fixed and sightless as a trapped rabbit's. Tim, what shall I do. Tim, come back and help me. A motorist who failed to stop . . .

The door opened.

"Now, here is the eight o'clock news for today, Friday, August the twenty-seventh—"

"Oh, *there* you are, Caroline," Lady Trevis said. "Why on earth don't you come down to breakfast? Why sit mooning up here? Listening to the news, what a peculiar thing to do, as if it meant anything to you, you silly girl. Stop fiddling about with that brush and come along; I'm fed up with sitting by myself. No Flora, and Hilda away for the night—I've been up since half-past six . . ."

Nagging, compelling voice, I thought I had escaped you once; shall I ever be free from you again?

She switched off the radio and put the brush down on the dressing table.

"Yes, Mother," she said. "I'm just coming."

Harry began to tidy up the cottage; a sudden enthusiasm had possessed him to have it appear really charming for his visitor. He bustled about, tossing old newspapers into a box, picking a bunch of flowers, dusting, washing the dishes that seemed to have accumulated from several week-end visits. He had never done much about furnishing the place—some straw matting, a table, and a couple of wheelback chairs. In a fit of energy he had once painted white over the wallpaper to make the most of what light there was. Really it was a pleasant little retreat if you didn't object to the hill brooding so close behind. And so conveniently isolated, considering that it was hardly an hour's drive from Bridpool.

He ran a carpet sweeper over the matting, and grinned as it occurred to him how much young Mr. Brodie of the Bridpool *Chronicle* would like to have a picture of him engaged in such a domestic occupation.

Now, glasses, drinks . . .

He had never taken so much trouble for Hilda. But then he and Hilda had recognised a chemical affinity in one another from the first moment. Neither bothered to put up a show for the other; there was no need. That was why he had enjoyed her so much.

They had met four months ago, during a burst of superlative warm May weather. Harry, who had recently taken a lease of Whistle Cottage, through an agent, under an assumed name, was lying in the neglected little garden on an air-bed, half asleep, enjoying the unaccustomed heat of the sun one Saturday afternoon. All of a sudden a large unrestrained dog crashed through the gappy hedge and trampled over him.

Harry loathed dogs at any time, and to have his sacred peace disturbed in this uncouth way was more than he could tolerate. He snatched up a stick and struck the dog; it bit his arm.

On to this scene of rage and hysteria came Hilda, wandering nonchalantly up the track. She wore denim jeans and a shirt; a dog-leash dangled from her wrist.

"Are you the owner of this dog?" demanded Harry, white with passion. "Do you see what he has done to me?"

As he was still holding the stick, Hilda remarked with unruffled placidity,

"Well, if you were so stupid as to go for him with a stick, what can you expect? Normally he's a good-natured animal, only a bit retarded. But if you take a stick to him he sees red—he has a thing about them."

"He was in my garden!"

"Nobody's lived here for such ages that he looks on it as his. Oh, do be *quiet,* Rhiny!"

"Do you know who I am?" stormed Harry, forgetting his cardinal rule in exasperation at her insufferable calm. "I'm Hari Lupac, the violinist!"

"Never heard of you," Hilda said, unimpressed.

"My hands are insured for thousands and thousands of pounds! If that bloody animal of yours has injured me badly, I can tell you I shall sue! And you will be very, very sorry!"

"Oh, why bother to sue if you can collect the insurance?" Hilda said lightly. "Anyway it only looks like a tiny scratch to me. Here, I'll tie it up for you if you like."

This Harry was quite glad to let her do, as he loathed the sight of his own blood. She tethered the dog to a tree; then Harry led her upstairs to the rudimentary bathroom which he had made the agents put in before he would take the cottage.

Hilda washed the bite, which was half scratch, half bruise and, even Harry could see, very trifling. But he was still furiously indignant, more so as he had needlessly given away his identity to this insolent girl who lived in the wilds and hadn't even heard of him. Could such a thing be possible?

"Sit on the edge of the bath if you feel faint," Hilda said with kindly contempt. "Have you any bandages or plaster in the place? No, don't move, tell me where, I'll find it. Hold your arm over the basin."

"Lupac," she said, when she came back from his bedroom with the roll of bandage. "Now I come to think of it I had heard of you—just. You were the one who escaped, weren't you? That picture of you in your bedroom reminded me—it was the one the papers used. I don't know anything about music I'm afraid—that's why I wasn't interested. I hope your vanity will get over the shock. Anyway you were making such a ridiculous fuss over that tiny nip that you needed taking down a peg."

Mingled feelings of outrage and attraction boiled over

in Harry; he slapped her face with his unbitten hand. She smacked him back with equally uninhibited vigour, and from this to a violent embrace, and to Harry's bed at the other end of the uneven little passage, were two inevitably brief stages. They stayed in bed most of the afternoon; meanwhile the dog, cause of all the trouble, philosophically went to sleep under the apple tree.

Later Hilda cooked Harry some bacon and eggs and agreed, rather scoffingly, to come back next day and cook him some more, in case his wound should still be troubling him. So the arrangement had been perpetuated, much enjoyed by both parties.

Yes, he would certainly miss Hilda, he thought; she had been fun and a great convenience. But she could be replaced; the world was full of girls.

This one he was expecting, now . . .

Tim was met at London Airport by Uncle Sean's assistant with a Daimler.

"Thank God your plane was on time; the old man's been working himself into a lather in his hospital bed, thinking it would be held up by fog; he doesn't trust anyone else not to make a shambles of the talks."

"Nice to be valued," Tim said, wrily, wondering if it was worth it, remembering how, six months ago when Caroline was ill, he'd been the only person his uncle had trusted to tidy up the chaos after the Ras al-Abdan explosion. The family system of keeping him strictly as a junior executive while he learned the business from the bottom was one in which he heartily concurred, but it tended to break down in times of crisis. To be sure, six months ago, the work had been a relief in many ways, an anodyne, but all the time he'd been torn, thinking of Caroline ill and wretched, needing him perhaps, emerging from hospital at last with nowhere to go but Woodhoe House and that old harpy of a mother. On its face, a reasonable arrangement, but even then he'd had his doubts . . . only Hilda's letters had reassured him with their constant reiteration that Caroline was settling, was putting on weight. At least now he'd have the chance to judge her state for himself, and if her progress didn't satisfy him, nothing, not mothers, sisters, nor the whole medical profession was going to prevent him from taking her away.

"What time's the meeting?" Tim asked, altering his watch to British summer time. Ten a.m.

"Not till two."

"Oh, that's fine. Then I've time to make some phone calls."

Woodhoe House gave the engaged signal, so he rang Caroline's doctor, who was occupied with a patient, and arranged a time to call again later. There was no reply at all from the Cadwallader School for Girls, presumably closed for the holidays, so on an impulse he tried the Lady Graduates' Club in Bridpool.

"Have you a Miss Hume staying there at present?"

No, they said, but they happened to know that she was in London attending the Headmistresses' Conference; she might be reached at the Melbourne Hotel.

Tim then telephoned his mother, after which he tried Woodhoe House again. Still engaged.

Giving up for the moment he allowed Uncle Sean's assistant, who by now was showing unmistakable signs of impatience, to whisk him off in the Daimler.

"Oh, Tim, my boy—" Uncle Sean shifted with angry impatience on his pillows. He was a heavily built, gloomy-looking old man, grey-haired, his thick black brows jutting over dark eyes, very like Tim's father. "It's grand to see you. Sorry to saddle you with this job, but James is in California, and Waters is such an ass he'd eat out of anybody's hand. Anyway you'll be glad of the chance to see Caroline. How's it going?"

"Fine," Tim said drily. "We got the new rig up this week; we ought to bring in the fourth well by the end of the month."

"I know that! With you out there it's bound to be going along as it should. I meant you personally. Looking tired. What's the news of Caroline?"

"I'm going down to see," Tim said.

"Good. Take a fortnight off. You've earned it. Nicolson can keep things going that long can't he? Have a second honeymoon, eh? Now's a sensible time, when you're both over the worst. Go to Madeira or somewhere. We don't want the youth and promise of the firm cracking up. Your father would have said the same, I'm sure."

"Thanks, Uncle Sean."

"It was a bad business," the old man said, looking at him with difficult, inarticulate affection.

Tim's face clouded. Seeing this Uncle Sean, heavily tactful, steered the talk to a different subject and began to brief him for the conference.

"Where are you staying?" he asked presently. "Got yourself fixed at an hotel, or is Rosa putting you up?"

Tim said that he was seeing his mother that evening but might then go straight on to Bridpool by a night train.

"Fine. Fine. Use my car if you like—eating its head off otherwise. I'll see you after the meeting anyway. Will you stay and have a bite of lunch with me first?"

"Thanks, Uncle Sean, but I arranged to ring Caroline's doctor at twelve; I'd better go and do that now."

"No, not at all, Mr. Conroy," Dr. Galbraith said. "Glad to be able to reassure you. When I last saw her, your wife was going on quite well. Physically just about recovered."

"And mentally?"

"Well—maladjusted a little still as you'd expect—feelings of insecurity—perhaps a slight tendency to dwell on painful episodes in childhood and adolescence as a means of escape from her more recent trouble. Quite normal, of course."

"She seems to have been worrying because she still has amnesia about the period of—of our son's death."

"No use worrying about that; the memory will come back in its own time as I've told her time and again. The fact that it does will be a sign that she is ready to face it," Dr. Galbraith said rather impatiently.

Tim sighed. Whoever picked this doctor for Caroline, he thought, could hardly have picked anyone less sympathetic. But perhaps sympathy was not a primary requisite in a pyschiatrist; he didn't know.

"You haven't had the impression that anything in her *present* surroundings was causing her distress?"

"Why no," Dr. Galbraith said. Then he checked himself and corrected. "She did on one occasion say something about a feeling that people hated her, but this is such a common state of mind among patients that I was not inclined to pay any particular attention to it."

"In her last letter to me she said 'Something terrible's happened to me but I'm not allowed to tell.' What do you make of that?"

Galbraith took a minute to reply.

"It sounds like another bit of regression to childhood," he said at last. "The child's sense, you see, of being under authority, so that any feeling is not the patient's responsibility but that of the adults in charge."

"But Caroline is a highly responsible person! That was the main trouble—she reproached herself so bitterly for having come out to Ras al-Abdan, for having allowed—"

"*Superficially* that might appear so," Dr. Galbraith corrected. "In fact that feeling of responsibility was what she has been trying to shed—to avoid the feeling of guilt over the child, and over tying you down in matrimony, by this amnesia in regard to the actual—ah—occurrence."

Tim's anger burst out. "Good Lord, what a lot of poppycock! Do you really expect me to believe that Caroline's mind works in this elaborate, tortuous way?"

"Oh, dear me, yes," Dr. Galbraith said patiently.

"Well, if her mind's in such a tangle as that I'm surprised you discontinued her visits."

"Every mind is in a tangle," Dr. Galbraith said. "It seemed to me that your wife would benefit from a period of being on her own. She was ready for a step of this kind. But if you are anxious about her, if you feel she needs more therapy, by all means bring her along to see me again."

"No, by God," Tim said, "she doesn't need any more

therapy of that kind. What she needs is love and care and to be back in her proper place. And I'm going to see that she gets it." He made to jab the receiver down, but then contrition overtook him.

"I'm sorry, doctor," he said. "I'm worried sick about her, and I was travelling all night and working all the night before—I'm a bit frayed, I suppose. But I shouldn't have bawled at you. The truth is, I blame myself for leaving her by herself in England."

"Please don't worry," Dr. Galbraith said, sounding quite detached. "It is natural to feel the way you do. As for leaving her in England—I understand you couldn't help it. She certainly does not blame you. Anyway, bring her back for another consultation if you aren't happy about her. I am sure, though, that you will find she is going on most satisfactorily."

When Tim had rung off, he had another try at ringing Woodhoe House. But the line was still engaged.

"Going out, Caroline?" said Lady Trevis, meeting her daughter in the hall.

Damn. "Yes, Mother."

"Take Rhiny, will you, sweet, he's terribly in need of exercise. Really, Hilda seems to be hardly ever at home these days. Which way are you going?"

"Up Hunter Hill," lied Caroline.

"Oh, you could just as easily go down to the village, couldn't you? I'd like you to take some flowers to Gladys Vernon. I meant to send a wreath but I forgot."

Oh no, no, pleaded Caroline soundlessly. Aloud she said, "You don't need to, now, surely? Hilda and I sent a wreath." Her voice was low and she looked down at one of her moccasin walking shoes, centring it on the worn place in the stair carpet.

"Don't be so damned negative all the time, will you, sweetie? If I say I want you to take some flowers, just take them, why not, without all this argy-bargy. It quite gets me down.

"In heaven's name, where has Hudson got to? I've

been standing with my finger on this bell for quite five minutes."

"Yes, ma'am?" said Hudson, appearing by her shoulder. His white hair looked as if he had spat on a palm and hastily flattened it; his pouched, contemptuous old eyes slid away from her. "Yes, m'lady? Did you want something?"

"Oh, Hudson. Find Rhiny, will you. Miss Caroline's going to take him out."

"I daresay he's in the cupboard, ma'am. He seems to like to go there, nowadays." The old man turned and plunged into an evil-smelling cupboard under the stairs, which housed raincoats, old umbrellas, hockey sticks, and also, it appeared, a moulting bull terrier. "Here's his chain, Miss Caroline," Hudson said. "He won't be too strong for you?"

At the suggestion of a walk the dog began to show maniac enthusiasm, nearly knocking over each of the three in turn.

"Of course he won't!" snapped Lady Trevis, fending off Rhiny's advances. "Come on, Caroline, I'll walk past the herbaceous border with you and find some flowers; I'm not going to have you slipping off, pretending there weren't any."

The front door slammed behind them, loose panes rattling. Hudson stared after them for a moment, muttering:

> "Like one that on a lonesome road
> Doth walk in fear and dread . . .
> Because he knows a frightful fiend
> Doth close behind him tread."

Then he spat very deliberately into the marble urn at the foot of the stairs, before plodding back to his pantry.

Lady Trevis's eyes flitted over the unkempt garden bed and she collected a large, awkward bundle of mixed flowers and thrust them into Caroline's unwilling arms.

"Don't let Rhiny loose, will you. He chases sheep nowadays; Kenealy swore he'd shoot him next time it happened." Now the real purpose of Caroline's errand came out. "While you're at Gladys's, ask her when she can come up and wash the curtains."

"Mother I can't ask her yet, so soon after it happened," Caroline said desperately.

"Rubbish. She probably needs some occupation. She can't stay moping at home for ever. Mind, I mean that; they should have been done in April."

Lady Trevis stood watching as Caroline fumbled herself, the dog, and the toppling bouquet out through a shabby, white wicket gate into the drive. Having made sure that her daughter departed in the right direction, she walked back to the house, staring with detestation at its decaying façade. "Mammoths," she muttered. "That's all it wants, a mammoth head on each side of the front door. God, what a prehistoric dump."

The flicker of spirit derived from persecuting Caroline had left her. She looked to make sure the telephone was off its cradle, so that it would not disturb her by ringing, toiled upstairs to her room, and sagged on her bed with a couple of illustrated magazines, wondering when Hilda would be home. Unfortunately for Lady Trevis, drink did not stimulate her in the least.

Caroline paused to loop Rhiny's chain twice round her wrist, and leaned back with all her strength against his eager drag. They proceeded down the river path towards the village. Every now and then she hitched up the slipping flowers as best she could with her left hand. It was a close, stifling, airless afternoon, as the radio had promised. She felt deathly sick.

At the entrance to the village she passed a small, pale, stout man in glasses, who was wheeling a scooter and looked sorry for himself. He glanced at Caroline as if he meditated asking her the way but she, longing to avoid all unnecessary contact, crossed the road towards Gladys Vernon's house, and he made for the Post Office instead.

*   *   *

"It's extremely kind of you to have made time for me, Miss Hume," Tim said, gazing with repectful interest at the bird's nest of grey hair perched over the Duke of Wellington's profile. He sipped at his glass of ferociously dry sherry wondering what it was; a large sticker with TH had been slapped over the original label.

"I always take a private bottle with me when I stay at a hotel," Miss Hume explained. "Don't trust hotel sherry."

She, in return, carefully scrutinised Caroline's husband and liked what she saw. "You're certainly not a young man to let grass grow under your feet," she said approvingly. "I think you did quite right to come to England so fast. I'm sorry I can't give you longer just now" —she glanced at her lapel watch—"but I'm lunching with the Warden of All Saints' in five minutes. What would you like me to tell you?"

"Tell me again about the impression Caroline made on you."

"She seemed oppressed—harried. She said she kept forgetting things and losing things. During her breakdown, while she was in the Beaumont Hospital, she had written me a letter—did you know that?" Tim shook his head. "I have it right here as a matter of fact; I've been so worried about her in the last few days that I took it out again."

Tim studied the letter with horror. "Caroline wrote this? She's better than that *now*, isn't she?"

"Oh, good gracious, yes. The breakdown was of very short duration. I am sure that, fundamentally, Caroline is a most stable person. It is just that events lately have been too much for her."

"Why didn't she *tell* me she couldn't bear to go home?" Tim burst out. "I'd have fixed it somehow."

"Oh, my dear boy, she didn't want to worry you, I daresay. She was very distressed about *your* distress."

"You haven't heard from her in the last day or two?"

"No, and this is what worries me. Professor Lockhart has written to her and I have; neither of us has received an answer. I have also tried to telephone without success;

once, the line was engaged, once it merely rang and no-body answered."

"I'll go down as soon as I've seen my mother," Tim said.

"I think you are very sensible. Ah, there is the Warden —silly man, why will he wear such peculiar trousers? Goodbye, Mr. Conroy, and please keep in touch—I shall be most anxious to hear from you. I am greatly relieved to have met you; I consider that Caroline made a very good choice."

She gave Tim a warm smile and moved with dignity to meet her guest.

"Here's my hubby coming now, I believe, Inspector," Gladys Vernon said, hearing the creak of the front gate.

Inspector Gleason nodded, glad that his uncomfortable tête-à-tête was over. He glanced round the dusty parlour, sighing, wondering if Gladys Vernon had always been a slut, or was it just that she had gone to pieces in the last few days? It was excusable, of course. The brief pomp of the funeral was over, nothing remained but one or two heart-breaking unwanted toys in the cupboard.

The house felt bereft; and it smelt dismally of potatoes, woodsmoke, and damp linoleum.

The footsteps halted at the front door instead of going round to the back, and they heard a light tap. Gladys went to answer it, glancing automatically at her face as she passed the chiffonier mirror. Her cried-out blue eyes were beginning to recover their colour; the blonde beehive of hair maintained its improbable flaxen perfection above her flabby features.

"Miss Caro, love," she said warmly. "It's ever so nice of you to look in."

"Hullo, Gladys—Mrs. Vernon," Caroline said. "You're looking better. I'm so glad." She hitched Rhiny's chain on to a rusty hook in the wall of the house.

"Come in for a moment, Miss Caro. Inspector Gleason's here, waiting to see Joe. I was just going to put on the kettle for a cuppa."

"No, I won't stop, really," Caroline said. "I'm going

for a walk. Mother sent these flowers with her love and said——" But faced with the baldness of her next message she allowed herself to be persuaded into the parlour where Inspector Gleason, kindly, shrewd-eyed, and stocky, was looking with discomfort at the ornate sympathy cards on the mantel.

"Oh, that's ever so kind of Lady Trevis. Aren't they lovely, Inspector," Gladys said. "You know Mrs. Conroy, I expect? Lady Trevis's daughter? I'm sure I don't know what's keeping Joe. He just stepped down the road. Can't seem to settle to any jobs at the moment so he said he'd go for a walk."

A little flustered, she picked up the teapot and looked uncertainly from one of her visitors to the other.

"No hurry," said the Inspector kindly. "Joe all right, is he? Are you looking after each other?"

"Oh yes, thank you ever so. There, that kettle's just on the boil." She took the teapot out to the scullery.

Caroline and the Inspector stood in silence; Caroline still helplessly holding her bouquet, stared down at its wilting petals. I could tell him *now* if I hadn't promised Hilda; it would be so easy to say, Inspector, I saw the man who killed Garry Vernon, I recognised him.

But Hilda said he wouldn't believe me. The people in the village think I'm hysterical, mad. The lawyer will know I'm telling the truth, though, won't he? Only an hour or so to wait, and then I can tell the whole story. I wish it didn't mean going to that place, though, she thought with a shiver of revulsion and dread.

"Back home on a bit of a holiday are you, Mrs. Conroy?" the Inspector said heartily. "Your husband's overseas, isn't he?"

Gladys, returning with the tea, wished it were permissible to kick her husband's superior on the ankle. For the Inspector, a Barlock man, plainly hadn't heard the village gossip about Caroline.

"That's right." Caroline's throat tightened. She looked down at the flowers and to her horror saw a tear splash on them, and then another.

"Let me put these in water," she muttered, and fled to the scullery.

"Here's Joe at last," said Gladys with relief, and followed her.

Police Constable Vernon came in, his pleasant open face miserable and harassed. "Couldn't seem to settle to any of the things that needed doing, so I walked up the valley road and had another look where it happened," he explained heavily to the Inspector. "I didn't really expect to find anything, I knew you'd had the place gone over thoroughly at the time, but I did find this bit of rag in the bushes. I reckon it might—"

Gladys and Caroline came back just as Joe passed it to the Inspector—a soft cloth, which had once been white and was now stiff with dried blood and coated with dust.

"What's that?" said Gladys, her eyes dilating. Joe put a protective arm round her.

"Don't take on, lovey. I didn't mean for you to see it."

"Did you find it—along *there?*"

He nodded and Gladys's face crumpled.

"Oh burn it, burn it!" she sobbed. "I can't bear to look at it!"

"We can't burn it, Mrs. Vernon," said the Inspector gently. "It might be evidence, you see. Someone threw it into those bushes—it didn't get there by itself. It might tell us something about the person who ran over your little boy and then left him there in the road. I'll take it in to the lab and let them get to work on it."

Gladys was crying in great choking gulps, her hands clenching and unclenching. Caroline, herself white as death, put an arm round Gladys and helped her upstairs.

"Take it to the lab," wept Gladys, "what's the good of that? Whatever they do it won't bring my Garry back."

Caroline administered tea and aspirin, and looked unhappily round the stuffy cottage bedroom. She opened the window. A teddy bear lay on the window seat. She carefully avoided touching it.

"I'll be all right now, Miss Caro, thank you ever so

much," Gladys said presently, blowing her nose. "You go for your walk. And I'll be up this evening for those curtains."

"Oh, no, for heaven's sake, don't; I'm sure Mother didn't mean it seriously. You want a bit of a break."

"I don't," Gladys said. "I want something to take my mind off."

Caroline held her hand tightly for a moment and then slipped down stairs. For the life of her she couldn't go back through the room where the men still were with that bit of rag. She went into the scullery and through to the brick wash house, where there was a copper, and a clothesline, and a pile of kindling, and a door leading to the vegetable patch. There was something else, too. Caroline halted, momentarily unable to go on. The wash-house floor was dirty, covered with coal dust and wood chips. In the middle, as if some despairing hand had just flung them down, was a pile of child's clothes. Small threadbare jeans, torn sneakers, ravelled sweaters, and several agonisingly familiar T shirts.

"Oh God," whispered Caroline soundlessly. "Oh, dear God—"

Blind with shock she almost ran out of the door, round to the front of the house, where Rhiny was half strangling himself in his efforts to get loose and massacre the dog next door. Unhitching him, she turned back along the village street, oblivious of the fact that his chain was cutting deep red weals across her hand as he leapt and snarled. She felt as if someone were hammering with vicious strokes at her brain.

Oh, please heaven, she thought, let that rag be the man's handkerchief or something that will tell them who it was. I ought to have told that Inspector, I know. I ought not to have waited. Those T shirts. I ought never to have let Mother give them to Gladys. I ought to have been able to stop him before he ran down the hill.

She walked back distractedly through the village, un-aware of the curious, sympathetic glances that came her way, and took the path by the brawling river. A sort of shudder was running through her mind, a sort of dreadful anticipatory stirring, as if a door were about to open, and she was racked tight with the apprehension that what came out would be too bad to be borne.

But I don't remember. All I know is that they wouldn't let me see him. They said there was nothing to see. Nothing.

I must not think. I must go to Whistle Cottage.

Rhiny jerked and dragged at her wrist. And the hammer strokes beat on without mercy.

"Mind you, I shouldn't think it will tell us anything," Inspector Gleason said. "But it could be that the chap used it to try and wipe the blood from the—your son's head. And then got scared when he saw how badly he was hurt, and threw the rag away before driving on. I'll certainly take it back to Barlock with me, it's just possible the lab boys will be able to get something from it."

The two men stood unhappily drinking their tea.

"Mrs. Conroy looked pretty upset," Gleason remarked.

"Thinking about her own boy, I reckon," Joe said heavily. "She came home when he died, you know, six months ago. Calling in here will have brought it back to her, poor thing. They do say—" He moved nearer, and the Inspector's kind, country face clouded as Joe told him the local rumours about Caroline.

"Poor girl—poor girl."

"A child's death comes hardest on a woman." Joe sighed. "Though I miss the little chap something cruel . . . What is it, sir?"

Gleason was sniffing in a puzzled way at the rag. It was an old bit of sheet, torn square. "Smell reminds me of my dad," he said frowning. "Can't think why. He's been dead these twenty years."

"Your dad?" Joe said curiously. "I wonder why."

"Can't make it out," Gleason said, sniffing again. "I know the smell, but I can't put a name to it."

"What did your dad do, sir?"

"Had a little music shop, Bournemouth way."

*　　　*　　　*

It was an unmetalled earth track, and the grass grew long and drooping at the verge and on the unworn strip in the centre. Her feet made little sound on it, as she placed them one after another along the baked, whitish soil. The banks on either side were steep, and she could not see over them, but there was the smell of young trees all around, and the wide, swinging flight of gulls high overhead suggested the sea not far off. Flowers on the banks grew thick: late, dropping foxgloves, buttercups, Queen Anne's lace—

"Archangels," she said cautiously, aloud, stopping to touch a yellow flower with her finger. "And, bedstraw, bindweed, scabious."

But if she could remember all these, why couldn't she remember her own name?

She looked at her shoes, her hands, as if they might give some clue to her identity. Shoes—well-worn, white with dust. Hands—ringless, thin but unwrinkled; a young person's hands. She felt her face; it felt smooth; pulled a strand of hair forward to look at it. Darkish soft hair, not very long. There were no pockets in her tweed skirt or cotton shirt; tucked in her waistband was a handkerchief. Initial C.

Who was she?

Doing her best to fight down a surge of panic she went on walking slowly uphill. Her thoughts spun about trying to fix on this memory or that—house? room? someone who is dear to me? It was no use. She felt as if she were walking in a fog, a bright sea mist with the sun behind it, tantalisingly close, in which objects were thinly but completely veiled.

It's summer. I'm a girl. I'm in the country. In—in England? It felt like England. I am not hungry. Nor tired. My head aches a bit but I don't feel exactly ill. I don't feel unhappy or frightened. Nobody else is anywhere near. It is quite silent. When did I start walking up this path? Where was I going?

She looked at the watch on her left wrist—a square, plain watch with no initials or ornaments. It said ten past six. Then she rubbed with slow, puzzled fingers at two deep, painful bruises over the back and side of her hand. What did that? Could I have caught it in a door? Have I been in an accident?

At the word accident a little warning light seemed to flash redly and momentarily somewhere deep in the veiled recesses of her mind. But no, the bruise was nothing serious; and her forehead was cool, and the lane, between its decreasing banks and the ramparts of young, planted trees, was too shady for sunstroke to be a possibility.

If I go on, she thought, I shall reach the place I was making for. I don't feel I had come out idly; I feel I had a purpose; I'm like someone who comes into a room and stands in the doorway thinking, "What did I come here for?" Sooner or later I shall remember.

Don't worry, she adjured herself, don't panic, there's nothing you can do to hurry things.

She went on walking.

"Resin," said Inspector Gleason. "Of course. Powdered resin. Off the strings of violins. Or cellos."

He stood beside Saunders, the lab assistant, and tipped the slide up and down. "You put it on your bow. I knew the smell had some association for me."

"Of course it's used in lots of other ways too," Saunders pointed out. "And unfortunately there's nothing else on the rag except dust. It's the Vernon boy's blood group as we expected. Doesn't really get us much further, even supposing you knew you were looking for a cellist —and it might just as well be a chemist."

Gleason nodded, sighing. "It's funny, all the same. Resin's not all that common."

"D'you suppose there's any connection between the child's death and the old girl who fell off the harbour wall?" Saunders said. "Two accidental deaths in a tiny place like Woodmouth inside of four days seems quite a coincidence."

"It does," Gleason agreed. "But I don't see how there can be a connection. We always do get more deaths in the summer. More traffic—people swimming, climbing the cliffs—and so far as I know old Miss Tidbury never had anything to do with the Vernons, except that Mrs. Vernon sometimes helps up at Woodhoe House."

Gleason's assistant put his head round the door and said,

"You're wanted on the phone, sir. Bridpool Central."

"Well, thanks, anyway, Saunders," Gleason said, and went back to his office. He picked up the phone.

"Gleason here. I beg your pardon. Yes. Miss Hilda Trev—, oh yes. Has been *what?* Good Lord. Yes. Yes of course. Right away. I'll go up there. It's only twenty minutes from Barlock by car—better than phoning. Quite. Have you any idea—? None. In Bridpool. Just so. Found a what? A tin? Could you repeat that word? A string— a *violin* string?" He paused, staring down at his desk, while an expression of great astonishment slowly grew on his face. "What a curious thing. Yes, I'll go up to the mother right away. You'll want her to come in for identification? Tomorrow? Naturally. Goodby."

He glanced at his watch. It was six. Being a methodical man, he signed the day's letters and reports before calling for the car. As he was driven across country to Woodhoe House, his mind went over the facts again and again. One old lady fallen off a harbour wall. No sign of foul play. Two hit-and-run deaths. All three victims from the same village, two even from the same household, although one of the deaths had taken place in Bridpool. Surely this was more than coincidence?

Of course such accidents did occur all the time, every day—but then the resin, and the violin string found twisted round the dead girl's finger? Didn't they add up to something? Three deaths in five days . . .

If only I had a third bit of connecting evidence, he thought, we might begin to get somewhere.

The conference lasted for over four hours. When Tim reported back to the hospital, feeling as if his eyeballs had been rubbed in more sand than lay between Aden and Bahrein, Uncle Sean let him off with a brief celebration glass of champagne before sending him off to Addington Square in the Daimler.

His mother met him in the door of the flat and embraced him.

"Darling," she said, "before—"

Then she took a careful look at him and changed her mind. His eyes, always deep-set, were sunk into his skull like sockets with fatigue, the vertical lines on either side of his mouth might have been scored with a chisel.

"Off with you into a hot bath this instant minute," she said, "while I mix you an egg nog. You look like an old shoe and I don't wonder, stravaging round the world the way you've been doing."

Tim knew his mother's edicts were not to be ignored, and he staggered off gratefully to the unspeakable comfort of a boiling bath in a civilised bathroom.

"I kept ringing Woodhoe House as you asked," Mrs. Conroy said when half the egg nog was safely swallowed. "I had to try five or six times before I got through. Someone's a terrible talker in that household—the phone was engaged solid all afternoon."

"That's what I found," Tim said. "Did you get Caroline?"

"No, Lady Trevis. I can't stand that woman."

Mrs. Conroy was a small Irishwoman, white-haired, with an air of great charm and distinction. She was very unlike her son in appearance, but their voices, eyes, and manner of expressing themselves were exactly the same. From her look of distaste now she might have been watching a hunchbacked toad hop across the room. Tim grinned in spite of his anxiety.

"How's Caroline? You didn't speak to her?"

She looked up compassionately at the eagerness in his voice. "I'm afraid there's worrying news, Tim dear."

"What is it? She's not worse? Did you speak to Hilda?"

"Darling, that's what's so awful. They've had two deaths in that household in the last three days. No—not Caroline. Hilda was run over and killed—"

"*Hilda* was? No! When?"

"In Bridpool, just last night."

"Good God," he said blankly. "What an appalling thing. You didn't mishear? You're sure?"

"Of course I'm sure."

"Sorry—being tired makes one so thick. Wretched Hilda—what a fearfully sudden end. She was such a dynamic sort of girl. I can't imagine her gone. Hey—" he said, suddenly harking back. *"Two* deaths, you said. Then who—?"

"No, not Caroline," Mrs. Conroy said quickly. "It's the old aunt, cousin or whatever she was, Miss Tidbury. I never met her, she came there just about the time your father fell ill—"

"She's died too?"

"Fell off the harbour wall in a thunderstorm two days ago and broke her neck."

"But—good Lord, how absolutely macabre." Tim frowned. "I don't like it, Mother."

"I know dearest, positively House of Usher, I'd say. Of course the two incidents were totally unconnected— poor Hilda was knocked down in Bridpool—but even so, ghastly for Caroline if she's still in a nervous state."

"That settles it," Tim said. "I'm not leaving Caroline alone at Woodhoe with that old witch, Lady Trevis. That would be enough to drive most people round the bend I should think, whatever state they were in before. Can you possibly put us both up here for a few days? I'll go and fetch her right away. Lord, though, poor Caroline, poor kid; to have this on top of the other—"

"But darling," his mother said, "that's just what I was going to tell you."

"What?"

"Caroline's missing. She went out with one of the dogs, and the dog came back at supper time but she didn't. The police are looking for her now."

Tim stared at her, his face whitening under the tan. "She knew about Hilda?"

"No; that's the curious part. She'd gone out before the police came with the news—quite a long time before. She'd been upset because a little boy in the village had been run over and killed last week and it had reminded her—"

"Ah, don't," he said under his breath.

His mother watched him, a line of worry creasing her smooth brow.

"Quite between ourselves," Lady Trevis had croaked confidentially, "Caroline has been so very odd lately that I shouldn't wonder if she'd gone completely off her head. They're going to drag the rivers—. That would really be the best thing for your Tim, wouldn't it? Of course *I'm* absolutely *shattered*. Two daughters at a blow—and Hilda was really devoted to me—let alone poor old Cousin Flora who was a shattering bore but adored us all—I just don't know *what* I'm going to do with myself now. I certainly can't afford to live here on my own so I'll have to sell the house and perhaps move to Mentone; all the dogs will have to be sold or put down, poor darlings . . ."

Mrs. Conroy had listened in a sort of fascinated horror and rung off as soon as she politely could, begging Lady Trevis to let her know when there was any news. But what a vampire the woman was; not a flicker of real feeling or concern, save for herself.

Tim put on his jacket.

"What are you doing, darling?"

"I'll get on a plane—charter one if necessary—and fly straight down."

Harry was growing restless and disturbed. Half an hour late already—what could have happened to delay the girl? He gave a last glance round the unwontedly neat room and then walked out impatiently, crossed the little patch of wild garden, and started down the track; he had no real intention of going very far, his whole picture of the forthcoming interview demanded that it should be held indoors, but inactivity was something he found hard to endure.

After fifty yards or so he stopped abruptly and stood listening, tense as a bowstring; his sharp musician's ears had caught a sound that jarred against the accustomed

natural background of bird calls and wind in leaves; yes
—there it came again. He turned sharply off the path,
forced his way through a thicket, and nearly fell over
the body of a man who was crouched down among the
bushes in a very odd position, almost on his knees,
propped against a young oak and retching his heart out.

"Here, what the devil's going on?" Harry said, violent
with anger and surprise. "These are private woods, I'd
have you know—if you must get drunk and make a pig
of yourself, please be so good as to go and do it elsewhere!"

Slowly, at these words, the man lifted his head and
looked up, supporting himself with an arm against the
tree; the face revealed was that of Mr. Todd.

For a moment Harry was utterly taken aback. His
face went ugly, slack, open-mouthed with shock. Then,
collecting himself, he noticed Mr. Todd's frightful appearance, sodden, sweating, his hair, what there was of
it, matted into dank points, his skin the colour of lead,
his tie and cardigan dabbled with vomit.

At once Harry felt more at ease; it was still a devas-
tatingly inconvenient and dangerous intrusion, but the
sight of somebody else in pain or difficulties never failed
to put him in a good humour; his first suspicion, that this
was some form of highly ingenious trap, began to abate;
he said, sounding amused,

"Hullo, if it isn't my friend the bookseller! You really
will have to learn to lay off the strong drink, Mr. Todd, if
it has such a bad effect on you."

Apart from one flaming glance of scorn, Mr. Todd
made no response to this pleasantry; crouched forward,
with his arms round his knees, he was rocking to and fro,
giving little high-pitched moans at the apex of each
movement.

"Oh, do be quiet!" Harry said impatiently. "Have
some self-control, man, can't you? What is the matter
with you?"

Harry's voice, so full of dislike and so totally lacking
in sympathy, jolted Mr. Todd into a momentary aware-
ness; making a tremendous effort he mastered his agony,

looked up at Harry out of yellowed, blood-veined eyes, and whispered, not without dignity,

"I'm a teetotaller, I should inform you. Never partook of beer or spirits in my life. The trouble's my gastric ulcer—think I must have ruptured it. That long scooter ride over bumpy moorland road—ghastly meal in Woodmouth—should never touch fish and chips but what was I to do—no other choice—going without meal is equally—equally bad—"

His voice failed for a moment and Harry, watching, was interested to notice that he dug his fingers quite a long way into the ground, fighting a new advance of pain; he went on with difficulty,

"Tramping round village all day—up through woods—I'm not cut out for this type of work—that's the truth of the matter. Minnie—have to understand—" Then he curled his arms tight round his knees once more, bowed forward like an embryo, and called out in an extraordinary hoarse, choked voice, as if from his very bowels,

"Oh—my—God—"

"Well, *I* never asked you to come out here and pry into my concerns," Harry said coldly. "Which I assume is what you've been doing. And I'm pleased to think you'll have found out remarkably little in the village, where they hardly know of my existence. By the way, many thanks for your note; I'm sorry you had the trouble of blowing up the bank, as it was the wrong one. Maybe I should have mentioned that I have accounts in several names."

Mr. Todd did not appear to be listening; his whole attention was concentrated on drawing a series of long, gasping breaths; at the end of each he clenched his hands and waited, frowning with effort, before painfully expelling it again.

"Morphia," he brought out presently. "For God's sake—can't you—give me a shot of morphia?"

"My dear fellow, why should you imagine I have any?"

"You were—an addict—at one time."

"What utter rubbish," said Harry lightly. "That just

shows the sort of exaggerated rumour that gets spread around. No concert performer of my calibre could afford to be an addict."

"For God's sake, Lupac—I'm *dying*. For God's sake. Do something."

"All the more reason why not," said Harry. "I don't want your dead body found with an unaccountable puncture in it. Old Dame Nature's way is best."

"Then"—anger made the sick man's articulation suddenly much clearer—"kindly get away from here and leave me—die in peace."

Harry, who had been squatting down as if humouring Mr. Todd's foible to conduct the conversation at ground level, now stood up. "Oh, you tiresome, tiresome, silly fellow," he said irritably, "how the devil can you expect me to leave you to die in peace not a hundred yards from my front door? You are a thorough inconvenience to me, I can tell you."

Mr. Todd's face stretched in a ghastly rictus of malice.

"Awkward—isn't it? Too many—unexplained deaths—round Woodmouth already."

Harry frowned at this; then he said smoothly, "All the more reason why yours shouldn't take place here. Well, my friend, the problem isn't insuperable. There's a fine bit of bottomless bog on the moor not five miles from here, which has probably swallowed plenty of bodies in its time. How did you say you came here, by the way?"

Mr. Todd made no answer.

"Oh, I recall now, you said you came by scooter. Left it down by the road, out of earshot, I suppose, while you played William Tell in the woods. So that's another nuisance that will have to be dealt with. Well, I'm sorry not to ring for an ambulance, but you hardly deserve it, do you? And as you've probably discovered, I'm not on the phone, and the wall telephone in the post office is rather too public for my taste; I expect you found that out too. But you're decidedly *de trop* here, there's no denying; I'll have to take you indoors."

"Leave me be!" Todd gasped in fury, but Harry ruthlessly pulled him up and carried him through the bushes to the cottage, casting several anxious, wary glances, as he did so, down the track, which was still empty. He did not halt in the parlour but went straight on up the narrow stairs, half dragging Todd, who was only semiconscious by this time, and into the bedroom. Here he let Todd's body slump to the floor, stood regarding him for a moment with pursed lips, and then picked up a bottle off the wooden chest which served as dressing table.

"Come on now—open your mouth and swallow some of this down. You ought to be grateful—it's just as expensive as morphine and far nicer. Caroni rum, ninety proof. You'll be so drunk you won't know when you go."

A good tumblerful splashed into the open mouth of Mr. Todd who gave a violent shudder and let out an inarticulate, gargling sound of protest.

"No good, old boy," Harry said. "It is rather a waste of rum, I fear, but you might as well enjoy it because you've got to have it," and he slopped in another tumblerful. Mr. Todd's eyes opened at him in a vacant stare.

"Tell me, my friend," Harry asked him confidentially, "did anybody else know that you were coming here?"

Todd's face, which had been pale, now flushed a darkish purple and a stream of rapid syllables began issuing from his mouth; Harry listened intently.

"Wife Minnie—told me scout around village—don't approach Lupac till more information—told her—wasn't feeling well—" His dignity had left him, he sounded plaintive and self-pitying.

"Oh, so wife Minnie knows about your trip, does she? I wonder what else wife Minnie knows. That rules out disposing of you in the bog or over the cliff then; it would be rather too near home. Your body had better be found a good long way off, on some lonely roadside, where you had dismounted from your scooter when you came over too ill to proceed. You had with you a bottle, with which you brightened your last moments—here, have another drink. I must say," Harry muttered, frowning as he poured more spirit down Todd's unresisting throat, "I would very much like to know how you got on to this place."

But Todd was beyond making any reply. He lay limp and inert, dribbling from the corners of his mouth, his eyes turned up horribly. Harry left him, shutting the bedroom door and locking it from the outside.

"Now all will be well so long as the tiresome fellow does not start to shout or snore; if he does I shall just have to explain that it is my aged Uncle William who has the misfortune to suffer from delirium tremens; however let us hope that he dies during the next hour or so." Harry ran downstairs beginning to whistle, but broke off to exclaim impatiently, "Where the *devil* can that girl be?"

Minnie Todd was a woman of routine. She left the Secondary Modern School at twenty minutes past four every day, bought figs, yoghurt, muesli, and frozen nut rissoles at a health food store, and caught a bus back to Barlock without waiting for Basil, who never got home until nearly six. So today she reached The Nook as usual at ten to five, washed up the breakfast dishes, did some work on her syllabus for next term's sixth-form maths, and made supper, poaching a bit of haddock for Basil, who found nuts hard to digest. While she worked, she listened to a radio programme of regional news which contained information about new traffic regulations, warnings against confidence tricksters, descriptions of wanted men, and other material of a topical and instructive nature, often useful to Mrs. Todd in her work.

Tonight they were giving amplification on an earlier bit of news.

"The body of the woman who was killed in a hit-and-run accident in south Bridpool last night has now been identified as that of Miss Hilda Trevis, of Woodhoe House, Woodmouth. If anybody saw the incident, which took place near the junction of Grenville Road and Bath Crescent, or can give any information about it, will they please contact the police, telephone number Bridpool 9000. I will repeat that . . ."

Minnie Todd nodded grimly, pressing her thin lips together. Here was a demonstration, if one were needed, that Lupac was a ruthless and dangerous fighter, prepared to defend his position by any means. How surprised, she thought, not to say incredulous the police would be if they could hear the recording of his conversation with Hilda.

But Mrs. Todd had no intention of going to the police at present.

She glanced irritably at her watch and put the haddock in the oven to keep warm: Basil was going to be late for the choral society if he did not turn up soon.

The girl was nearly an hour late now, where on earth could she have got to? Thoroughly bothered by this departure from schedule, Harry flung from side to side of the room like an irritated bluebottle, looking at his watch, rubbing vexedly at his eyelids, biting his lips. Ten minutes, he said to himself, I give her ten minutes. What to do if she did not appear during that time he had not considered, but before this decision must be made there was a light tap at the door and Harry hurled himself at it with the enthusiasm of a child welcoming the postman at Christmas. Would she be surprised to see him? She must recognise him at once, of course, and he had his opening words of welcome all ready:

"My dear Mrs. Conroy! You will be surprised, no doubt . . ."

But the girl on the threshold looked at him without the faintest glimmer of recognition in her eyes.

"It is Mrs. Conroy, isn't it? Caroline? Hilda's sister?"

"I—I don't know," she said. "I'm sorry to bother you, but I'm lost. I've lost my way and I've forgotten who I am. Please could you ring up a doctor?"

He looked at her blankly: a small, fragile girl, fine-boned, with feathery darkish hair. Not a bit like Hilda; that said nothing, though, for Hilda had told him that she and her sister were quite different in appearance. This girl smiled at him tremulously.

"It's so silly, isn't it," she said. "Silly, but it's a bit

frightening for me. I should be so grateful if you could phone someone."

"I'm not on the telephone," he said.

He was wild with annoyance. Was she Caroline? Was she bluffing? Had she recognised him at once and guessed the danger? He looked at her again, narrowly. If that were so, his only course was to outplay her; she could hardly keep it up for long.

"Come in and sit down," he said, forcing a friendly, easy manner. "You must be tired and terrified. I'll give you a drink and we'll think what's best to be done."

He watched her like a hawk as she came into the small room, remembering Hilda's tale of the younger sister found here with her boy friend by the angry mother. But the girl made no sign. She hardly glanced at her surroundings, simply sat down like an obedient child in the wheelback chair he pulled out for her. A violin lay on the table but her eyes moved past it indifferently to rest on the jar of flowers. "It's so absurd," she said with a note of apology in her voice, "I can remember what those flowers are called but not my own name."

"Can you remember anything about yourself at all?" Harry asked. He had his back to her, pouring out an extremely stiff gin.

She shook her head. "I can remember a few *things*— a leather needlebook, and a picture of mountains, and a dressing gown with rabbits on the sleeves—I suppose I had it when I was small. Nothing else."

"Here, drink this," Harry said, giving her the glass. He rummaged in a drawer and found a couple of snapshots of Hilda. "Do you know that person?"

He watched her acutely as she studied the picture. Not a muscle moved in her face; they might have been portraits of the Infanta of Castile, for any sign of recognition she made. Disappointed, he took them back and, tearing them in half, dropped them indifferently into the grate.

"Do you think you've had some sort of shock or fright?" he asked carefully. "People sometimes lose their memories for a short time when they're subjected to a lot of strain. It's called fugue—a kind of running away from trouble."

"I don't know," she said. She pressed her fingers against her eyelids. Was there anything hidden inside her —fear, like an evil old man with a candle, lurking at the back of her brain? Fear of what? Of whom?

Harry's eyes, studying her, were as bright and opaque as sequins. He compressed his lips and two long vertical creases appeared in his cheeks. He could not decide what to do. It seemed so likely that this girl was Caroline. He felt tempted to go ahead with his original plan to finish her off and dispose of her body in Piper's Patch, the stretch of quaking and odoriferous bog up on the moor. She could pickle there undisturbed; no one would find her body there. If this girl was Caroline no one would even begin to know where to look, since he had been so careful to ask her not to tell anyone where she was going. Her recent odd behaviour would be borne in mind; it would probably be assumed that she'd gone off her head and either jumped into the sea or wandered away. The whole of England would be searched. Meanwhile the unknown tenant of Whistle Cottage would in due course give up his tenancy, quietly depart, and sever all connection with the district. No one would have any cause to associate a missing unbalanced girl with Harry Lupac. In order to keep his identity concealed from the locals he had always bought his week-end food in Bridpool, and had nearly always contrived his arrival and departure at night.

He was now more than ever inclined to regret his encounter with Hilda, but not to a serious degree; Harry had too much self-confidence to worry unduly about any of his past actions.

But if the girl were not Caroline? Suppose her to be some wild-life enthusiast, or one of a party of motorists or hikers who had strayed away from her friends and bumped her head on a tree? They would all be out looking for her like a pack of wolves. Supposing she were a local girl who had said to her family that she was going for a nice walk past Whistle Cottage for a change; a local girl subject to fits of amnesia, who always told her mother where she was going. . . .

"Drink your drink," he said irritably. "You've hardly touched it."

"It's very strong," the girl said. She sipped it. "Please, don't you think you'd better take me to the nearest hospital? I'm sorry to be a bother but I'm sure that would be best. If my—if anyone is looking for me they'd be sure to get in touch with hospitals."

"Slowly, slowly," said Harry. "For all we know, your mother, your grandfather, your husband, and three of your aunts may be coming up the lane searching for you at this moment. It would be silly not to give them the chance of putting in an appearance."

She smiled faintly. She looked very young and vulnerable. Harry tried to remember if Hilda told him Caroline's age. Twenty? Twenty-one? He knew she had not been married very long. Hilda had still been nursing the raw, savage resentment over Caroline's under-age marriage, and he had drawn it all out of her one evening, half teasing, half inquisitive at uncovering such a bitter stratum of hatred.

"Child marriage—so sweet—hardly out of the nursery —ugh, that smug little prig! Why, good grief, Harry, she's not even particularly pretty. I suppose men find that lost-child look intriguing, though I can't imagine why —there's nothing behind it. Father used to coddle her with a whole lot of mawkish nonsense—his beautiful daughter, my God! And hypocritical! All the time, while Mother was nagging at us and hounding us off to dances and dinning it into our heads that if we didn't hurry up and catch a man we'd be on the shelf, clever little Caroline was sneaking up here to meet Tim on the sly. Boy-and-girl romance. Met at dancing class, so pretty and suitable. Mother was livid when she found out how long the affair had been going on—she almost withheld her consent to the marriage. Of course, in public she was all over it—done so well for herself, his people are very well off—ahh, it makes me sick to think of it. Caroline had all the luck all the way—she was the one who was sent to the good school to make nice well-bred friends while I had to go out to work as a sort of lady stablehand."

"That was the place where you got the sack for seducing the son of the house? And then Caroline has the luck to make this nice advantageous marriage with a rich young man. Sour grapes, eh?"

His voice was not very amiable. She turned and sank her teeth in his shoulder.

"You needn't think I'm pining for tedious Tim, even if he does end up an oil magnate. He's a dead bore. Dull, steady, reliable—bone from neck up."

"Well then, don't begrudge him to your little sister." He grinned. "You really loathe the poor girl, don't you? Would you like it if she died?"

"Good heavens, no. Dying would be an escape for her; it's far worse being back at Woodhoe," Hilda said, her eyes brilliant with satisfied malice.

Now Harry tried to fit this girl into that picture—hiding her adolescent romance from the hostile mother and sister, stealing off to this haven in the woods to meet her lover. And then the inevitable discovery. Yes she fitted in very well, she would be well cast as Juliet.

He was almost sure she must be Caroline.

"Try and recall your childhood," he urged. "I think that would be the way to bring memory back. Begin with anything you can remember and make yourself spin a little web around it—of details, of fancies, it does not matter."

She looked at him helplessly. "I can't," she said.

"Now think again." He was friendly, persuasive, encouraging. "I will start you. Your nursery when you were small. Toys, pictures—a doll, perhaps? The dressing gown with the rabbits. Think of the things you used to do —sitting on your mother's lap, roasting chestnuts at the fire?"

Her face registered nothing.

He went on, "Think of walking to school—you must have done that. Picture yourself—your heavy satchel cutting into your wrist as it hangs over your arms"—his eyes flickered from her bruised hand to her face and back again—"the sun is shining, the hawthorn hedges are green, it is spring. Think. Think of the shouts of other children in the road, children scattering to the side as a car comes by"—again his eyes darted to her face, bright, rapacious. He beat a little tatoo on the arm of his chair.

"I think," she said in a troubled voice, "I do remember something. There was a boy . . ."

"Take another sip of your drink. A boy, yes?"

"He used to call out, 'Who's Medusa?' "

"Who's Medusa?"

"I was frightened of the other children. They used to tease me. And one day I called, 'I'll set Medusa on you.' They thought it was a tremendous joke and after that—oh, for years—this boy shouted 'Who's Medusa?' whenever he saw me."

"Who were you?"

"I know I was ugly—someone—someone used to keep telling me so. I used to wish that I was so ugly that if I looked at them when they were teasing me, they would turn to stone."

"Who were you? Who told you that story?"

She frowned with concentration, holding her breath, pressing her fingers against her forehead. But her eyes when she looked at him again were hopeless.

"It's no good. It doesn't come."

"Drink your drink. It will help you. Make you relax. I wish I could hypnotise you. Do you think I could?" His eyes bored into hers and for a few moments they sat so, motionless, staring at each other. Then Harry burst into a soft giggle. "How absurd we must look, sitting staring at each other in a tiny room in the middle of nowhere. What a ridiculous situation this is. Do you not find it so? Rather piquant, don't you think? Shall I tell you my name? It is Lupac, Harry Lupac. I am a violinist, quite a famous one. Does that name mean anything to you?"

He came to an abrupt halt, staring at her covertly. But she was plaiting her fingers together and gave no sign.

"Do you think," she said presently, "that I could have

something to eat? I'm hungry and I think I feel rather faint."

"Of course, of course," he said, plunged back from exhilaration to annoyance. He wanted to smack her head, punch her, beat knowledge out of her somehow. This guessing game would be amusing to play with an unknown girl on a desert island, but time was getting on, dark was coming—

He went angrily to the larder and clattered with plates and corned beef. Miserable girl—she would be leaving fingerprints everywhere, and that would have to be attended to afterwards. If she was Caroline.

Then he remembered something Hilda had said. *One of those thin, dark girls, the type you don't care for.* Certainly, although there was no actual resemblance, this girl was similar in type to his own sisters, enough to put his hackles up, make him feel irritable and edgy. She *must* be Caroline!

"When you walked to school," he called through the open door, "were you by yourself? Was your sister not with you?"

"No," she said at once. "My sister was older. She was away from home then."

"Ah!" he pounced. With triumph in the curve of his back he bent and set the plate of bread and corned beef beside her. "Now wait"—as she moved to take it—"what was your sister's name?"

She thought for a moment. "Dee. It was Dee."

"Dee? Not Hilda?"

She sat rigid, and then put her hands over her face in a gesture of despair.

"Oh, I don't know. I can't remember."

"Never mind." He patted her as if she were a good dog. "Eat your sandwiches. We're getting on famously."

Seven

Friday, August 27—evening.

"Tim darling. How wonderful of you to come so fast," Lady Trevis said, but there was no cordiality in her voice. She looked haggard. Her eyes were very sunken, very bright, and there was a flush on each cheekbone. Her lips were crusted. "What *can* I say? It's too shattering for words. I'm a wreck, literally! Dr. Campbell has given me some stuff and I was just waiting till you came, to see you, and then I shall take it and get a bit of sleep, otherwise I'll never be able to face that ghastly ordeal tomorrow. Oh, I forgot. This is Inspector Gleason; his people are out searching for Caroline, he's come in to use the phone or something. Inspector, this is my daughter's husband."

"Sorry to disturb you again, ma'am," said the Inspector, who had plainly taken an extreme dislike to Lady Trevis. "No news yet, I'm afraid. I'm just ringing back to the station at Barlock for some more equipment." He went into the annexe and juggled with the old-fashioned wall telephone.

Tim looked round the familiar hallway with horror. He was deadly tired; all his perceptions were painfully sharpened by his exhaustion. It seemed to him that there was a miasma of despair about this house, behind the well-remembered smell of moulting dogs, dry rot, stagnant flower water, decaying leather upholstery. . . .

The antlered heads on the walls were more moth-eaten, the rugs more holey than on the last visit. He could see no other difference. It looked as if no one had flicked a duster or opened a window since he had come to discuss wedding arrangements four years ago.

How could Caroline ever have recovered in this house, how could he ever have allowed her to come here? If the doctor hadn't been so insistent that she should remain in England away from the scene of the tragedy—if he himself hadn't been so desperately overworked after the oil fire—

A girl's figure appeared outside the glass-paned front door and with a leap of the heart he thought, It's Caroline, and moved to let her in. But of course it was not Caroline, this girl was a good ten inches taller, a big, buxom, curly-headed girl.

"Lorraine," he said without pleasure, and then, courtesy demanding it, "Come in, won't you?"

"Tim! My *dear!* How *marvellous* to see you!" She came in with hands outstretched, her face split in a wide grin. "I'd absolutely no idea you were com—" Slowly, as she took in the tableau in the hall, Lady Trevis haggard as a tragedy queen, the Inspector patiently jiggling the phone, she appeared to realise that something was wrong. She glanced round, nervous and bewildered. "What's happened?" Lady Trevis threw up her hands. "My God, you come to this house and you ask what's happened? What *hasn't* happened?"

All my pretty chickens, thought Tim sourly.

"Caroline's missing," he explained to Lorraine, whose big plum-coloured eyes were fixed on him so intensely that he wondered if she was taking in what he had told her. "She went out just after lunch with one of the dogs, six, seven hours ago now—"

"But it's not only Caroline, it's Hilda!" broke in Lady Trevis shrilly. "Had you heard, Lorraine, did you know that darling Hilda—"

"No! No, you don't mean to say—" Lorraine was aghast. "Hilda, too? How on earth—"

Irritated to snapping point by their excited strophe

and antistrophe, Tim turned away from them, nearer to the Inspector, who had got through to the station at last. He tried to catch what Gleason was saying.

"—another hundred feet of rope. Have to try along the cliffs."

"Caroline's been behaving so bloody oddly these last weeks," Lady Trevis said in her penetrating croak. "Delusions about all sorts of things, suspicions, persecution mania. Flora's death probably just tipped her over. I believe she must have had some sort of brainstorm and jumped in the river or something like that."

Meeting Tim's eye she faltered slightly but then, rallying, exclaimed, "Well, you were here yourself the other day, weren't you, Lorraine, when she was making that song-and-dance about Flora's death, blaming herself. And all the fuss about her tonic, saying the pills made her giddy. Ridiculous rubbish."

"But, well, she *was* giddy," Lorraine said. "She did fall into the water on Tuesday—"

"She should have had the sense not to go swimming—"

"She didn't particularly want to," Lorraine said contritely. "I'm afraid I persuaded her—"

Tim was half attending, half trying to hear what the Inspector was saying into the telephone.

"Dragnets, too, for Wemmary Pool, on the moor. Got that? This line's terrible."

When they find her, vowed Tim, she shan't stay in this place a night longer, if it means sleeping in the police station. He looked with hate round the high, dark room. Imagine having to see those terrible Victorian canvases of St. Bernards every morning when you came down. I've made such a mess of it, Caroline, my darling. If only, if *only* they find you, I'll do anything, take a year's leave, throw up the job if Uncle Sean won't let me; we'll go away to Greece, somewhere, anywhere. Oh, darling, come back, please don't be lost . . .

A dumpy, faintly familiar figure came in, its face swollen with crying, carrying a tray of tea.

With an effort he remembered her: Gladys the maid,

who had left to marry a policeman; she had always been rather fond of Caroline.

"Oh, poor Miss Caro, sir," she said. "Oh I do hope she's all right. I couldn't rest at home thinking of her, and it was all my fault in a manner of speaking because if I hadn't gone and got upset this afternoon it wouldn't have unsettled her, like. Oh I do wonder where she can be. I keep blaming myself."

"Nonsense, Gladys," Lady Trevis said. What was there in her tone? Satisfaction? Something malicious that gave Tim an unpleasant feeling. "It wasn't your fault. Don't try to make yourself important. Miss Caroline had been getting odder and odder, there's no use blinking the fact. Look how she'd been losing things—clothes, keys, money, jewellery, those pills—she couldn't keep anything. And walking in her sleep—Hilda said she'd met Caroline half a dozen times, wandering about the house, and next day Caroline wouldn't remember a thing about it. And seeing snakes—she said she saw one in the bath last week, it was only a bit of rag. She was definitely growing more and more unbalanced. Did Hilda tell you about her tearing pages out of books?" she said to Tim.

"Pages out of books?" He felt sick; this was a nightmarish affair. And why had Galbraith known nothing about it?

"We had to put away all the books because if there was anything about children or babies she'd tear the pages out and burn them."

Tim stared at her in horrified disbelief, but Gladys interrupted.

"Oh no, m'lady, it was Miss Hilda did that."

"*Hilda?*" said Lorraine, pop-eyed.

"What nonsense," Lady Trevis said angrily. "You don't know what you're talking about."

"Yes, I do 'm," Gladys persisted. "I saw Miss Hilda do it once. She was tearing pages out of a book and burning them. I came into the room while she was at it, and she said, 'I'm doing this so's Miss Caroline shan't be upset. Anything that reminds her is bound to upset her.'

Rather quick and short she was; I thought it a bit funny at the time."

"You're dreaming," Lady Trevis said. "You'd better go and get on with packing up Hilda's things. The girl's little better than half-witted," she told Tim when Gladys had gone. "She lost her own child a few days ago; Caroline had some unbalanced, fanciful idea that they were sisters in misfortune, and she insisted on taking a bunch of flowers to Gladys and working her up into a state; working herself up too."

The Inspector ended his telephone conversation by saying, "I'll wait here with the small car till you come, then," and rang off. Lady Trevis rather ungraciously offered him tea and he accepted a cup. Tim silently poured a cup for Lorraine. Her eyes, moist with sympathy and sentiment, met his as she took it from him; uncomfortably he looked away.

"You're quite sure you can't think of any particular favourite spot where your daughter might have gone?" Inspector Gleason asked. Lady Trevis shrugged.

"She used to walk for miles all round here. It's a wild part of the country."

"There wasn't anything special that you recall about her behaviour during the last twenty-four hours? At breakfast, or last night, or during the day?"

"At breakfast she was sulking; as usual. Last night she got all steamed up; I told you she seemed to think it was her fault that my cousin had fallen into the river. (Caroline ought to have been looking after the library, only she developed one of her imaginary ailments and asked Flora to do it for her.) After supper she had a long argument with me, insisting that she was well enough to go out and join her husband; of course we didn't know then that you were on your way here," Lady Trevis said, breaking off and giving Tim a sudden, disconcertingly artificial grin, squarely baring every denture. "So I turned on the radio to stop the row, and then she burst into tears and ran out of the room."

"I see," the Inspector said. "What time last night

would that be? Did she go straight to bed? Could she have gone out and met anybody?"

"I'm afraid I couldn't say. It was just after Hilda rang up to say she was stopping the night in Bridpool and wouldn't be back. Caroline took the message."

"Miss Trevis rang up, did she?" The Inspector was suddenly alert. "You hadn't mentioned that. You're sure you can't remember the time of the call more exactly—it would help pinpoint Miss Trevis's time of death."

"Oh dear, how can I tell? Caroline answered it, she wasn't on the line for more than a minute, and it was after that we had our row and I turned on the radio. I know, you can find out from the Radio Times; I remember what I turned on—it was some ghastly violinist playing classical stuff—Lucas, Lustig, some such name."

"Violinist?" The Inspector put down his cup and saucer abruptly.

Wearily humouring him as one who probably didn't understand the term, Lady Trevis found the place in the Radio Times. "Here you are. Hari Lupac, ten-fifteen."

Tim suddenly could not stand the inactivity in the room another moment.

"I'll go out with you, Inspector, if I may, when you leave again? In the meantime, Lady Trevis, do you mind if I go up and have a look at Caroline's room? Maybe she kept a diary or something—I might get some ideas, perhaps."

"Certainly, if you want to," Lady Trevis said coldly. "Inspector, don't think me unfeeling, will you, but I've identified poor darling Hilda's things and there's nothing more I can do till tomorrow except wait about like a spare part, so I'm going to take my tablets and get some sleep. You'll excuse me, won't you, Lorraine?" she said, raising her plucked brows as if wondering why Lorraine was still with them anyway. "Ask Hudson for anything you want, Inspector—make yourself *quite* at home."

The irony of her intonation was not lost on Gleason, who replied, "Thank you, Lady Trevis," without joy. Lorraine hesitated, ill at ease, unwilling to go, uncertain whether to stay.

Tim stood for a moment looking up the dark stair well that occupied the core of the house, with its smell of mutton and huge pictures of great shaggy dogs engaged in improbable rescues. Actually he had never been in the upper part of the house, never seen the bedroom of Caroline's childhood. But he was not going to ask Lady Trevis where it lay. He waited until her light nervous tread had died away.

An old, white-haired man passed him, muttering angrily.

"Do you know—" Tim began.

Hudson turned and looked at him vaguely. Tim saw that tears were running down his cheeks.

"I knew how it would be!" he said. "I tried to warn her. I knew that scheming bitch would drive her to summat desprit sooner or later. I done what I could, I chucked away those pills, but what's the good; she's gone, and she was the only decent one of the whole bunch. Bloody useless dog come back, oh yes, but she won't come back no more. Let them what tormented her rot in hell, *I* say." He gave Tim a blear-eyed glance and declaimed, quaveringly, *"An orphan's curse would drag to tell A spirit from on high,"* before going on his way and disappearing through an archway. Tim stared after him for a moment, and then ran softly upstairs. At the top he met Gladys with a suitcase in either hand.

"Can you show me my wi—, Miss Caroline's room?" he said.

"It's along this way, sir, next to Miss Hilda's. I'll be next door, packing up Miss Hilda's things, if you should want me for anything."

"Packing them up?"

"Lady Trevis said to pack up all Miss Tidbury's things, and Miss Hilda's, and get them out of the house. She doesn't want to see them no more. She's—she's very upset," Gladys said inadequately.

"Yes."

Tim went through the door she showed him and switched on the light in Caroline's room.

It was square and old-fashioned, with a brass bedstead

and white counterpane, violet carpet the colour of cheap boiled sweets, and china utensils with wicker-bound handles. The atmosphere was chill and dank; the room smelt of mildew.

His own photograph smiled at him with false cheer from the bedside table; apart from this there was no trace of Caroline save a pair of sandals forlornly in the middle of the carpet, like deserted children in an orphanage playground. Her clothes were in the drawers, though.

Tim sat on the bed and stared about him, trying to pick up some vibration to tell him what Caroline had been thinking, intending. It might have been a room in a dubious hotel, it said nothing. He opened a shallow drawer in the flimsy little bedside table and found a sheet of airmail paper with three words on it: *Tim, my darling*.

At that he groaned, and, leaning sideways, pressed his face for a moment against the uncomforting darkness of her pillow. Oh, sweetheart, he thought, what has been happening to you in this house?

There was no reply here to his question. The chill of the room began to penetrate his bones. Next door he could hear Gladys bumping about, so he went to speak to her.

Hilda's room resembled Caroline's, but was made intimate by a scattering of cosmetics, jewellery, letters. At present it was heaped with clothes which Gladys had taken out of drawers. It wore a sad, dishevelled, breaking-up air.

"You said you saw my wife this afternoon, Gladys?" he said.

"Yes, sir." With Gladys's honest grief and worry there was mingled more than a touch of self-importance at having apparently been the last person to see Caroline alive. It was obvious that she was telling her story for the fourth or fifth time, and the words had taken on a ballad-like slant of doom:

"It was the sight of that dreadful bit of rag that turned her, just like it done me. White as a ghost she was. I was laying down on the bed, see, and she gave my hand a kind of squeeze, and, my heart! I thought, the minute she'd gone, what did she mean by that? She run off through the gate, crying her eyes out, with that great brute of a dog tugging at the chain, and no one hasn't seen her from that minute to this. So when I heard tell, I come up to ask if there wasn't nothing I could do, like. Well, I ask you! She and Miss Hilda both! Isn't that a dreaful thing for poor Lady Trevis?"

She had filled the two cases and now climbed on a chair and dragged down a third from the top of the wardrobe. It was locked. She vainly snecked at the catch, then opened it with a key from a bunch she had found in a drawer.

"Well, there's a funny thing," she said, staring down at the contents. "That's Miss Caro's silver slipper that she lost. Or, no, I s'pose this is the other one. Miss Hilda likely put it away so's not to upset her."

"That's Caroline's cameo brooch," Tim said, strolling up and looking over her plump shoulder at the miscellaneous jumble of articles in the case.

"She lost that too, last month. Real miserable she was —gracious! you never think Miss Hilda had it all the time? She must have found it lying somewhere—and what the dickens is that ugly thing doing here, I wonder?"

"There's Caroline's address-book—and that's her fountain pen—and her purse. These are all Caroline's things," he said.

They stared at each other over the little heap. There was a black plastic snake, of the kind sold in joke shops, and an alarm clock; absently, Tim picked this up and wound it, looking at the time: nine-thirty.

"You never think Miss Hilda—oh no, that would be wicked!" Gladys said.

"What was that business you were telling downstairs about tearing pages out of books?" Tim's unease in the presence of Lady Trevis had prevented him from grasping the full import of this incident and he listened carefully now, twiddling the hands of the cheap clock, while Gladys repeated the story.

"And there was something else about pills—pills that made her giddy?"

"I don't know about that, sir."

It all seemed to hang together in a horrible way—the cache of stolen articles, the pages from the books, Caroline's desperation, Hilda's bright, nurselike letters to him saying that Caroline was coming on rather slowly, was still jumpy and odd—

"Deliberately trying to drive her into another breakdown?" he said, looking down at the clock's shiny, self-satisfied face. "But why? Why should Hilda do such a thing? Did she hate Caroline?"

The clock in his hands suddenly sprang into maniac life and shrilled out a loud peal in double rings, artfully pitched to sound like a telephone bell.

"Peculiar thing to have," Tim said, startled, staring at it. "You'd think it would lead to a lot of confusion—oh, I see. There's its box. Joke alarm clock. Endless laughs and puzzle your friends. I wonder how she used *that*."

Gladys's round, pink face was shocked into shapelessness, her mouth an oval of horror. "But Miss Caroline used *always* to be running to answer the phone and when she'd get there, whoever it was had rung off. So disappointed she used to be. In the end she didn't always bother to answer—I reckon she thought she was just imagining the bell."

"My God," said Tim. "If that isn't criminal—"

"It's downright wicked! And Miss Caroline still so upset and grieving over the—over little Master Punch. We was all so sorry about that, sir." Embarrassed, she looked down again and took out the last things from the bottom of the case: half a dozen LP records. "Would these be Miss Caro's too, sir?"

"Shouldn't think so. She left her records at Ras al-Abdan. What are they? Mozart violin concertos? I expect they were Hilda's—better pack them up with the rest of her stuff. I'll take this lot."

Inspector Gleason put his head round the door. "Just off, now, Mr. Conroy, if you care to come along?" His eye fell on the pile of records. "Hari Lupac . . . Whose are those?"

"Miss Trevis's, we think."

"That's interesting. Put them on one side, will you, Mrs. Vernon, for the moment. "I'd like to have another look at them. Now, Mr. Conroy—"

He nodded kindly to Gladys.

Tim followed the Inspector's solid, reliable back downstairs, wondering what Gleason's reaction would be if he told him that Hilda seemed to have been deliberately trying to drive Caroline out of her wits.

Lorraine was still standing awkwardly in the hall like an unwanted child, her mouth drooping.

"Can I do anything?" she asked Tim eagerly.

He tried to be kind. "I don't think so, thanks a lot, Lorraine. I should run along home."

Her hopeful look sank. She turned disconsolately towards the door.

"I'll ring you if there's any news," Tim said. "And you might give Lady Trevis a call tomorrow—see if there's anything you can do then."

"Okay," she said flatly.

"Lorraine," he said on an impulse, "do you think Hilda liked Caroline?"

"Hilda? Good Lord no, she *loathed* her!" Lorraine blurted. "It stuck out a mile. I think she always had, from when they were small. When Carey was little Hilda was always teasing her about how ugly she was, till the silly kid believed it."

"I see," Tim said slowly. Gleason beckoned him from the police car. "Well, goodbye," he said to Lorraine. "Anyway, thanks for writing. If only I'd known all this before—"

He slid into the car, forgetting Lorraine at once, his mind switching back to Hilda—cool, hating, calculating Hilda. Why had she done it? What was her motive? Just sheer love of tormenting? Jealousy? And then as the car turned, briefly illuminating with its headlights the ragged front of the house, perched over the white turmoil where the river Tebburn flowed into the Tare, an inkling of Hilda's motive dawned on him; it was to prevent Caroline escaping again. Four years ago she had managed it, triumphed, against all probability, and run off to a happy marriage, leaving the elder sister still a prisoner, hag-ridden by Lady Trevis's moods. Hilda was making sure it wouldn't happen twice. Everyone was to have been persuaded that Caroline was too unstable to take up the threads of her marriage again. And in the end perhaps she would have been.

Hilda's character fell into place before him and again he flailed himself inwardly. "How could I have been so blind as to trust her?"

Inspector Gleason interrupted these thoughts. "We'll try the cliffs out to Pennose first," he said. "There's all sorts of ledges where people get stuck at bank holidays; Lord knows why your wife should have gone climbing but we have to try everything."

The steep green banks flashed past hypnotically in the headlights as Tim struggled with his desperate weariness.

The girl had finished her sandwiches. When Harry wasn't looking she pushed the unfinished drink behind his carefully arranged vase of wild flowers.

"I really do think—" she was beginning when he brought her a pencil and paper.

"Write your name," he commanded. "Just scribble it down quickly."

She took the pencil. It felt long and awkward in her fingers. She gave an apprehensive look, first at Harry, then at the rough, ruled paper. Quickly and clumsily, in the centre of the page, she wrote *Punch*. The word stared back at her from the page. It gave her an unhappy feeling, she didn't know why. Punch—Punchie—my lamb—

"Punch," said Harry irritably. "That can't be your name, you know. Write something else—anything that comes into your head." With a pretence at ease he stuck his hands in his pockets and strolled to the french window, where he stood balancing on his heels and toes.

Then he started.

"Hey!" he yelled. "Who the hell are you? What are you doing there?"

The pencil rolled from her fingers. Astonished at the

fury and suspicion in his voice she jumped to her feet. "What is it? Oh, what is it?" she said, and crossed the room to look past him.

The garden was a tangled wilderness of unpruned roses and raspberry canes and brambles, running down to the edge of the abandoned railway cutting. With a jaunty flip of black-and-white, a magpie wheeled off into the woods beyond. Then she saw what it was that had roused Harry's anger. Slowly and timidly a small boy was making his way towards them through the weeds. He held a red-stained chip basket, and, in the late evening light, his eyes were big shadowed pools of fear. His legs were scratched, his face grubby; a bloodstained handkerchief was tied round one knee. There were blackberries in the basket.

"Oh—" the girl said. She pushed the back of her hand against her forehead. Something was coming through now—the oil derrick and the hot, brown, hazy sky— Punchie's red-and-green T shirt—he always had a graze and a bandage on one knee or the other—

But Harry was not attending to her.

"Who are you?" he said furiously to the terrified child. "What are you doing in my garden? Don't you know this is private? Come on, answer me? What's your name?"

The boy's lips parted soundlessly. She looked down then, to be spared the sight of his terror, and at once her eyes fell on the violin. At the sight of it her mind performed a sort of violent somersault, and all the odd memories which had been assailing her slid into place. Lupac! Of course this was Lupac! But what was *he* doing here? And where was Hilda—and the lawyer—hadn't Hilda said she was bringing a lawyer?

The torn photograph of Hilda caught Caroline's eye again. Why did he have those pictures? And—now she came to think of it—why had he been behaving so oddly, working and working to ferret her identity out of her when the natural thing would have been to take her straight to the nearest doctor or police station? Caroline's mind moved slowly back over the conversation. He had been expecting her—he had said, "It *is* Mrs. Conroy, isn't it? You will be surprised—"

He must somehow have got wind of Hilda's plan and managed to come down ahead of her. Then, did he *know* Hilda?

"I was only pickin' a few blackberries," the little boy said desperately. "I didn't know this house belonged to no one! Down in the village everyone thinks it's empty."

Everyone thinks it's empty. This house. Whistle Cottage. All at once a feeling of the most cold and deadly terror took possession of Caroline; irrational it might be, perhaps, but she could not shake it off. She was in a lonely house with the man whom she had seen kill a child. Of course he didn't know that—or did he? But he didn't know who she was—*or did he?*

"Hey," said Lupac in quite a new voice to the little boy. "All right—never mind about the trespassing, forget it. I am sorry. I did not mean to scare you. Now, take a look at this lady. Do you know who she is?"

Caroline caught her breath.

"Yes, I knows her," the boy said directly, rather puzzled. "I seen her in Woodmouth."

"But what's her name? Who is she?" Harry asked sharply.

The boy looked baffled. "I don't know her *name*. She gave me sikkençe once."

Harry struck his hands together in an exasperation almost beyond control. Then his cunning returned, and his mind began to race. It was Caroline, it must be: she lived in or near Woodmouth; she gave the child sixpence; that all fitted. In any case he couldn't afford to wait here any longer, they would soon be searching for the girl, and moreover he knew that his judgment was slipping; he knew that if he was subjected to any more unexpected stresses his caution would desert him completely and his actions would become irrational; this had happened before. It had been a mistake, already, to call in and question the boy; now he would have to be disposed of as well. Thinking coldly, clearly, and with lightning precision, he said to the boy,

"Is there a doctor in the village?"

"Yes, sir, Doctor Campbell. He lives by the church."

"Good, then I'll get out my car and run you both down there. This lady's ill, and it'll save you a long walk home—it's nearly dark. I daresay your mother is worrying about you as it is."

"Thank you, sir," the boy said, bewildered by this sudden turn of events.

Harry went through to the shed at the back, opened the doors, and ran out his car. He also slipped a gun from the tool box into his pocket. He much disliked using a gun but there were times, like the present, when it was more reliable.

"Please don't bother to drive us down," Caroline said, when he went in the front door again. "Truly I'd rather walk. Bill will show me the way. It might do me some good—bring back some of my memory." She forced a trembling smile. What was Lupac going to do? She felt that at all costs she must avoid getting into that car.

"Oh, no, I insist," said Harry. And she could see that he meant it.

"Just let me bandage Bill's knee then," she suggested hurriedly and then, realising her slip, "You said your name was Bill Davey, didn't you?" The boy nodded, bewildered. "He shouldn't go about with that dirt on it," she told Harry. "May I use your bathroom? Do you have one upstairs?"

"For God's sake—another ten minutes like that won't give him tetanus!" Harry exclaimed, but without listening she hurried Bill up the stairs. On the landing she tried a door which was locked, then turned to her left and caught a glimpse of a bathroom with open door at the end of a short, dark passage. She and Tim had never used the upstairs; in those days the room had been merely a closet, damp because it backed into the side of the hill.

No use thinking about that time, though.

Locking herself and the boy into the bathroom Caroline turned the taps full on and began dabbing at the small bony knee. She *knew* her instinct was not mistaken—she had seen something like murder in Harry's eyes as she looked back from the stairs. Her own murder and the murder of the child as well—he could not afford to leave alive a witness who had seen her with him at the cottage. But how could they escape? What could she do to save them? Was it possible to explain to the child without terrifying him out of all reason?"

"Sit on the bath," she ordered, and steadied him. The feel of the small jerseyed body gave her courage and determination. "Bill," she said, "can you be pretty brave and sensible? Are you a scout or anything like that?"

"I'm a Wolf-Cub, miss," he said, looking up at her with intelligent, seven-year-old eyes.

"Oh, that's grand. Well, listen—I don't trust that man downstairs. I think he means to do us some harm; if we go in his car I think he might take us off to—to somewhere we don't want to go to."

"Like in *Kidnapped,* on the telly," Bill said, nodding.

God bless television, Caroline thought. No doubt seven-year-olds shouldn't be accustomed to the idea of cruelty and violence, but if it's seen as make-believe—

"Yes, like the telly. Now look—you could get out through the window—it's big enough for you but not for me, do you see? It's only a step to the ground here, because of the hill, and you can creep off into the bushes while I pretend to be still washing your knee—"

"And run down to the village and get help," interrupted Bill enthusiastically. "Okay, miss, just give me a hand up and I'll go now. Will you be all right, though, miss?"

"Yes, I'll be all right. You go to Mr. Vernon—you know Mr. Vernon the policeman?" He nodded again. "And say Miss Caroline's here with Mr. Lupac and to come quickly. Mr. Lupac who ran over Garry Vernon. Can you remember that?"

"Coo," he said, and repeated "Loopatch" carefully after her. She glanced round quickly—what could she give him? She pulled her handkerchief out of her belt. "Here, this'll show you're not telling a story—it's got my initial on it. Now then, up with you—take care and go quietly. Not scared?"

He shook his head at her, grinning, and wriggled through the tiny square window.

"Hurry up!" came Harry's impatient call from the top of the stairs. "Anyone would think he'd broken his leg off."

Caroline waited till the small figure had disappeared into the dusky bushes, then sank on the edge of the bath, weak with reaction. Thank God, oh, thank God. In a moment she must pull herself together and try to find some means of escape for herself, but thank God at least the child was safe. Not another child. Not a third.

For the last ten minutes she had been aware that if she chose she could now look back; the barriers her illness had thrown up against memory were crumbling under this new assault of tension and fear. Quite deliberately, then, she turned and faced the day of her son's death.

It was Miller, the garrulous old Yorkshire time keeper, who had pleaded so hard for the little boy to be allowed to watch the drilling; Punch would be sure to bring them luck, he said. In the end Tim, persuaded by Caroline, had reluctantly agreed; and Punch had been so proud. It was his third birthday. They were working on Bertha, the number-two well, at that time, and expected to meet the oil at any minute. Miller had taken Punch on ahead in the Landrover. And then Caroline, dressing in the bungalow, had heard the explosion, had dropped her hairbrush and ran, hatless, down the sun-scorched sandy road to the rig. How could she ever have forgotten that half-mile of road?

Colossal flames like giants' torches were raging straight upwards, the men racing about the site were puny black ants. Detached clots of fire burst out of the central mass and fell, still burning fiercely. Where could the Landrover be? Then, dry-mouthed with horror, she realised that what she had taken for a pile of burning wreckage *was* the Landrover. The men were trying to get at it, to open the doors. She had tried too, struggling and screaming, till they dragged her away. She saw Nicolson, Tim's assistant, also dragged back from the flames; someone knocked him down and threw sand on him. "Punch? Where is he? He can't be in there?" she said frantically, first to one, than to another. Nobody answered, she could not have heard them if they had; the noise of the fire was a steady roar, louder than any gale. Then she had seen Tim coming toward her, had seen the expression on his face.

She had sat by Nicolson's stretcher in the ambulance while Tim stayed to direct the fire-fighters and try to get the blowout under control. She had tried to comfort the young man, terribly burned himself. "Don't, Peter, don't. It was quick. They can't—can't have known." She had no tears, she felt numb and stupid, hardly noticed her own burns. At the hospital she had fainted; a confused nightmare followed, delirium, anguish, narcosis, delirium, anguish, haunted by Tim's drawn, desperate face when he came and sat holding her hand.

Then the air ambulance back to London; Tim had accompanied her as far as Aden, but had to race back to deal with the chaos resulting from the fire. Not a word had been said about Punch, not then at least. Never for one moment had Tim suggested that Caroline was in any way to blame. That was left to Lady Trevis.

She bowed her head over the basin. Who would care if Lupac did murder her? Tim would be better off without the sight of her to remind him; Hilda had so often said that Tim would never want to live with her again—

"You weren't the type to marry in the first place; you're not sufficiently well-balanced. Tim needs someone solid and dependable," and it was true, true. Lorraine had said something of the sort, too. No wonder Tim's letters were so short and infrequent, very likely by this time he had started divorce proceedings and they were keeping it from her.

What was there to look forward to? The musty, hateful house, the bitter voices, Mother and Hilda, shrill with contempt for her failure. Couldn't even keep a husband when she got him, couldn't look after her own child. In a way I suppose it would be only fair if I stayed at home now, to let Hilda get away for a life of her own, I know she longs to; Mother relies on her so much, she'll have a terrible struggle to get away. Of course Mother's fonder of Hilda than she is of me, but I might just do. Oh, should I try to escape for Hilda's sake?

"Merciful heavens!" came Harry's furious voice outside the door. "How much longer are you going to be?"

He rattled the latch. Caroline turned off the taps, shot back the bolt, and faced him breathlessly, holding her dripping hands in front of her as if they were some protection.

"He's gone!" she said. "You—you scared him. I think he thought you were really going to take him to the police. He wriggled out of the window."

Harry switched on the light and stared at her. His nostrils were pinched and white, she noticed that he was breathing very fast, without any sound.

"Gone!" Harry said. "And you didn't try to stop him? You let him go on purpose, didn't you? Why?"

"I couldn't stop him."

His eyes fell on her wet hands, he took hold of her wrist and suddenly flung it down, bruising it against the side of the bath.

"You're a bad liar, aren't you, sweetie," he said. "Let us understand one another. You have remembered, have you not, that you are Caroline? Come along; you shall accompany me in the car and there will be plenty of time to overtake that child as he plods his weary way to the village. It is a pity about what I shall have to do to you both, but it cannot be helped."

"I don't understand you!"

"No? But you understand this, perhaps?" Looking down she saw the gun he had taken from his pocket. He gestured her to precede him down the stairs. With insane courage she pushed his hand aside and flung herself through an open door opposite. The gun exploded as the door slammed, and the key jarred in her hand. He was shooting into the heavy lock. She could guess that it would hold only for a moment or two, and she ran desperately to the window and threw it up.

*   *   *

"Sacred to harmony, sacred to harmony, sacred to love; Sacred to harmonee, and love," sang the choral society in a final triumphant rallentando. Then there was a shuffling of books and stacking of chairs; the society dispersed with mutual congratulations and Minnie Todd walked home rather irritably because it took twenty minutes on foot from the Oddfellows' Hall to The Nook whereas it would have been only three on the scooter. Had Basil come home and decided to go straight to bed?

The house was all in darkness, the door locked.

When she found her candlewick spread still neat and smooth, no Basil in the double bed, Minnie became more seriously perturbed. Basil was generally so reliable. What could have happened to him?

For more than ten minutes she sat carefully revolving the various factors in the situation. If some scandal broke, prematurely exposing Harry Lupac's darker side, she knew that her authorities would be seriously angry with her; Lupac would be no further use to them. On the other hand, Basil *had* been complaining that he felt unwell; his nonarrival might be due to an unexpectedly bad attack of pain from his ulcer. For the first time Minnie felt a shade of remorse for her cavalier treatment of him in the morning. After all, party loyalties were only party loyalties, but a husband was a husband; she would be lucky if she ever replaced him.

At last, her mind made up, she went to the telephone and dialled Bridpool 9000.

As Gleason shuttled the police car smoothly through a series of narrow lanes, Tim's mind, weighed down by weariness, tried again and again to follow Caroline through the dark reaches of fear in which she had been so unchartedly adrift. What was the "dreadful thing" that had happened, of which she was not allowed to speak? Who had not allowed her? Hilda? Was it connected with the child who had been run over? Or the old woman who had fallen off the harbour wall?

Where could she have gone to? Who would she have turned to?

Endless tree trunks flickering past lulled him into a sort of waking dream: he thought he had met Caroline as usual in Whistle Cottage. It was pouring with rain and a savage wind hissed through the cracked window; a puddle was accumulating on the floor. "This is a bit bleak, isn't it?" he said. "How about getting back to your place?" "Oh no, darling it's so awful there." "Well then, why not come home with me?" "That would mean invitations, and your family knowing about me, and then you'd have to be asked back—" A sharp gust of rain slapped his face and he saw that Caroline was locked inside the cottage looking at him through the window. "They've locked me in," she called to him despairingly, "because I left Punchie in the woods. Oh, find him, darling, please—it's long past his bedtime and he'll be so frightened—"

Whistle Cottage, Tim thought. Might Caroline have gone there? Very unlikely, but it was just worth a try when all else had failed.

The car stopped with a jerk.

"Here we are," the Inspector announced. "You'll be wanting a torch, I expect, sir; we've plenty of spares. If you'll take the top path we'll go along the lower one by the rocks; watch out for yourself, there are some treacherous stretches on these cliff paths."

He moved carefully along, shining his torch this way and that, catching the flickered reflection, sometimes, from the eyes of wild creatures, but never seeing what he hoped to find. Down below the sea creamed and sighed; the lights of the other party shone, sometimes, on white curdled water.

"Caroline!" he called. "Carinney! Where are you?" and the echo came drifting back, "are you . . . are you?"

"Well, nothing here," the Inspector said, materialising beside him after an hour. The men from the other car were there as well, and one who had just arrived on a motor bike. "We've been right round the point as far as the next bay. We'll go back through the village now, call in at Vernon's to see if any messages have come in there, and then out the other way on to the moor."

"You don't think there's any connection between Hilda's having been run over and Caroline's disappearance?" Tim asked as they turned back towards Woodmouth.

"Don't see how there can be, without telepathy. Your wife was already missing when I went up to Woodhoe House to tell Lady Trevis about the other sister. Your wife had been very upset about Miss Tidbury and the little Vernon boy, I do know that; I thought myself this afternoon that she looked as if she had something badly on her mind."

Tim nodded. "We lost our own boy six months ago—in very tragic circumstances—I don't know if you'd heard. She couldn't help being reminded." His throat felt tight. Determined not to let silence grow, he went on, "It's an odd coincidence, surely, that there should be two such similar hit-and-run accidents. Do you think the same person could be responsible?"

"It's odder than you think. Miss Trevis was found with a violin string round her finger. Why? She didn't play the fiddle. We can't trace who she was with last night; friends in Bridpool, Lady Trevis said she mentioned when she spoke to your wife on the phone, but the people she usually stays with hadn't seen her. Also she said, apparently, that she was going to the cinema, but the last house would have begun long before. And now some woman's rung up, it seems, to report that her husband's missing, might have come out to Woodmouth. Secondhand bookseller from Bridpool, name of Todd. What's he doing out here?"

"Do you think Hilda could have been having an affair with some man and keeping it dark?"

"Possibly," the Inspector said, slowling down a narrow, twisting hill. "She was a close kind of girl, I gather, kept herself to herself. No local affairs, no gossip about her. I shouldn't wonder if she had a secret or two."

"Should you be surprised to learn that she had deliberately been tormenting her sister, trying to disturb her mind?" Tim asked, and told the Inspector what he had found. Gleason whistled.

"What do you suppose the pills were?" Tim said. "You don't think she was trying to *poison* Caroline?"

"Not necessarily, from the sound of it. There's plenty of drugs will make you feel giddy and ill. Nasty, though, isn't it? Human nature's an odd mix-up. When you hear something like that it makes you wonder what else is going on behind closed doors unbeknownst to anybody. Worrying thing for you to discover. Well, we're doing all we can to find your wife, that's one comfort. You'll be glad to get her away from there."

Tim was comforted by this calm assumption that they would find Caroline; as the Inspector had meant him to be.

"The violin string round her finger," he presently said. "That pile of records in Hilda's case—they were all violin concertos."

"That's right, they were," said Gleason, turning his face a moment from the road. "I noticed that. I'm going to have a look at them when I get back."

"Well I can tell you one thing: they were all inscribed on the sleeves, H from H."

"Were they?" Gleason incautiously jabbed on the accelerator and the car shot forward. "H from H? You're sure of that? And they were all Hari Lupac records?"

"Yes, they were—oh," said Tim, "you don't suppose *Lupac* gave them to Hilda, do you? She didn't know him, did she? Caroline never mentioned such a thing."

"Lupac," Gleason said. "There was powdered resin found on the bit of rag near Garry Vernon's body. Hilda died with an A-string round her finger. Caroline burst out crying when her mother turned on the Lupac recital just after Hilda phoned up—which must have been just before her death, incidentally; she was found at ten-thirty. Hilda had a pile of Lupac records inscribed H from H. There seems to be a connection."

"If there isn't," said Tim, "I don't understand it. What's Lupac got to do with the Vernon child's death? Or with Caroline's disappearance? He hasn't ever been down here, has he?"

"Not so far as I know," Gleason said. They were among the lights of the village now; he pulled up outside a cottage. "I'll just call in here; I told them to leave messages with Joe." He peered at the lighted porch. "Mrs. Vernon's back home again, I see. Seems to be expecting us."

Gladys was waiting in the doorway. "Oh, sir, I'm glad you've come—" She and the boy who was with her spoke together and the Inspector found it hard to disentangle their words.

"Easy, son. You say what? You've seen Miss Caroline? Yes, where? Whistle Cottage, near the old lime kilns? By gum, the one place we haven't looked yet!"

"And she's in deadly danger, sir," Bill said earnestly. "She give me her handkerchief"—he flourished it—"and said to come as quick as possible. She's going to be kidnapped by Mr. Loopatch."

"Mr. Who?"

Bill repeated the name and added, "He's foreign. I bet he's a spy, sir. One o' them secret agents."

But the Inspector was already running back to the car.

There was a tiny Victorian leaded balcony outside the window. Caroline scrambled out and peered over, but the drop was daunting. At this lower end of the house the ground sloped away, and in the half-light it looked about sixteen feet down. No sense in being picked up by Harry with a broken ankle. She turned to survey the roof. The window she had come through was in a gable, and from the corner of the balcony a gully ran up to the roof-ridge. Without a second's hesitation Caroline began cautiously going up the angle on toes and fingers, trying not to make the slightest sound. If she could work her way along to the other end, where the house nearly met the hill—

She heard a muffled crash below. The bedroom door had given way at last and, in a moment, though she couldn't see him, she knew Lupac was on the balcony; she heard him grunt, and the scrape of his feet on the leads. She was on the roof-ridge by now, frantically clambering sideways; her arms and legs seemed weighted down, unused to the demands she was making of them. It was like a nightmare—she could not go fast enough. Would Lupac think she had jumped down from the balcony? Could she dare to hope that? No—there! A dark blob, his head, appeared above the slant of the gable, she saw a flash, and something cracked on the roof beside her. A tile went clinking and slithering down.

"You are an easy target, there, Caroline, do you know?" he called. There was an almost caressing note in his voice.

Caroline did not reply. She threw herself over to the far side of the ridge and hung there by her hands. Could she work her way along like this? The tiles were wet with dew, and one hand slipped. Then she heard another shot; a bullet whacked the ridge between her hands, and bits of tile flew into her face. Automatically she let go with both hands and felt herself begin to slide slowly, horrifyingly. How much of a drop was there on this side of the house? She would fall on a bit of stone terrace outside the french window . . .

Then, unbelievably, something stopped her. She had come to rest perched on the ridge of a dormer window. Crumpled over it she did nothing for a moment but take deep gulps of breath. The blood pounded in her ears like a waterfall; air tasted like blood. What was Lupac doing? No sound came from the roof; she guessed he was climbing down and would come round to the terrace in a moment. She had got to move, and fast.

She tried to climb back up the roof, but it was too slippery. Her numb and shaking limbs would not take her up, and she clung on the cold tiles like a terrified fly. She must think of some other plan, but what? The window in the dormer. Was the window open?

It was open, and there was only a foot-span between the dormer roof and its broad sill. With a final jerky effort, Caroline pushed herself across and then huddled paralysed on the sill. Supposing he had expected her to do this? Supposing he was inside the dark room, waiting to pick her off as she climbed in?

She could not stay on the windowsill, though; she inched her way through and crouched on the floor inside, her breath caught, her heart thudding.

She was in a bedroom. It smelt closely of hair oil, and of leather and tweed. There was another smell, too, spirits of some kind, very strong. No voice, no shot; she listened fiercely, passionately, until she could hear her own fingers moving on the fabric of the rug. The house was too full of silence, packed with it, bulging with it; silence and darkness hung in the corners, leaked through the cracks of the door. Where was he waiting for her, secure in the knowledge that she must come his way? She flogged her petrified mind to think. He must be indoors somewhere. Once she was out she was safe; there were twenty impenetrable hiding places in the undergrowth outside. He must know, then, that she could get out only by passing him. That was why he was not troubling to come and search for her.

The stairs. He would be on the stairs, waiting for the door to open and present her to him, confident that her self-control would give way first, and that she would make a panic-stricken dart for safety.

Caroline stood up, took a deep, calming breath, and began to move slowly, with the utmost caution, towards the dark end of the room where the door must be. Before every step she stood still, listened, and felt before her with her hands, reining in the thought that she might put out a hand and touch *him,* motionlessly waiting for her.

Her foot struck something soft; it might have been a cushion. Stooping to feel, she bit back a scream by a hair's breadth. The horrible fancy had come true: she had touched a human face, an open mouth. Not Harry, it could not be Harry, she realised next moment, taking a desperate grip on her dissolving courage—there had been a moustache on this face. But who could it be? A stranger? A corpse? Somebody else that Harry Lupac had decided to tidy out of his way?

Crouching down, she stared fiercely at the dark shape

on the floor and, mastering her repugnance with an extreme effort, touched the face again. It was cold, clammy—dead? But now that her head was on a lower level she caught a long, labouring breath, and the fumes of spirit even stronger, sweet and sickening. Whoever it might be, friend or enemy, was inaccessible under drink or drugs, neither refuge nor danger.

Just the same it took all her self-control to edge round the shadowy form and move on, leaving it behind her. Had there been a faint scrape at the door, or had she imagined it?

After ten minutes she reached the wall opposite the window.

Step by step to the right—no, that's the side wall. The door must be to the left, then. Yes! Her left hand brushed the ridged newel post and flickered over the panelling. The door was not quite shut, but she did not try to open it. She tiptoed across and stood pressed against the wall, so that when it did open she would be behind it. Now, wait! Don't move. He wants you to move, he wants you to come out, so just wait, and keep as still as death.

What can I do to keep me still and calm, to keep me awake?

I won't think about Tim, or Punch, nothing that might make me move or tremble, or even breathe faster.

But I can think about Punch now, she realised. And I know why: because I have been punished enough for his death. I was to blame—partly, not entirely—and I have acknowledged it and atoned. Now I can forgive myself and turn my mind forward, and start again. Tim, I will do better if I ever escape from here. I won't be afraid in so many stupid, needless ways, now that I have seen the face of fear itself.

Why did I refuse that job with Professor Lockhart? I can easily do it. I'll ring him up as soon as I get home.

Half an hour went by.

Every muscle in her body was begging and imploring leave to give way and let her sink to the floor. She made herself rigid and fought off the drowsiness that came over her in waves. If I can get out of this house alive, she thought, prodding herself to wakefulness, I can do anything in the world; the future is not dead for me if I can do this.

No sound in the house. Not the faintest footstep or murmur. Perhaps he's become scared and given up, run off into the dark?

Then suddenly, shattering her composure, the front door banged. Brisk footsteps crossed the hall and a light flicked on somewhere. She could see its reflection in the crack of the door. For a moment she felt sick with despair. Had he really been outside the house all this time, looking for her in the bushes? Had her whole elaborate game of hide-and-seek been a futile manoeuvre while she could have been escaping?

She heard Harry's cough downstairs, rather loud, the scrape of a chair being pushed, the clink of a glass. He was in the kitchen.

Now what?

Then it struck her that the noises were too loud; he was not the sort of man who banged or scraped or coughed. He *meant* her to think he had just come in and sat down. Why?

Now there came the unearthly squeak and scroop of his violin tuning; her nerves screamed in silent protest at each squalling note. She pictured him sitting below, a smile on his mobile red mouth and at the corners of his down-dropped eyelids, deliberately drawing out discordant sounds to torture her. After a few minutes of this he evidently had the instrument tuned to his liking for he began to play the Bach partita that she had heard in the Philharmonic Hall; the rigid, architectural music rose up in the house like barbed wire.

Caroline hesitated. Was this the moment for her to move? Had he really relaxed his watchfulness?

She put out her hand towards the door knob—and then snatched it back. She had felt the door slowly opening. He must be standing within a foot of her outside—and yet all the time the seesaw, contrapuntal music was coming from downstairs. He must have a record on, she thought, the devil, the unspeakably clever devil. To her exhausted mind it seemed utterly disproportionate that someone should devote all this ingenuity just to killing her. He must enjoy it. It must be even more fascinating for him than playing the violin.

Almost dispassionately she watched how a little pencil point of light stole forward across the floor. She heard a sound outside, a soft giggle, and the door swung silently towards her until it stood wide and he took a cautious step into the room.

Caroline hardly realised what she was doing until she had her shoe off and stood with it in her hand; then she slung it with all her force at the chest by the window. Something slipped and crashed; Lupac started and leapt forward—and in that instant Caroline whipped behind him out of the door. The stairs were to her left, opposite; she darted down them.

A moment's desperate fumbling with the front door, bolted and chained—she heard his steps turn and start down the stairs, and his voice, agonised, sobbing, "Caroline!" like the voice of a lover who sees his beloved slipping away.

As she pulled the door open and ran out a shot scuffed beside her on the path. The sharp gravel bit into her unshod foot and she thought hopelessly, "It's no good. Even now he'll get me."

But as she thought it she saw through the trees the beaconing light of Gleason's headlamps coming up the hill.